Books in the C~~~~~~ MW00333535
by Richard F. Weyand:
Childers
Childers: Absurd Proposals
Galactic Mail: Revolution
A Charter For The Commonwealth
Campbell: The Problem With Bliss
by Stephanie Osborn:
Campbell: The Sigurdsen Incident

Other books by Stephanie Osborn
The Division One Series:
Alpha and Omega
A Small Medium At Large
A Very UnCONventional Christmas
Tour de Force
Trojan Horse
Texas Rangers
Definition and Alignment
Phantoms
Head Games
Break, Break, Houston
Tourist Trap

Other books by Richard F. Weyand
The EMPIRE Series:
EMPIRE: Reformer
EMPIRE: Usurper
EMPIRE: Tyrant
EMPIRE: Commander
EMPIRE: Warlord
EMPIRE: Conqueror

CAMPBELL

THE SIGURDSEN INCIDENT

by

STEPHANIE OSBORN

STEPHANIE OSBORN

ISBN 978-1-7321280-7-1
Printed in the United States of America

Cover Credits
Model: Matt Shute
Background: Nikada
Composition by: Oleg Volk
Back Cover Photo: Fritz Ling

Published by Weyand Associates, Inc.
Bloomington, Indiana, USA
August, 2019

CONTENTS

STEPHANIE OSBORN

Ah, Youth

"You've read the materials, I assume, Mr. Campbell. The assignment was to apply them to yourself. So how would you add ten to fifteen years to your age?" the theatrical instructor asked his student, as the class sat in the specialized makeup room. Each "desk" was a makeup table, complete with kit and lighted mirror, arranged around the periphery of the room.

CSF Academy Cadet William Campbell studied his image in the mirror before him, mentally reviewing the concept on which he'd been working for the past several weeks. It was important that he get this one down; a failure in the all-important undercover disguise course — also known as Theater 501 — could scuttle him, washing him out of the Intelligence track at the Academy. And that was the track that excited him above all others; he could readily imagine spending his entire career in the Intelligence Division. Finally, concluding he was on top of things, he replied.

"First, sir, I'd close-shave the top of my head, to give the appearance of being bald. If I darken my hair to black, it'll automatically age me a little, since my skin tone and overall complexion keys to light brown hair, and darker hair than your natural color is aging. Then I'd add some silver to the temples, and maybe to the eyebrows. For a full-on change of appearance, I'd shave my beard, which for an older character would probably be necessary anyway; beard hair grows faster, and would have to be touched up with silver every day, possibly more than once a day, whereas the hair at my temples would only need touching up every couple of days." He glanced at the instructor, who was nodding, and whose face held an open, interested expression; Campbell gathered he was giving the instructor more than he'd expected. So he continued.

"Some crow's feet at the corners of the eyes — not too much, just a bit — maybe held in place with some liquid latex — or glue, in a pinch. Using the same technique, I'd add some forehead wrinkles between the eyebrows, maybe deepen the naso-labial fold on each side of my nose." He thought for a moment. "If I wanted to look even

1

more different from 'me,' I could add a scar here or there, with latex appliances and a bit of makeup to match my skin."

"That sounds like a plan, Mr. Campbell. Can you execute it?" the instructor asked.

"I can try, sir," Campbell declared. "I'm not sure I want to shave my head today, though... class photos are coming up in less than a week, sir..."

"Hah!" the instructor chuckled. "All right; I won't make you shave your head only to have it recorded for posterity, Mr. Campbell. Let me show you how to do something called 'soaping out hair.' If you soak a bar of soap in a small bowl of water, the soap softens into a gel or paste consistency, and you can use this to plaster the hair to your head and smooth it, then apply makeup, and it will pass. It won't necessarily stand close scrutiny, and heaven help you if you get caught in a rainstorm, but in a pinch, it'll do. This will take a little bit, but I have some soap especially intended for the purpose, so while it's softening in the water, we'll work on the rest of it..."

"No offense, sir, but I don't understand," Campbell observed, puzzled.

"What don't you understand, Cadet?" Rear Admiral Jacob Durand queried, as his student stood before the desk in the empty classroom.

"I thought I was lined up for the Intelligence track," Campbell pointed out. "Why is my next course TAC541 – Tactical Strategy Analysis and Simulation? And it's shared with the OCS?"

"That's an easy answer," Durand said. "You just finished at the top of my class for the entire year-long sequence. That puts you at, or near, the top of the Intel track, son. Which means you need to take TAC541. And... so do the officer candidates, for obvious reasons."

"I... I'm sorry, sir," Campbell apologized. "I still don't get it. Why am I required to take it?"

"Mr. Campbell, you show considerable promise," Durand said, "or you wouldn't have done so well in my course sequence. Therefore, like all students who do well in my course, you are being placed in a special sub-track. It's generally felt that intelligence agents who show a certain gift for counter-intel investigations need to get a taste of what they'll most likely be investigating. The bridge of every ship in the CSF is comprised almost exclusively of personnel from the

2

Tactical Division. So YOU need to know what it's like to be in a forward tactical position. You need to know what's required of them, what happens, the order in which they happen, and what's possible and what's not. Among other things."

"Oh," Campbell said then, the light dawning. "So I can understand what it's like on the other side of the fence, as it were."

"Bingo," Durand said, a slight grin spreading over his face. "Finally, he gets it! If, for instance, a ship has been severely damaged and there is risk to the power plant, the crew is going to be heavily involved in stabilizing it as much as they can, and then probably evacuating... or, more likely, evacuating the rest of the crew while the engineering team stabilizes. If you come in at that point and demand to have all of the electronic logs downloaded for you and handed over, investigation or not, you'll probably be told to go to hell... and possibly all but left on board. Which would NOT be good for you if the power plant blows."

"But if I understand that they have higher priorities at the moment, and know what those priorities ARE, I can simply request that the files be locked down, then come in and get 'em MYSELF," Campbell continued, thoughtful, "maybe with an intel team to spread out and help... only I can tell them how to do it and still stay out of the way..."

"Now you're catching on. So. We want you to see what it's like to be on a ship's bridge during a battle... without actually putting you on one. Because if you don't know what to do, if you don't understand up-front how they operate, you're only going to be in the way, in a real situation."

"Hm. Well then," Campbell decided, "this should be interesting..."

"That's one way to put it, all right," Durand noted.

OCS Cadet Marc Huber, formerly of Becker in the Outer Colonies, was confident as he entered the immersive VR simulation. He was, after all, one of the top students in the Tactical track for his OCS class, and he'd already completed his degree before ever coming to Jablonka, so he was head and shoulders past any of the Academy cadets.

Consequently he felt complacent about the exercise that was about to begin.

'CSS *Challenger*,' he thought with grim amusement, '"Captain Potemkin" is boarding now. Get ready, crew. We're gonna tear up the invader.'

Outside the simulator, Campbell studied the scenario he'd been given the day before, and smiled to himself. He'd spent a couple of hours the previous evening going over the candidate system — the Natchez system — in great detail, considering it not just from a tactical standpoint, but from an intelligence officer's standpoint. More, he'd gone into the portion of the intelligence database available to cadets and pulled out strategic data about the Natchez system, and as a result, he had a good grasp of the overall system.

'And a plan that might just work, even if it IS a little crazy,' he decided. 'It feels odd being the enemy aggressor, but hey... that's what war games are about in the real world, and even though this is a class, it's a war game. Maybe if the professor sees what I'm attempting, even if I fail, he'll go off and discuss it with others in the Tactical Division, and it'll help with planning.'

With that, he entered the simulator for the ESN *Columbia*, a 'battle destroyer' in Earth's fleet; the ship designations and classes used for the simulation were kluged craft composed of pieces-parts of actual classes; each was small like a destroyer or light cruiser — to allow for less for the students to keep up with, so early in their careers — with the beam weaponry and range of a battleship, and the acceleration of a destroyer. The idea was to keep the cadets thinking, since the simulated spacecraft weren't like any real ships anywhere, but they had to work with their assigned 'ship' as if it was. The bridge crew promptly snapped to attention.

"'Captain Nelson' on the bridge," his assigned XO announced.

"At ease," Campbell noted, heading for his chair. "As you know, our target system is the Natchez system; the target locus is the manufacturing facility on Natchez 5d. We have been in hyperspace en route for the last several weeks, and are coming up hard on the system periphery. Man your stations; sound general quarters, and prepare for hyperspace transition."

"Aye sir," his XO and helm responded at the same time, even as the general quarters alarm sounded. "Trajectory?" the helm officer asked.

"Zero mark zero on the target," Campbell said. "Five light-hours outside system periphery."

"Light-HOURS?" the XO wondered.

"Good copy, XO. Five light-hours."

"Zero on the target," helm read back. "Five light-hours outside."

"Count it down," Campbell ordered.

"Coming up in five... four... three... two... one... mark."

"Begin hyperspace transition."

"Sir, all departments report ready to transition," the XO confirmed.

"Set maneuvering warning," Lutzdorf said.

"Maneuvering warning set, sir."

The low-g warning light on the bulkhead lit, and the alarm system rang three bells.

"Set hyperspace warning."

"Hyperspace warning set, sir."

The hyperspace warning light on the bulkhead lit, and the alarm system rang four bells.

"Reduce hyperspace thrust to zero, helm."

"Reducing hyperspace thrust to zero, sir."

"Hyperspace thrust at zero, sir."

"Engineering. Reconfigure drive for transition."

"Reconfiguring, sir."

"Drive reconfigured for transition, sir."

"Execute hyperspace transition sequence, helm. Call 'em out."

"Executing hyperspace transition sequence, sir. Powering up hyperspace field generator... hyperspace field generator nominal, sir. Projecting hyperspace field... independent hyperspace field bubble forming... hyperspace field bubble stable. Activating forward thrusters at 10%... entering hyperspace field bubble now. *Columbia* is completely enclosed in the bubble. Modulating hyperspace field generator to separate hyperspace field bubble... hyperspace field bubble separating from hyperspace... hyperspace field bubble separation complete. Shutting down hyperspace field generator... hyperspace bubble dissipating."

The deck beneath them shuddered slightly.

"Returned to normal space. Hyperspace transition sequence complete, sir."

"Stand down hyperspace warning."

"Standing down. Shall I flip ship, or continue inbound?"

"Coast, Helm. We're going to coast."

"...Yes sir."

In the CSS *Challenger* simulator in a different part of the simulations building, helm looked up.

"'Captain Potemkin,' sir, I show hyperspace transition in the outer system," she reported.

"Ah. Here they come," Huber noted, calm. "Location?"

"Roughly five light-hours straight out from Natchez 5d, sir. Out near Natchez 8."

"Mm. Probably looking to see how I've set up my squadron... that I don't have," Huber decided. "Keep an eye on 'em, but we have plenty of time yet."

"Aye, sir."

"Very good," Campbell decided, casting a knowledgeable eye on the sensor readouts. "Let's drop and activate that drone we brought along."

"Drone?" the XO wondered.

"Drone," Campbell repeated.

"Drone dropped and activated, sir," helm reported. "Inbound toward system target."

"Good. Now, let's ease behind Natchez 8, so... move to eight mark zero on the target, current distance."

"Done, sir," helm noted a few minutes later. "We are hidden from Natchez 5d behind Natchez 8."

"Excellent. Hyperspace transition, please. We are aiming for one hundred twenty-two minus seventy-three on the target. One-half light-minute out."

"What the hell...?" the XO murmured.

"Trust me, Pete," Campbell replied to the murmur in an undertone. "We may or may not win this one, but I'm not pulling this out of my ass."

Cadet Peter Thomas, the *Columbia's* executive officer and an OCS student, shrugged, grinned, and went along with his crazy captain.

"They're inbound, sir," the *Challenger's* helm officer noted. "Shall I sound general quarters?"

"From that distance? It'll be a while," Huber pointed out. "Must be one of the non-Tactical cadets. Put the crew on alert, and monitor their inbound progress. Maintain patrol."

"Standard patrol?"

"The one I set up, Helm."

"...Aye, sir."

Columbia exited hyperspace very near a large comet — Comet Naatali Bingham, named for the signer of the Commonwealth Charter from Natchez — that Campbell's pre-exercise homework showed him would be there. It was inbound below the ecliptic at very nearly the maximum velocity for a comet, and was currently nearing closest approach to Natchez 5. According to Campbell's research the night before, within twelve hours, it would reach closest approach to Natchez 5... and that was precisely what he wanted.

"What the hell?!" Thomas wondered, staring at the comet on the screen.

"Excellent," Campbell declared, intensely satisfied. "It's between us and them. Helm, slide us up the ion tail toward the coma surrounding the nucleus."

"Aye, sir."

Once the *Columbia* was close enough to the nucleus to scan it, the crew realized it was a 'potato,' an irregular, multi-lobed chunk of mixed ices and rocky debris.

"Perfect," Campbell declared, pointing at the image. "Ease the *Columbia* into the niche between those two protuberances, just above the nucleus. Match velocities with the comet; we're going to ride it."

"Above, relative to the ecliptic, sir?"

"Affirmative, Helm. That way, the coma surrounds and obscures our signal, with the ionization creating a kind of natural sensor scrambler field. We're gonna ride it right on in to our target. Oh, and stand down from general quarters, but keep the crew on alert. Settle in, guys; we're here for a few hours."

"Shall I bring up a systems display, sir?"

"Please."

As the helm changed the screen view, executive officer Thomas moved to stand beside Campbell.

"No disrespect, sir, but I'm not sure this is a good plan," said Thomas. "We're playing 'tag' with a hostile by hiding right where any ship's captain with any common sense KNOWS we have to be? Captain Potemkin isn't stupid, from what I've seen of his file entry..."

"Look, Mr. Thomas," Campbell said. "Pay attention to his maneuvers. Where is he right now?"

"He's anti-sunward of the gas giant, sir. Planet 5."

"Exactly. Where did he come from?"

"Planet 4..."

"Via what route?"

"In..." Thomas slapped his forehead. "...The ecliptic plane. He's thinking exclusively in the ecliptic plane, because that's where all the planets are, when a stellar system is three-dimensional."

"Exactly. And where are we, Mr. Thomas?"

"Coming up from below the ecliptic. Riding a damn comet."

"Right. It'll never even occur to him that we're stupid enough to try it, much less do it and get it right."

"We're gonna hand him his ass." The XO shook his head. "On a platter."

"That's my plan, Mr. Thomas, that's my plan."

"Wow," one of the bridge crew of the *Challenger* murmured. "This is gonna take a while, if we have to wait for the enemy to fly in from Natchez 8. Should we, maybe, go out to meet 'em?"

"NO," Huber declared, in no uncertain terms. "That would leave the Natchez 5 system undefended. We remain here. Don't worry; they'll come to us."

"But what is their rationale for not spacing all the way to the system boundary before making transition?" the XO wondered.

"Most likely inexperience and a lack of tactical knowledge," Huber noted, unconcerned. "Remember, the class is composed of officer students in more tracks than Tactical, let alone ordinary Academy students."

One of the bridge crew — who happened to be an Academy cadet in the Intelligence track — shot Huber an angry glance.

"...Steady as she goes," Huber continued. "Whoever she is, she'll come to us."

It was fully twelve hours. At the end of that time, and given the comet's high speed for such a body, the *Columbia* was almost ten light-seconds away from their desired target — Natchez 5d.

More, as they'd tracked the *Challenger*, they noticed its patrol pattern executed periodic sweeps on both sides of the gas giant around which their true target orbited. And that pattern now brought the *Challenger* to within eight or nine light-seconds of their position.

"Sonovabitch. This is gonna work," XO Thomas murmured, and Campbell gave him a broad grin.

"Sound general quarters," Campbell ordered. "Man battle stations."

"Battle stations," XO Thomas responded seconds later. "*Columbia* ready."

"Send the signal to the drone," Campbell ordered. "Hyperspace transition to closest point, maximum acceleration into the system. Power to all shields. Come to heading zero mark five at one light-second. Maximum acceleration."

"Zero mark five at one, sir," Helm averred, as the acceleration alarm sounded.

"Firing plan C4. Guns free. Fire at will."

"Target acquired. Firing all guns," the weapons officer declared.

"CAPTAIN POTEMKIN! The ESN ship is right under us!" the helm officer cried. "She was hidden in the comet!"

"WHAT?! Come about! Bring up shields!" Huber barked the orders. "Guns fr—!"

But before his crew could respond, the simulated weapons struck the *Challenger* amidships.

The bridge screen washed red, and words in big block letters appeared:

CSS CHALLENGER DESTROYED WITH ALL HANDS

"Damn," Huber breathed.

Within fractions of a second, the simulated CSS *Challenger* 'blew up' on the viewing screens of the ESN *Columbia*.

"Set course for the target," Campbell ordered. "Come to heading one-seventy-three minus sixty-eight on Natchez 5d, seven light-seconds out. Maintain maximum acceleration. Firing plan D5. Guns free. Fire at will."

"Coming to heading one-seventy-three minus sixty-eight on Natchez 5d, sir." Helm nodded.

"Guns ready; six kinetic energy projectiles ready," the weapons officer added. "Unmanned drone just came out of hyperspace and will rendezvous with us in five; guns up."

Moments later, the ESN *Columbia* dropped half a dozen kinetic energy weapons and opened up her guns on the simulated fourth satellite of gas giant Natchez 5. The drone also targeted the manufacturing facility. Within seconds, nothing was left but a series of smouldering craters.

The main screen washed green, and a message popped up:

**CONGRATULATIONS ESN *COLUMBIA*.
MANUFACTURING FACILITIES ON NATCHEZ 5D HAVE
BEEN DESTROYED.
MISSION ACCOMPLISHED.**

"That... was a damn interesting plan," Thomas decided. "What the hell made you think of...?"

"I'm Intel," Campbell said with a grin. "Sneaky is my stock in trade."

"Never mind observation," the helm officer agreed.

"That was an interesting infiltration," Vice Admiral Colin Takala, the sims course instructor, noted to Campbell in his office in the Academy the next day. "It definitely required patience."

"Well, sir, when you're doing intelligence work, sometimes you need patience," Campbell pointed out. "I've studied tactics, certainly;

but I figured it didn't hurt to try putting my intel background to work on the thing."

"It was excellently done," Takala decided. "I'm giving you the maximum score for this midterm exam. You're at the top of the class, Mr. Campbell. We've never had an Intelligence track student achieve that before."

"Thank you, sir."

The code names for the ship captains, along with instructions to the students, were intended to prevent identification of any given student as commanding a particular ship, and all of the students rotated through the captaincy of the two simulated spacecraft. Still, when the class rankings came out, Huber suspected.

And was not happy.

The final exam simulation saw a rematch, but this time Campbell was Captain Horatio, in the CSS *Columbia*, while Huber, once more as Potemkin, was attacking Parchman in the ESN *Challenger*.

This time, *Columbia* hid in the rings of a 'tipped' gas giant and jumped *Challenger* as she flew past, taking her out.

Huber was furious.

"No, son, I'm sorry," Vice Admiral Takala told Huber in private, in his office in the Academy building. "You're a fine pilot, but you don't have what it takes to make it in a battle. We can't put you into the main Tactical track. That said, since you ARE a fine pilot, we're putting you into the shuttle fleet. I think you'll do an excellent job there."

"But sir—"

"No buts, Mr. Huber," Takala said, and his tone told Huber that there would be no further discussion, let alone appeal. "I'm sorry. I know it's disappointing for you. But the matter is closed. You'll be transferred to the shuttle pilot training track, effective tomorrow. Dismissed."

As a deeply disappointed and angry Huber headed for the pilot-training wing of the Academy to get his courses for the next semester, he overheard a group of his former classmates in a conversation as they walked between classrooms.

"Did you hear? Campbell topped the class! An Intel track student topped out the Tactical Simulations course!"

"No shit? I didn't think he was that smart."

"Oh damn! You should have been on the bridge with me when he was mopping up 'Captain Potemkin' back at midterms! No wonder the prof gave him a new code name for finals!"

"What happened in the finals?"

"I dunno; I wasn't assigned to his ship that time."

"I was," another student declared. "He went up against 'Potemkin' again."

"And?"

"He handed 'Potemkin' his ass! AGAIN! It was brilliant!"

Huber stopped dead, staring after the cluster of students.

'Campbell,' he thought. 'That damn Intel cadet from the Academy?! And HE was the one who took me out, both times? Damn.'

He continued on toward the pilots' track offices. But as he headed for the elevator, Cadet Campbell rounded the corner. Huber glared at him in anger and hate so intense, his vision temporarily washed red.

He stepped to one side, and Campbell, who was studying something on his personal electronic display unit, slammed his shoulder into Huber.

"Son of a bitch!" Huber snarled. "Watch where you're going, dammit!"

He spun on his heel and stepped into the elevator.

Campbell stared after him in surprise, as the elevator doors closed on the other student.

"What the hell was THAT about?" he wondered.

He never did figure out what caused the sudden falling-out with Huber. Not that the pair had ever really been friends, but in the few classes they had together, they had at least been on amicable terms. Now, however, every time they encountered one another, anywhere on Sigurdsen, Campbell decided that if looks could kill, he'd be dead several times over. Never mind the tendency for unexpected collisions, or elbows to the ribs, or the like. 'Bully' seemed to be the operative term, Campbell decided.

Finally Huber disappeared, and Campbell figured he'd finally graduated from OCS and been assigned... rather to his relief.

Bill Campbell was smart, and he was skilled, and he could be crafty when needed. Consequently, he did well in all of his classes, especially those required for matriculation into the Intelligence Division, and ended up by graduating in the top ten percent of his cadet class overall.

His family showed up for his graduation: his father, Dr. Peter Campbell, professor of history at the University of Jablonka, Stabljika; his mother, Dr. Martha Strahan Campbell, economics department chair at the University of Jablonka, Stabljika; and his sister, Cadet Sara Campbell, who had just finished her plebe year at the Academy, a few years behind Bill. They all sat in the stands with the rest of the families, and screamed themselves hoarse when the Superintendent pronounced the cadet class new ensigns.

Then, with Bill on leave for twenty-four hours to celebrate with his family, and Sara having received permission to attend provided she returned to her barracks by midnight — she would be going home with her parents, on leave for the summer, in two days — Peter and Martha Campbell took them both out to dinner.

Campbell was so proud he thought he might damage the fastenings of his uniform.

But two days after graduation, only hours after his parents and sister departed on the suborbital shuttle headed home, newly-minted Ensign Campbell's world fell apart.

He had already moved out of the cadet barracks and into the apartment assigned to him in the Intelligence Division housing, and was still putting away his things. He'd just opened a box of textbooks and was debating about whether to shelve them or store them, when the knock came on the door. He went to the door and hit the intercom button.

"Who is it?" he asked.

"Commander Julian W. Thompson, military police. Is this Ensign Campbell? William Campbell?"

"Yes, it is."

"May I come in?"

"Sure. Hang on while I suss how this security system works; I only just moved into the place yesterday, and I'm still figuring things out."

"No problem. Take your time."

After a moment or two, Campbell got the door unlocked and opened it, to reveal Thompson standing just outside. The military police officer stepped inside, then took the door from Campbell and closed it.

"What's wrong, Commander?"

"Son, I'm afraid I have some very bad news," Thompson noted, unhappy. "There's been an accident. The mass transit shuttle to Stabljika, Flight 298 with scheduled arrival to Stabljika at 16:47, crashed upon experiencing a failure of two out of three main engines. There... were no survivors."

"Wait," Campbell said, feeling the blood drain from his head. "That's... that was... Mom and Dad and Sara were on Flight 298! I saw 'em onto it just this morning! Sara had only just finished her plebe year!"

"I know, son," he murmured, laying a light hand on Campbell's shoulder. "They've already been identified. As the nearest of kin, you'll need to head for Stabljika as soon as possible to, ah, identify and claim the bodies — they've already identified 'em via DNA, but you still have to ID and claim them — and set up the memorial service."

"Oh, dear God," Campbell whispered, and sat down hard in the nearest chair.

First thing the next morning, Campbell sent a text to his new supervisor, Commander Ryan Byrne, in charge of case assignments in the Investigations Section of the Intelligence Division, letting him know of the disaster and of the need to return to his hometown to claim the bodies and initiate the proceedings for cremation and memorial. Moments later Byrne responded with automatic approval of bereavement leave, condolences, and encouragement.

Numb, Campbell then prepared for the day. Half an hour later, and having eschewed breakfast lest it come back up, he headed out of his brand-new apartment, en route to the commissary. There, he got several sets of black mourning sleeve bands and purchased them, immediately donning one. Then he headed back to his new quarters to begin the process of packing for an extended stay in Stabljika.

He spoke to no one.

Being military, he was given a standby seat on the next commercial shuttle to Stabljika out of Jezga, by the same company his parents had flown. Said company was extremely solicitous, and when they realized he was next-of-kin to no less than three of the fatalities in the disaster, his standby seat was immediately upgraded to high priority, first class. He was given first-boarding privileges, as the gate attendants held back all the other passengers out of respect. The silence, as he boarded, was deafening.

Given Stabljika was on the far side of Jablonka, on the western shore of the Voda Ocean, it was a several-hour ride, but Campbell said nothing, did nothing, the whole way, save stare at the bulkhead in front of him. When the flight attendants came around with refreshments, he declined everything except a bottle of water.

At last they landed at the spaceport in Stabljika. Campbell grabbed his small duffel out of the overhead stowage, then, while the flight attendants explained the situation to the rest of the passengers, who remained seated, he was allowed to be the first to debark the shuttle. Again, the silence was so loud to the young ensign's ears, it was painful. He made his way to the hatch and exited as swiftly as he decently could without bolting.

At the gate, a woman stood holding a sign: CAMPBELL. He drew a deep breath and headed straight for her.

At the morgue, the woman representing the shuttle company, Anna Gann, took care of the bureaucratic matters, then stepped back, remaining in the waiting room. Soon Dr. Philips, the coroner, was taking Bill back to a special holding area where the victims of the crash were being kept, pending claim by next of kin. Philips scanned down the display on his electronic display unit, then headed for the body drawers in the corner, mentally counting off the drawers, if the slight gestures of his index finger were anything to go by. Finally he stopped in front of three drawers, stacked vertically.

"Here we are," he said. "Campbell family. Two adults, one male, one female, and one pre-adult female?"

"That's correct," Campbell choked out in a hoarse voice. "My parents and my sister."

"Right. Okay, we just need to make a positive ID, you can sign some paperwork, and then we'll release 'em to the crematorium. It's up to you to make arrangements for a memorial service, unless they had something already set up."

"They did," Campbell averred, still badly hoarse. "I guess I just need to set it in motion. And add Sara into it."

"All right, son," Philips said, gentling his voice. "Hang in there. This won't be as bad as you think."

He opened the bottom drawer and pulled back a cover which had been fastened down with hook-and-loop material, exposing the face of an older man. He had a full head of brown hair, though it was rather salt-and-pepper. The jawline was strong, the nose straight, forehead high, brow high. The body beneath the cover was recognizably humanoid, though the odd contours indicated the extent of the injuries.

"Dad," Campbell choked. "Um, Peter Campbell. Dr. Peter Campbell. He taught history at the University of Jablonka, Stabljika."

"U.J.S. professor of history. Got it," Philips said, annotating his electronic display unit.

"Do they know what caused it, yet? The accident?" Campbell ground out.

"Unfortunately, yes," Philips said. "Poor maintenance. I did hear that the tech involved was rather fond of his drink, and that likely contributed. He's in a world of trouble, and his job is gone. He may get charged with multiple counts of death due to willful negligence or the like. Which, if convicted, means he won't be doing much for a long time... except maybe breaking rocks." He shrugged. "I know it's no help to hear it, but it was just damn bad luck of the draw for your family."

"Cause of death?" Campbell managed to force the question through his lips. He didn't really want to know, but he had to know.

"Oh. Blunt-force trauma. No external ruptures; all the injuries were internal, but there were plenty of 'em. That's... pretty usual in a crash like this, unless there's fire."

"No fire?"

"No. Not on this one. It just... dropped out of the sky, when two of the three prop units failed while carrying a full load, from what I was told."

"Damn."

"Yeah."

'So they knew what was coming, the whole way down,' Campbell thought, sick at heart, as the coroner covered his father's head, closed the drawer and pulled open the next one above it before jerking down the top of the cover to expose an older female face. It was heart-shaped, with delicate features and what was once called dishwater-blonde hair and brows, lightly tanned, and the beginnings of frown lines on the forehead. Like her husband's, the body hidden beneath the covering was humanoid, but distorted, mute testament to the force of the crash.

"Mom," he managed to rasp out, then choked again. Philips pulled a chilled bottle of water out of a pocket of his lab coat and gave it to the younger man; Campbell promptly opened it and took a sip, trying to relax and moisten his throat. It didn't seem to help a lot. Finally he elaborated, "Um. Dr. Martha Strahan Campbell. Also a professor at U.J.S., but in the economics department. In fact, she was the department chair."

"Mm-hm," Philips said, annotating his records on the electronic display unit again. He covered the face, sealed the hook-and-loop fasteners, and closed the drawer. "All right, son, this next one isn't quite as pretty, I'm afraid."

"Oh no," Campbell murmured, his heart sinking.

"Are you going to be okay?"

"Do I have a choice?" Campbell asked, bitter.

"Well... no, not really, I don't guess," Philips admitted, rueful. "But we can take a break if you need to."

"No. Let's... let's just get this over with."

"Okay. Hang in there. This last one... well, the blunt force DID cause external rupture."

He opened the top drawer and pulled back the covering, and Campbell gasped.

The young woman inside was essentially a younger version of her mother, with delicate, heart-shaped face and medium blonde hair, though her tan was somewhat darker. But the side of the head was flattened above the ear, and the smooth, unlined brow was grotesquely deformed by a hideous split that ran from the flattened part of the skull, down almost to the bridge of the nose. Not only was the flesh laid open, but the skull was cracked as well, exposing brain tissue. Blood had trickled down her face for a time before her heart had finally realized she was dead, and the rivulets had stained the skin a dull reddish-brown.

Campbell let out a cry of anguish, and turned away, then started to gag. Philips quickly closed the drawer, not bothering to replace the cover for the moment — that could be done later — and grabbed the nearest open waste receptacle, thrusting it under the distressed ensign's face.

Nothing came up, likely thanks to the fact that Campbell hadn't eaten since dinner the previous night — which had been before Commander Thompson had arrived — and Philips led him out of the holding chamber to his personal office in the morgue facility. There, he pushed Campbell into a chair, then eased his head down between his knees. Philips fished the water bottle out of the cargo pocket of Campbell's shipsuit, then fetched a straw from someplace, shoving it into the opening, before kneeling beside the chair and holding it under Campbell's face.

"Here," he ordered, "drink. Slowly. There's a reason I ensured it was chilled."

So Campbell sipped the water gingerly, allowing a few small swallows to trickle down his throat, then waiting to see if it would stay put. When it did, he sipped a bit more.

"There," Philips said. "That's good, good. Slowly, now. Good. So... that was your sister?"

Campbell nodded.

"Sara," he said. "She was seventeen; would have turned eighteen in a couple-three months. She had just finished her first year at the Academy."

"Which, by the look, you just graduated from," Philips said, and Campbell nodded again. "You're... what? Nineteen? Twenty?"

"Turned twenty about four months ago," he said. "They were on their way home from my graduation. She was going home on summer leave with Mom and Dad."

"Aw, damn," the coroner said, sympathetic. "I'm so sorry, son. Do you have any other family close?"

"A few cousins, most of whom I've never met, because they're on other planets in the Commonwealth," Campbell noted. "Frankly, I probably wouldn't recognize them from a fence post. Nor them, me."

"So you're alone now."

He shrugged.

"I'm in the CSF," he noted. "They're my family now. I'll manage."

"I assume they left a will, and instructions for how to handle disposition of their bodies and effects?"

"Mom and Dad did, yeah," Campbell murmured. "I guess I'll just see if I can extend all that to Sara, and take care of it all at once."

"All right. When you're a little better, here, I'll need you to sign some release forms, so I can send them to the crematorium. You'll have to talk to the crematorium staff about what to do with the ashes. They have a nice selection of urns, if you want to keep the ashes. Or you can go out to sea and pour out their ashes, or put the urns in a memorial garden..."

"Yeah," was all Campbell said. After a few more moments, he eased back to an upright position in the chair, and took the water bottle from Philips, continuing to sip. Philips rocked back on his heels and watched in silence for long minutes. Finally Campbell focused on him.

"Let me see those release forms now," was all he said.

A few days later, Campbell found himself in a memorial service in the chapel of his parents' worship center. A table in front of the minister contained three small urns, and he pondered them while the minister read words of comfort that he could not, in those moments, hear. Instead, in deep pain, he wondered how such rich, full lives, such strong active bodies, could be condensed down to such small containers.

At last the service was over, and he rose and moved to the table in front, thinking he might take the urns and quietly head back to the house in which he had grown up, but the service's attendees had other plans.

"Oh, sweetheart!" a plump, motherly woman he only half-recognized exclaimed, coming up and hugging him tight. He stiffened, as a receiving line promptly formed behind her. "I'm so sorry, Bill! Martha was my closest friend! I don't know what we're going to do without her and Peter, and young Sara! But you call me if you need anything now, you hear?"

Campbell pasted on a smile that didn't reach his eyes, and nodded, wondering how he was supposed to call someone whose name he couldn't even recall.

It went on like that for over an hour, with an entire church full of his parents' "best friends," while Campbell desperately wished someone would rescue him and let him slip out a side door... but no one did.

Finally, as the line dwindled, he looked up from the latest middle-aged-stranger-woman hug... and froze.

Instantly he jumped to attention, saluting the figure in top-brass uniform who now stood before him.

"Rear Admiral Durand, sir! What are you doing here?! I didn't— I mean, I hadn't..."

"At ease, Ensign," Durand murmured with a smile. "I'm sorry I didn't manage to get closer to the front of that receiving line; I'd have rescued you from the perils of overly-motherly women you don't know. But my shuttle got delayed by a storm coming into Jezgra, so I got here late and had to sit in the back."

"I'm sorry, sir," Campbell tried again, having moved into the 'at ease' position, though his body and mind were anything but. "If I'd known you were coming, I'd have reserved..."

"Stop that," he said, voice soft. "I had something I needed to do for Academy Superintendent Walters, in any case. I was supposed to see this all done with military honors, but the weather put paid to that, and I'm betting it was a little easier on you, that way. So. This came down from on high. Which one is Sara Campbell? Oh wait; I see the names on the urns." He leaned over and placed a single gold bar on the urn marked 'CSF Academy Cadet Sara Campbell.'

"She... they made her an...?" Bill Campbell tried.

"Yes, son. They posthumously made her an ensign. Congratulations; there are now two of you in the family." He laid a light hand on Campbell's shoulder. "We'll have the plaque changed to read, 'Ens. Sara Campbell, CSF.' And I'll see that the cost of the change gets handled."

Campbell blinked several times, then dropped his gaze. Finally he choked out, "Thank you, sir. Thank ev—" It was as far as he could get. Durand nodded, understanding.

"I'll take care of passing that on to the right people," he maintained, glancing back at the dozen or so people left in line. Then he lowered his voice. "I'm betting you want to get out of here, the worst way."

"Oh boy, do I."

"Do you have a vehicle here?"

"No sir. My parents have — uh, they had one, but I can't find the starter fob. I'm betting Dad had it on him when the shuttle went down, but it wasn't in his effects. The luggage is so much trash. So I guess I'll have to have one made. Not that I have any reason to keep it, I suppose."

"Ensign," Durand said, raising his voice, "please gather up your family's remains and attend me." The remaining people in line stirred, startled, and began to murmur.

"Um, but sir," the minister began; he had been presiding over the receiving line with a beatific smile. "There are more in lin—"

"Padre," Durand addressed the minister, "are you seriously trying to tell me that I cannot give my ensign an order, when I require his attention elsewhere?"

"Well, no sir, but..."

"Good. Ensign Campbell, I need you to come with me. Get your family's remains and attend. That IS an order, Ensign."

"Yes sir!"

In short order, the minister had helped Campbell gather the three small but fairly substantial urns into a specially-provided carrier, and Campbell trailed behind an imperious Rear Admiral Jake Durand as he headed out of the chapel into the sunshine.

But somewhat to Campbell's surprise, instead of seeing him into the front seat with the driver, Durand had the young ensign sit with him in the rear seat.

"Um, sir..."

"Stop that, son," Durand said then, holding up a hand. "I understand. This is NOT an official visit, so relax. I'm guessing you don't much remember me from your childhood; I WAS out and about on various assignments a lot, in those days. Not to mention offworld a good bit of the time."

"Uh..." Campbell thought back to his childhood, and suddenly a memory of a sunny summer day with lemonade and ice cream, and a tall man in a uniform who smiled a lot and slapped his father on the back, kissing his mother on the cheek, floated to the fore. "Oh!"

"That did it, eh?" Durand chuckled. "No, I'm not here because you're Ensign Campbell, Bill; I'm here because your parents were dear friends of mine, and I wanted to pay my last respects. Given that, and since the school year just wound down and he's still trying to dig out from under, Bill Walters, the Academy's superintendent, asked me to handle your sister's... promotion, or he'd have been here, too... and that WOULD have been official."

"Oh. Um. Well, no offense, and please don't tell Admiral Walters, but..."

"You're just as glad it worked out the way it did?"

"You didn't hear me say that, sir."

Durand chuckled, wry.

"Didn't hear a thing, son. Listen, I don't know if your parents ever told you, but the Durands and the Campbells have known each other ever since there was a colony on Jablonka; our forebears were among the First Colonists, and came to Jablonka on the same ship."

"Oh wow," Campbell murmured, surprised. "I remember Mom and Dad saying something about First Colonists in the genealogy, but..."

"Well, when they realized you wanted to go into service, I expect they quieted down about it. They knew I was an up-and-coming officer, likely to be in a position of authority over you at some point, and they didn't want to risk accusations of nepotism or the like. Which is also why I've kept my distance and not tried to pull any strings for you. You deserve to find your own way, and to get there by the sweat of your own brow. That's the honest and honorable way to do it, and I didn't want to do anything that would ever risk tainting that for you."

"Thank you, sir. But the class at the Academy..."

"I was already in the rotation to teach it," Durand explained. "And I treated you like any of the other cadets. You never even recognized me."

"...No sir. Well, I knew who you were, and that Mom and Dad knew you, just... not that you were such a close friend of the family."

"All right. Glad to be out of the chapel?"

"Immensely, sir."

"Terrific. Now, the rest of this visit is completely off the record. Did you hear that, Sam?"

"Hear what, sir?" the driver said, glancing into the rear-view mirror with a wicked smirk.

"Good man. So. Bill... have you been staying in the family home while you've been here?"

"Yes sir. I didn't really have anywhere else TO stay in Stabljika, unless I went to a hotel, and that just seemed stupid."

"No doubt. But has it been a pleasant experience, or is the house filled with too many ghosts?"

Campbell considered that for a bit.

"Too many ghosts, sir. Too many memories. I mean, they're all GOOD memories, but..."

"It's too damn painful right now."

"Yes sir."

"Then may I offer an invitation?"

Campbell blinked.

"What, sir?"

"I'll be staying with my kid brother Ted and his wife Diane," Durand explained. "They have the family house, since I went into the service. But they knew your parents, too — they'd have been at the memorial with me, except the baby had a doctor's appointment, and the older kid had a ball game — and when I discussed it with them, they told me that you were welcome to come back with me and spend the rest of the time with them. You don't have to stay in your parents' house if you need some emotional distance."

"I... don't know what to say..."

"Don't say anything. Think about it for a few minutes, and let me know. We can drop you off at your parents' house, or we can simply swing by and let you grab your things, then head for Ted's place."

Campbell did as Durand had recommended, pondering in silence until Sam the driver pulled up in front of the venerable Campbell house on the edge of the city, which still overlooked the surrounding countryside even after all these years, thanks to certain ordinances regarding expansion and zoning. Campbell looked up, to see Durand watching him, expectant.

"Let me go in and gather up my things," Campbell decided. "I'll only be a few minutes."

"We'll wait, son," Durand declared.

In the end, it proved a useful connection, as Theodore Durand offered to function as Campbell's agent in Stabljika.

"Because it's going to take you a while to sort through all their possessions and such like, and figure out what to keep and what to sell," Ted Durand pointed out. "And it gives you time to figure out what to do about the house, too."

"Well, I don't need it," Campbell noted. "Not as a career CSF officer. But I hate to see it go out of the family... it's the original colony house, just with a few add-ons and updates..." He paused. "But I guess you already know that."

"We do. YOU might not know it, but Diane and I keep up with some of your aunts, uncles, and cousins," the younger Durand brother revealed. "I do happen to know that one of your cousins was looking to move his family back to Jablonka, but wanted to live here in, or at least around, Stabljika, only..."

"Only the zoning ordinances were probably making it difficult to find a place," Campbell realized. "And if they move into the property, it's taken care of, it stays in the family..."

"Exactly," Theodore Durand agreed, as the admiral watched in approval from across the room. "I think it would be a win-win, frankly. They have the money to buy a place, they just didn't have a place to buy. And that nets you some money for the future."

"I think maybe we have a plan," Campbell decided.

In the end, Campbell simply told the younger Durand brother what items he wanted to keep, and Ted Durand offered to handle the sales, sorting out the items on Campbell's list and either shipping it to him, or keeping it in storage until he wanted it.

"And that ought to take care of things pretty quickly," Admiral Durand noted, "because Ted's never been one to let the grass grow. I'd say the whole matter will be taken care of within a month or two, especially if his kids and your cousins help."

"And they will," Ted Durand averred. "So we got this, Bill. You can go on back to Jezgra with Jake if you want to."

"Well, it would probably look better if he went back commercial, rather than coming back with me on my personal shuttle," the Admiral pointed out.

"I don't have a problem with that," Campbell noted. "The shuttle company treated me really nice on the way over, I guess maybe because they were afraid of lawsuits or something. Or maybe they're actually just decent people, and something bad happened. I dunno. I guess how I get treated on the way back will determine which one of those they are."

"Heh," Jake Durand chuckled. "Smart young man."

"Savvy, too," Ted Durand agreed.

It turned out to be a little of both. Campbell got placed on standby again, because he was military and needed transport, and the first shuttle for which he was in the standby line was full, but the second one was not. More, the gate crew recognized him, and made sure to upgrade his seat.

He didn't get to board first, but frankly, that was something of a relief; he hadn't liked all the attention, especially in the circumstances and given his deep grief.

So he slipped on board, stowed his duffel, and settled in for the trip back to Jezgra.

Upon arriving back on base, he went straight to his quarters and resumed unpacking and moving in more properly, and the next morning, though still wearing the mourning arm band, he reported in to Commander Byrne to begin duty as an ensign in the Intelligence Division.

His career in the CSF had commenced.

Recent History

Three years later found William Campbell still an ensign, but coming up on his time-in-grade promotion to lieutenant. He was still not on the active roll of investigators, rather to his disappointment, though he said little about the matter. That did not mean, however, that his abilities were not being put to good use.

Campbell entered full immersive VR and opened the recording of the relatively recent Battle of Saarestik. The recording had been made from consolidating all the sensor data of the surviving ships... which, in this instance, included perimeter system sensors and other ships in the system within sensor range, since only one ship, the CSS *Nils Isaacson* defending the system, survived the battle.

He had yet to be assigned his first investigative case, even though he was part of the Counter-Intelligence Investigations section, even despite the fact that he had assisted several experienced investigators on nearly a dozen cases, as well as assessed some two dozen 'situations' — battles or fights of various sorts — and reported his conclusions on them. At this point, he wasn't entirely sure if the lack of case work was why he had yet to be promoted, or if the lack of promotion was why he'd not been given solo case work. 'Or a little of both,' he thought. 'Like that old Earth book, *Catch-22*. Damned if you do, damned if you don't.'

His latest assignment — which was still not a case, as such, but was needful, just the same, and by now his higher-ups knew he had a certain skill with it — was to study the details of the battle and see if he could ascertain which of the Outer Colonies had attacked; given none of the attacking ships survived the battle, this was an important bit of information that was lacking in the current analysis. So he was in the Class 1 secure facility in the basement of the Intelligence building, fully tied into the event. A few quick commands brought up a three-dimensional view of the system, centered on the Saarestik system's sun, facing the incursion's most probable target, Saarestik 4b.

He zoomed in on the only ship in the area, the *Nils Isaacson*, and watched for several moments as it maintained its standard cruising pattern, outside Saarestik's orbit and above the plane of the ecliptic. At his command, a small countdown clock popped up in his peripheral vision, counting down to the first appearance of the enemy spacecraft. As the clock neared zero, he zoomed out his view to take in the entire pertinent sector of the stellar system.

Then he watched as two unidentified spacecraft dropped into the system from hyperspace. The smaller of the two, a destroyer, remained near the hyperspace transition, while the larger, a light cruiser, headed in at high acceleration, its trajectory aiming for Saarestik 4, a gas giant... which meant its most likely target was the mining operation on the rocky satellite designated 4b.

'Which,' he thought, 'is just what Senior Tac Officer Childers decided, too. Except I can see it from an overhead view — it's making a beeline, orbital-mechanics-wise — and she was in the middle of things, where it can be harder to see.' He paused, pondering. 'I'd heard she was a brilliant tactician. Based on what I'm seeing, I think I'd have to agree.'

Thirty minutes later, which was how long it took the periphery sensors to relay the data, the *Nils Isaacson* powered up, maneuvered into position, and jumped into hyperspace.

Moments later, the enemy light cruiser killed its normal space drive, turned one hundred-eighty degrees, then reinitiated the normal space drive, and began to slow its progress toward Saarestik 4. Meanwhile, the destroyer that maintained stationkeeping near the original incursion point powered up.

'They saw the *Nils Isaacson* transition to hyperspace,' Campbell realized. 'So the *Nils Isaacson* is going to come out too far away, probably planet-side, though they wouldn't have been if the light cruiser had stayed on course...'

...Which was precisely what happened.

But the *Nils Isaacson* stayed in position only long enough to register what had happened before dropping back into hyperspace. Seconds later, she popped out of hyperspace directly behind the light cruiser well less than two million miles behind it, outside the light cruiser's beam range but inside the *Nils Isaacson*'s, and fired two salvos of all weapons. The light cruiser broke apart, and seconds later, its power plant blew up.

Almost immediately the destroyer dropped into hyperspace, and moments later, three heavy cruisers transitioned to normal space. But before they could react, the *Nils Isaacson* hypered out. Instantly the three heavy cruisers set up a defensive posture to their rear, and Campbell thought he noticed slight movement in two of the three ships.

Seconds later, and before the enemy craft could more than begin their maneuver, the *Nils Isaacson* transitioned back to normal space, amidships to port, and some forty-five degrees above. The *Nils Isaacson* promptly opened fire, and all three heavy cruisers broke apart, then blew up as their power plants exploded.

'Damn,' Campbell thought, 'I know the captain's calling the orders, but those orders are on Childers' recommendations and book tactics. One ship is mopping up an entire squadron. She IS brilliant. I'd love to meet her one of these days and discuss tactics with her.'

Straight off, *Nils Isaacson* dropped back into hyperspace, and Campbell watched as the ship's own data tracked it through the system to a point near, but slightly outsystem from, the point where the destroyer had transitioned to fetch help. It entered stationkeeping mode and waited for several minutes.

Abruptly, the destroyer, apparently concerned at the lack of comm with its compatriots, transitioned into normal space.

'Shit,' Campbell thought in disgust, 'you didn't even have the sense to change location before dropping out of hyper? Your C.O. was a genius, huh?'

The *Nils Isaacson* was on the enemy destroyer before it knew anything was wrong, and the destroyer became a rapidly-expanding cloud of debris.

Nils Isaacson transitioned into hyperspace, headed leisurely back to their original position, to continue patrols.

'Heh,' Campbell chuckled to himself. 'Yeah, no doubt about it — I'd love to meet this Childers. I need to look up and see what her rank is now; if that didn't garner her a promotion, I'd be surprised.'

'Hm,' Campbell thought then, 'let's go back and have a closer look at those three heavy cruisers, just before the *Nils Isaacson* took 'em out, so I can see what that was all about. I could have sworn they were maneuvering into a particular defensive perimeter. Not that it would have done them much good, if it's what I think; they just didn't have enough ships to do it, and do it right. But I might be wrong; they might have just been jockeying for sensor views, trying to spot the *Nils Isaacson* when it dropped out of hyperspace...'

He shifted the timestamp and zoomed in on the trio, then initiated the scenario at 1/10th speed, from the point where the *Nils Isaacson* hypered out, until it hypered back in, and noted that the three heavy cruisers were indeed maneuvering, though they did not have time to make it far before being destroyed, so swift had been the attack by the *Nils Isaacson*.

Campbell promptly ordered the VR computer to extrapolate motion based on the existing time segment, then extend it by sixty seconds. He watched as the three ships slowly shifted into a Y-shape, sterns toward a common center, bows out but separated by some 120° — a circular perimeter, forming a broken toroid of shielding and weapons angles.

'Not that it would have done 'em any good,' Campbell concluded what he had only suspected earlier. '*Nils Isaacson* came in above and amidships, and that maneuver wasn't going to help protect 'em that much, unless she'd come in directly in line with them... which was evidently what they expected. Still, I recognize that tactic. It needed at least a couple more ships to take it three-dimensional and be effective, ships they didn't have... but it was definitely a Kalakis maneuver.'

Admiral Kalakis was one of the better-known naval tacticians in the Outer Colonies, and hailed from Epsley... which meant it behooved Campbell to look for other signs of Epsley involvement.

'Like the debris,' he decided. 'If I can spot certain pieces-parts in the debris field, that'll be a dead giveaway... so to speak.'

But the debris itself didn't tell him much, no matter how close he zoomed; the pieces were too small, and the observing platforms too far away, for the resolution he needed to see pertinent details.

So instead, he backed out to a distance, then ordered the computer to play each explosion in sequence, while he watched.

That was when he realized that, when each power plant detonated, it generated a specific asymmetry in the 'shock wave' of vaporized material.

And that asymmetry, he recognized.

'Epsley,' he determined. 'That's typical of their overstressed ship power plants; they build 'em that way to help counterweight the drive on the other side. I have no clue why they think they need to build the damn things like that, but it's telltale.'

But it was still insufficient; other Outer Colony planets had access to Epsley-drive spacecraft, both legally and illegally, and might use a small force such as this to decoy suspicion onto another planet.

'Due diligence time,' he decided.

So the next thing Campbell did was to pull up the stats on the mining operations on Saarestik 4b. He found that in addition to copper and nickel, which the mining operations produced in quantity, Saarestik 4b was one of the richest sources of the platinum group of metals, most of which were used by spacefaring planets in quantity.

A quick double-check indicated that, of all the Outer Colonies, the Epsley and Melody systems were the primary sources of platinum-group mining... though neither produced it in the quantities that Saarestik 4b was able to produce.

'No wonder they wanted to take out the mining operation,' Campbell realized. 'It would make their metals production nearly twice as lucrative, if the Saarestik 4b operation was shut down.'

But there was one last step needed to determine whether the culprit was Epsley or Melody.

So Campbell pulled up a special database in the VR computer. All Commonwealth-flagged merchant ships that traded with Outer Colony enterprises echoed their sensor readings once they got back to CFP space, downloading everything they picked up while in Outer Colony systems into a common database on Jablonka. This database was scanned regularly for intelligence information, and was open — within certain classification schemes — to the Intelligence and Tactical Divisions alike. And for this assignment, Campbell had been given the maximum classification access. So he dug into it, searching for the last six months of data from the Melody and Epsley systems.

The Melody system data showed nothing off-nominal. Everything that was supposed to be there was there; nothing that was NOT supposed to be there was there, and nothing was missing that should be there.

The Epsley system, however, seemed to be missing some fleet patrols.

'Around half a dozen ships down, by my estimate,' Campbell decided, digging back into the database until he predated the Saarestik battle by a good six months. 'And there it is. Five ships gone permanently missing, along about a month, maybe a month and a half, before the *Nils Isaacson* encountered the interlopers in the Saarestik system. Just enough time to hyper between systems, then get wiped out by defenders as they attempted a less-than-strategic attack. Let's see if I can nail identities.'

In the end, he was only able to identify four of the five ships — three heavy cruisers, the *Hard Core*, the *Hard Times*, and the *Hard Knocks*, and one light cruiser, the *Hard Drive*. He could find nothing definitive on the destroyer, save an indication that at least one destroyer was missing. The light cruiser had just been replaced from their shipyards only a month or so prior to Campbell's analysis, and had been christened the *Hard Drive II*. Two more heavy cruisers were in work, and one had been delivered, the *Hard Core II*.

'Not that imaginative on naming,' he thought. 'Though I suppose it's difficult to come up with good themed names like that. But it sure as hell helps me out.'

Campbell used the VR system to write his report, effectively dictating it into the system, and laying out his reasoning and support for his deductions, then adding a recommendation to look for any of Rear Admiral Betty Cintra's staffers who originated on Epsley and ascertain their loyalties; there had to be a source of intel going between Saarestik and Epsley, and a planted mole on Saarestik was the most likely.

Then he applied the appropriate classification to the white paper, addressed it to his entire chain of command up through Rear Admiral Jacob Durand, and initiated classified transfer, adding quite a few security bells and whistles to protect the document from eyes that did not have a need to know.

Campbell closed the VR connection.

What The Hell Is This Game?

Captain Mary Rao was the planetary senior tactical officer for Sigurdsen Fleet Base on the Commonwealth planetary capital of Jablonka, just outside the capital city of Jezgra. She had been given the captain's silver eagle just one year before, and had been in the position of tactical officer for a scant seven months.

That said, she was good, and she knew her job.

When she could stay at it.

For a little over two months now, Rao had become increasingly ill, with all the signs of severe migraines — intense head pain, nausea, vomiting, blurred vision, lightheadedness, sensitivity to light, and more. She also tended to have itchy, watery eyes and irritated, red and angry skin, which was odd, since she had always had good, clear skin until then. When the migraines had begun, she had gone to see her personal physician, Dr. Harold Rathman, who had examined her thoroughly — to include the latest versions of MRI and CT scan — and found none of the expected migraine causes; her neurochemistry had not changed, she had had no head injuries, and the migraines occurred at all phases of her cycle, eliminating a hormonal influence as a trigger. Nor had her diet changed, nor any other part of her daily routine — she had picked up a new brand of makeup, she explained, but when the illness had begun, she had even put that away... not that it seemed to make a difference. So it was, he concluded, unlikely to be a true migraine, and no morbid pathologies presented.

"So, while I know it's not fun, I doubt it's anything serious," he had told her. "Sooner or later, this will all clear up."

Still, he gave her a prescription for Toclan for the nausea, and Amatrex for the pain, and sent her home to rest. Rao had followed the instructions for both medications religiously, but so far, had seen little sign that they helped. Instead, she had found ways to continue her work, thankful for the staff she had been assigned, who were knowledgeable and skilled, and who grasped that their superior was ill and trying to find the cause, and picked up the slack when she could not.

Finally, in desperation, she had given up trying to maintain a normal life outside work, and simply went straight home at the end of her shift and collapsed in bed, occasionally taking sick leave to extend the time she rested in bed. This, more than anything else, seemed to help — the longer she rested and hydrated at home, the better she felt. Weekends were especially good for this, and by Sunday, she was usually beginning to feel like her old self again.

But that particular Monday morning, fully nine weeks into the malady and well before lunch, Rao found herself in the necessary, leaning over the toilet, throwing up again. It was the worst such bout yet.

'This can't possibly be right,' she thought in dismay. 'I don't care what Dr. Rathman says! Something must be seriously wrong with me! I was getting well, I swear I was. I did fine over the weekend...'

She broke off the thought, eyes widening, as realization struck.

'...When I was away from my office.'

She thought hard. 'Never mind when it started LAST month... or the month before, I forget; I've been getting sicker for at least the last three weeks, maybe four,' she reckoned. 'That first Thursday, and then Friday was pretty bad... then I felt okay until the next Wednesday, and was sick all the way through until Saturday morning. But I had to work all that overtime anyway, for the emergency drill. By Saturday night, with some rest at home, I felt a lot better. Then I got sick again that next Tuesday afternoon, stayed home Wednesday, felt better, came back Thursday and got sick but had to work through Friday quitting time.

'And then I went straight home from there, got in bed, and didn't get out until Saturday lunch, when I felt much better. Ate well, had no problems with digestion or these damned migraines, and did great...

'...Until I came into the office today. And I haven't been in the office two hours yet, and I'm already throwing up into the toilet, and my head is just about splitting open. This isn't ME! There has to be something wrong with my office. Maybe something I'm badly allergic to? Oh! I wonder if I have 'sick office syndrome'? Well, I know how to find out about that, either way.'

She retched for several more moments, purging the last of her breakfast, then flushed the toilet as she pulled her personal comm unit from a pocket. She hit a number in the memory, then held it to her aching head.

"Rosalind? Rose, this is Mary. Is there any chance I can meet you for coffee at some point this afternoon? No, no, not my office, I don't think. No, it INVOLVES my office. I think I have a 'sick building' syndrome going on here, and I've been sick as a dog, and it's getting worse. I need to get OUT of my office for a while, and I need to tell you about it, then maybe bring you over here to see what's up. Can I come over to YOUR office? Oh? Wow. Yeah, that'll be great. No, chamomile for me; yeah, I'm in the necessary right now. Yeah, nausea, vomiting, migraine, the works. I've even got some skin and eye irritation, so I'm probably allergic to whatever it is; my eyes look like two fried eggs in a puke bucket, and my hands itch like a sumbitch; it's all I can do not to scratch 'em raw. No, Dr. Rathman has me on an antihistamine AND a steroid, PLUS a topical. Nope, not helping a bit. No, not then; there's an all-hands meeting with Vice Admiral Takala, and... oh really? Well, yeah, you have a point. All right. Look," she hurried through the response, as her stomach lurched again, "lemme tell you when I see you, okay? I'm — ugh — not done here, I don't think." She paused and listened, clearing her throat quietly against the bile trying to rise up in it. "No, that'll be fine. I'll be there. Later, ho-ugh!" she said, disconnecting the call as her belly purged again.

"Oh, wow, girl," Commander Rosalind Ramirez said from the comfort of a cozy chair at a corner table in her favorite tea room off-base, as Rao finished her explanations, even laying out the timeframes on her electronic display unit's calendar app. Ramirez was one of the ranking officers in the Facilities Division; she was specifically in charge of a significant portion of the Base Housekeeping Department, and more, she was a childhood friend of Rao's, which meant Rao felt safe discussing the matter with her, knowing she wouldn't be viewed as off the beam, or a hypochondriac. "Yeah, that sure sounds like sick building syndrome, all right. Now I understand why you needed to talk with me right away. You're sick, and getting sicker with every moment you spend in there."

"That's what it looks like to me, too, Rose," Rao averred. "I only just figured out the correlations this morning, and called you immediately. If you can check it out and find out what's wrong, then we can do whatever we need to do to correct the problem, and it would be great. I have an important job here, and I don't want to drop the ball because my office is making me sick. As it is, my team is off at a meeting with some brass, because I was too sick to go. I didn't tell them I was meeting you, as well."

"Not a problem, Mar'," Ramirez agreed immediately. "And if anything comes up, if anybody tries to get you in trouble, you call me; I know how to handle it, and it'll all be fine. That's really one of the main thrusts of my job, making sure that our facilities are suitably healthy for our personnel, and nobody gets nailed — in ANY fashion — for health problems due to facility issues. Is that helping any?" She waved at the cup of chamomile- mint tea blend from which the other woman sipped.

"Maybe a little," Rao said with a slight shrug. "I mean, it's staying put, at least. What-all is in here? I mean, I taste the chamomile I asked for, and maybe some mint... but there's other stuff, too..."

"Well, there's chamomile, like you suggested," Ramirez noted. "I think there's a couple different kinds of mint in there, yeah, and maybe some other stuff, like valerian... but I don't know for sure. It's a special blend the proprietress makes for people who need settling, whether their nerves or their bellies, she says it works as well for both. Then she adds a bit of honey for sweetening and a few calories, especially if the person has been barfing, like you have. If they're really REALLY sick, she adds just a smidge of cane sugar 'cause it helps calm nausea, but that's hard to get hold of, any more. It doesn't seem to grow well off Earth, which means exports..."

"Oh, okay, I get it. And yes, I think it's helping a little bit. The truth of the matter is, though, just getting away from the building helped more than anything, I think. It's almost like, like my whole body relaxed, as soon as I stepped outside into the fresh air and took a deep breath. I'm glad you had the idea of walking off base to this little tea shop. It's nice, and I think the walk helped me clear whatever gunk I got into at the office, judging by the way it felt." She shrugged again. "At least for the time being."

"It did you that much good, huh?"

"Oh yeah. I was kinda wobbly during the walk, especially the last couple blocks. But I swear, Rose, it felt like someone was sweeping out my insides. Lungs, eyes, nose, gut, everything."

"Hm. Okay. Do you think you could maybe handle a little toast? Or a scrambled egg?"

"I doubt the shop's owner would care for such a small order, Rose. And they're not on the menu."

"She won't mind," Ramirez said, waving at the older woman behind the counter and giving her a thumbs-up; the woman nodded purposefully and immediately ducked into the kitchen. "She's a friend, too. She used to be one of my people before she retired and bought this shop — well, not MINE; she was my superior before she retired. Anyway, I called ahead and explained the sitch. It sounded like you've been barfing your guts out most of the day, especially when you hung up on me mid-ralph, and we need to get some nourishment back into you, so you can go back with me and show me around, never mind giving your authority for me to sweep your office area." Ramirez raised an eyebrow. "What I DON'T want is you giving out on me, halfway back across the base, because you don't have any fuel in you, and collapsing on the sidewalk. You already said you got wobbly on the way here. And I didn't think to bring my ground car."

"All right," Rao agreed with a sigh. "I guess you're right. I'll try. I do feel a little better at the moment."

"There's my old poppet."

"I know they haven't started assigning investigations to you yet, Bill," Ensign Lily Martell of the Maintenance Division, one of their up and coming 'grease monkeys' for troubleshooting shuttles, and the go-to person when a mystifying problem came up, said to Ensign William Campbell, her significant other of only a couple of month's standing.

He sometimes found it interesting that he'd picked a shuttle mechanic for a girlfriend, especially in light of his family's deaths. He also sometimes wondered, had Lily been the maintenance worker on their shuttle, if they might still be alive. Campbell threw a surreptitious glance at three small urns on a nearby bookshelf.

"...But let's face it, you're smart, baby," Martell continued, startling him out of his train of thought. "When they do, you're gonna get ALL the hard cases! What if something happens? What if you have to, I dunno, go undercover? You could get killed! How will I ever know what happened to you?" she asked, as she snuggled in his lap on the sofa of his apartment.

"Calm down, Lily," Campbell told her. "You've been reading too many spy novels, honey. It doesn't really work like that. Oh, I suppose it COULD, if something screwy went wrong. And it could be possible that I'd have to go undercover once in a while, maybe, to investigate a political football or something. But I'll set things up with my superiors so that, if you need to find out if I'm okay, you can go to them and they'll give you enough info to set your mind at ease. I know there's a way to do that, because Captain Pike had to do that three months ago, when I helped him on that case; I'm just not sure yet HOW. But I'm sure they'll explain the procedure to us once I start doing my own investigations. Don't expect to be told all the particulars of my assignment, though."

"No, I get that," Martell decided. "I mean, I'd LIKE to, but I understand that I can't. I just need to know that you're okay."

"They might not even be able to tell you that much," Campbell pointed out, "because in intel, things can happen fast. But they can, say, let you know... in a roundabout way... that I'm not dead, if we've had to make it look like I am, while I do that undercover stuff. That's what you're really worried about, isn't it?"

"Well... yeah," she admitted. "That and..."

"And?"

She gazed at him solemnly. Martell was a beautiful woman, a tanned blonde whose hair was almost the same creamy tone as her skin, with soft blue eyes and a full, almost pouting lip. She was not incredibly knowledgeable about matters other than the mechanics of spacefaring engines, but she was brilliant where that was concerned. She also had a goodly degree of common sense, and her body was tall, lithe, and muscular without detracting an iota from her feminine attributes; if anything, Campbell thought, those same muscles made her even sexier... at least to him. Right now those eyes were worried, and the pout fuller, as she considered something that was troubling her. Finally she confessed what it was.

"Hata Mari," she murmured. "They wouldn't make you be a Hata Mari, would they, Bill?"

"A wha-? Oh, wait. You mean Mata Hari," Campbell realized. "You know she didn't do a tenth of the things in the legends that sprang up about her, right?"

"Huh? Hata Mari was a super-spy," Martell claimed. "She slept with everybody and convinced them to tell her all their secrets."

"Not... really," Campbell said, thoroughly stifling a laugh with considerable effort, and suppressing the grin that tried to take over his face. Martell was sweet, sexy, and just as importantly, trustworthy, and he was considering the possibility that listing her as his permanent companion might be in his future; the last thing he wanted to do right now was to hurt her, or just as bad, embarrass her. "That was the story that was concocted to convict her of treason and double-espionage, true, but history has proven that virtually all of that was false. Besides, that's... not the way I operate."

"Are you sure?"

"I'm sure."

"Okay, then," she said, accepting. She wrapped her hands around the back of his head and tugged gently. "It'll be okay. C'mere and let's get back to what we were doing; I gotta be at work early in the morning."

"I don't have a problem with that," Campbell agreed, bending his head to hers and covering her lips with his own.

The light meal that the tea shop provided for Rao — along with a slice of ham and cheese quiche with fresh fruit on the side for Ramirez — was impeccably done: two slices of golden white-bread toast and a perfectly-scrambled egg, not too runny, not too dry. Rao managed to get all of the egg, and one whole slice of toast in her, making serious inroads on the second slice before her belly decided she had best slow down. Rao pushed the plate back, then reached for the cup of tisane, sipping from it and finally able to savor the delicate floral flavors enhanced with honey.

"Better?" Ramirez wondered. "All done?"

"For now, yeah," Rao noted. "And yes, I do feel better. That tasted really amazingly good."

"Okay, Joan, check please," Ramirez called, and the proprietor brought the bill to her. "Thanks for the assistance in getting Mar' a little stronger, Joan. And Mar', you did great, hon. Protein and carbs; you should feel a good deal better for getting that into you."

"Thanks, Commander," the woman said with a smile. "Does your friend feel better?"

"Some, yes," Rao confirmed, "and I think once Rose here does her thing at my office, I'll feel better still. But let me have my share of that check, please."

"Nonsense," Ramirez said, picking up the check. "I have this. Besides, Joan only put a pittance on here for the egg and toast."

"It only cost a pittance, and as pale as the Captain was, I thought she needed it," Joan replied. "You always treated me with proper respect, Commander, and it's no trouble to help. A friend of yours is a friend of mine. And I DID head the department at one time, so I understand your job, all too well."

"Well, we both thank you," Rao murmured.

"No problem," Joan said with a smile. "Come back soon, and bring your friends."

"I will."

"All right, let's get this paid and get back across the base, Mar', so we can see what's going on," Ramirez decreed.

"I got it already," Joan said. "I just wanted you to see it, per our standard operating procedure, but I'll add it to your tab, Commander. You can pay at the end of the month, like usual."

"Thanks, Joan," Ramirez said with a smile. She grabbed a messenger bag slung across the back of her chair. "Okay, Mar'. Let's go."

"So you said your team was away at a meeting, covering for you?" Ramirez said, noting the empty outer office bullpen area.

"Right," Rao confirmed. "Vice Admiral Takala called a mandatory staff meeting to discuss something coming out of the Outer Colonies, and how he and Admiral Pachis wanted to respond. I hated to do it, to blow it off, but the way I felt, I think it would have been worse if I'd tried to go. I'd either have been barfing into a handy trash can — which is not good, when you're in your supervisor's office — or worse, jumping up and running for the necessary, so I

WOULDN'T barf in his trash can. Or before I could crap diarrhea all over myself, which I've had a touch of, too. And Brian understood all that; he said he'd take care of it."

"Brian?"

"Commander Brian Lee Gnad. He's my second, XO, chief of staff, whatever the brass is calling it these days. My right-hand man."

"Oh yeah, that memo that came down about the terminology," Ramirez remembered, reaching into a small kit she'd brought and pulling out some instrumentation. "Eh. They'll change it back six months from now, anyway. You'd think they'd have worked out those little nits by now, as long as the force has been in existence. Maybe they'll figure it out eventually."

"Eventually. Maybe. Every time somebody new comes into the head office, they gotta yank it around, put their stamp on it, though. So. What do I need to do?"

"Sign this, for starters."

Ramirez handed over her personally-assigned electronic display unit; a release form was displayed on its screen. Rao took the stylus Ramirez proffered and signed and initialed the form as needed, everywhere she pointed.

"Okay," Ramirez said. "That takes care of that. Now... how are you feeling in here?"

"What, in the bullpen?"

"Yes."

"So far, so good." Rao shrugged. "I'm still weak, but damn, I've been getting — and keeping down — only about half the food I usually get in me, for several weeks now. I'm GONNA be weak."

"But other than that?"

"Other than that, not too bad," Rao decided. "My face itches a little bit, and my eyes started stinging some when I walked in the door, but I don't feel like throwing up."

"All right. Sit here, near the door into the corridor, and let's leave it open, so you're getting air from outside this suite. Then I'll use my equipment to sweep the place for mold and chemicals and allergens and shit. No, no, you stay put," she ordered, when Rao started to protest. "Sit your ass in that chair and let me do my job."

"I outrank you these days, you know."

"Not in this instance, you don't," Ramirez retorted, donning a filter mask, goggles, and disposable, chemical-resistant gloves. "Have a closer look at the clauses you just initialed on that form."

Rao studied the document more carefully while Ramirez began to sweep the outer office with her instrumentation.

"Oh," Rao said after a moment of reading. "This... essentially puts you in charge of determining what's wrong, and what the ill party needs to do, to recover... including sending me to my physician, if you deem it warranted."

"Right. Here, doing this? I'M in charge. Now siddown, hush, an' let me work, girl."

"Okay."

Ramirez took her time, making good use of the fact that the office was empty and there was no one to get in the way... which had been as she wanted it, and why she jumped at the chance to do it immediately; that way, no one else could be affected by anything she stirred up in the process of the survey.

But the outer office showed very little in the way of anything over which to concern herself. That didn't mean, however, that Rao wasn't simply severely allergic to some cleaner or another; it just meant that the building was safe for everyone else.

Then she entered Rao's office proper.

"Oh shit," she whispered, looking at her instrument readout. "Oh, dammit to hell and back, twenty-gajillion times over. What the HELL has been going on in here?!"

"No, no, no," Ramirez decreed, when her scan was finished. "You can't stay in here until we get it cleaned out. Not AT ALL."

"But I have work to do," Rao protested.

"Then take it someplace else," Ramirez ordered, hustling her out of the room before closing and locking the door. She peeled off her protective gear, immediately pulled her comm unit, hit a speed dial, and waited. "Jim? Yes, it's Rose. Get your decon team down to the Tactical Division headquarters building, and head for Captain Mary Rao's office. No, JUST her office. I'm going to want a full report and eval when you're done. Be prepared to take samples, and to run forensics on 'em, so we can figure out what the hell has been going on." She ended the connection and turned to Rao. "Now come on. I'm getting you out of here."

"But I need stuff in there!" Rao protested.

Ramirez immediately began pulling out more gloves and another filter mask. "Then here. Put these on, and we'll go in and get what you need. Then you give it to me for decontamination — so make sure nothing's classified in what you get — and while I'm doing that, you go home, strip, and put the uniform you have on in a special bag I'll give you. Yes, decorations and all. I'll clean 'em and get them back to you. Oh, and then shower thoroughly at least three times. Face and hair, too. Three times. Use the strongest body detergents you have. Then put on clean clothes, and call me to come pick up the bagged uniform."

"Shit," Rao grumbled, donning the gloves. "You've gotta be kidding me."

"No, honey, I'm not. Trust me," Ramirez said. "If this had gone on much longer, you wouldn't be here."

"Wouldn't be here? What the hell does that mean?"

"It means it was killing you, girl! We need to minimize your exposure going forward, or it still could."

"What the hell?!" Rao said, shocked. "Damn! What's going on?"

"I'm not completely sure," Ramirez noted, "but apparently somebody got hold of exactly the wrong stuff to use as cleaning solvent in your office."

Rao stared at her.

When Ramirez came by Rao's home to pick up the contaminated uniform and hand over her decontaminated office items, Rao metaphorically tackled her.

"So if I can't work in my office, where the hell am I supposed to work?" she wanted to know. "Given what I do, I can't work just anywhere, you know."

"Don't you Tactical types have a secure facility somewhere in the building? With special links to the classified stuff you'd need?"

"Oh," Rao murmured, slapping the heel of her hand to her forehead. "Yeah, I'm just not with it; my blood sugar must still be too low. Duh. I'll go work in the Class 1 secure facility."

"There you go," Ramirez said in satisfaction. "You oughta be safe there, girl."

"Am I good to go now?"

"As long as you're feeling okay, I guess. Only a doctor could tell you for sure, but I'll need more info before I can send you to your doctor, anyway. When I leave here, I'm going to meet my people over in our lab and see if we can't verify exactly what we've got."

"Okay, then. Back to work."

"What you said."

And the two women headed out the door together, headed for their respective office buildings... if not to their respective offices.

Repercussions

Two days later, while she worked in the room assigned to her in the Class 1 secure facility in the Tactical Division headquarters building's basement, Rao received orders to report at once to Admiral Haden J. Pachis, head of the Tactical Division, in his office on the top floor of the Tactical Division headquarters building. Immediately she logged out of the VR system where she had been working, and headed out of the basement, en route to the top floor.

Pachis' receptionist, Lieutenant Commander Olivia Andre, hit the intercom as soon as Rao reported to her.

"Admiral? Captain Rao is here."

"All right, Olivia. Send her through."

A puzzled Rao followed Andre's unusually-brusque hand wave, headed through the door into the inner sanctum.

"Captain Mary Rao reporting as ordered, sir," Rao said, saluting smartly, once she stood in front of the Admiral's desk, where he studied paperwork on an invisible-to-her virtual display.

Admiral Haden J. Pachis was an older man, white-haired, with a craggy face and piercing gray eyes, nearing retirement age. He had had a long and illustrious career in the Tactical Division of the CSF, largely aboard ship, and the decorations on his uniform showed it. He was well known in the service, honored and respected by allies, feared by adversaries; when he noticed you, for good or bad, you knew it. If his notice was favorable, you were in clover. If not, your career could be over. If you were an enemy of the Commonwealth, you could be dead.

And now, Admiral Pachis looked up at Rao... and scowled.

'Uh oh,' Rao thought, heart dropping into her finally-quiescent stomach... at least, it had been quiescent until that point; now it was tying itself in knots. 'That ain't good.'

"Yeeeeesssss," Pachis drawled in profound displeasure, almost as if he could read her thoughts; it never occurred to her that he might be reading her nuances of expression. "Captain Rao. Would you care to explain to me why you went off-base on Monday to meet a friend at a tea shop, instead of attending Vice Admiral Takala's staff meeting with the rest of your team? A MANDATORY staff meeting?"

Rao felt herself pale, and wondered who had betrayed her — for that matter, who had even known she'd met Ramirez, let alone gone off base. But she remembered Ramirez' instructions, and nodded.

"Certainly, sir. It may not have come to the Admiral's attention as yet, but for the last several weeks — about a couple of months or so — my health has been less than optimal, sir. More, and worse, it has been deteriorating in the last two or three weeks. Monday morning, while I was in the necessary purging my digestive tract, it suddenly occurred to me that I was only getting sick during the work week, and always recovered during my days off. I called Commander Rosalind Ramirez, in the Facilities Division — she's one of the top officers in the Housekeeping Department — to ask about the possibility of an allergy to some of the cleaning products, or even a sick-building syndrome, and she insisted I come off-base to meet her, in case I was actually allergic. She specified the time and place, sir, not me."

"I see. And you have proof of this?"

"Yes sir. She came straight back with me to my office suite — she wanted to do it while the office was empty, so there would be less likelihood of cross-contamination or the like, never mind the potential of making more of my staff ill, so she insisted on the timing during Admiral Takala's meeting — and swept it for any sort of allergens or contaminants, and to see what was being used, so we could possibly have my personal physician test me for allergic reactions, then take matters from there, once we knew my sensitivities." Rao pulled out her electronic display unit and showed the Admiral the automatically dated, timed copy of the release form, which she had signed and Ramirez had later sent her. "She told me to refer all inquiries to her or her supervisor, sir."

"I see. What condition were you in when you went to meet her?"

"Not good, sir," Rao admitted. "I had a nasty migraine, and I swear by that point, I'd barfed up my pancreas, excuse the detail, sir. For the last two or three weeks, I've been wearing my shaded glasses in my office, with the lights off, just to be able to function."

"Hm. So you wouldn't have been able to participate in the staff meeting in any case, not with any degree of coherence."

"No sir. Not at all. And begging your pardon, but I didn't want to potentially barf all over the Vice-Admiral's nice, newly-renovated conference room, sir. Which," she added, "was a distinct possibility."

"But you still tried to keep working, around being sick."

"Yes sir. My job is important, sir, and I didn't want to risk possible disaster from an invading force just on account of a headache and some throwing up, no matter how bad." Rao pulled a sheepish face. "Though my wastebasket is probably a lost cause by now. I'll need to requisition a new one, I'm afraid."

"Commendable determination. And so did it help, getting off-base?"

"Yes sir. I sipped some sort of herbal tea that she specified from the tea shop's proprietor — I've known Ramirez a long time, and she knows how to get me settled when I'm sick, after all these years, though I gather the mix is the proprietor's secret — and though I don't know what-all was in it, it tasted good, and for a wonder, it didn't want to come back up... which, at that point, was a big deal, right there. And just the fresh air from the walk seemed to help. Like... like it cleared out my head, my chest..."

"I see. Go on."

"So while she had coffee and I had the... herbal stuff," Rao continued, "I told Rose-uh, Commander Ramirez, about what had been happening, and the timing, and everything. She even had me bring up my calendar and show her what days I got sick... and transfer it onto HER electronic display unit, I suppose for her report on the incident. Then she insisted I eat a scrambled egg with toast — because I'd lost all my breakfast that morning, and couldn't even begin to eat lunch, and I guess I was still wobbly, and it showed, sir, pretty badly — so that I could walk BACK across the base with her without passing out or something, so she could scan my office."

"I see." Pachis scanned her up and down. "Hm. You do look rather thinner since the last time I saw you; we may need to have your uniforms re-tailored. And you're a bit pale, yet. Sit down, please, Captain."

"Yes sir," Rao said, hiding the titanic sigh of relief as she realized he believed her. She eased into the visitor's chair across the big desk from the Admiral, but couldn't hide THAT sigh, as her still-weakened body all but slumped into it. She immediately squared her shoulders and straightened her back, but the Admiral saw, and lifted an eyebrow, a hint of concern crossing his craggy face.

"Captain, are you still unwell?" he asked then.

"Well, not so much, sir, though I'm still a little weak yet," she explained, "because on Commander Ramirez' instructions, I gathered my work materials, let her decontaminate them, decontaminated myself, and I've been working in the secure facility in the basement for the last two days. That seems to have helped, a lot." She shrugged. "I'm not having migraines or throwing up any more, so now it's more a case of just rebuilding my strength and getting food into me. It's not unlike I've had an intestinal bug... for over two months. But I'm being careful — easy to digest foods, nothing spicy, plenty of fluids... you know the drill, I'm sure, sir."

"Yes, and that seems wise, Captain. So. You moved to the Class 1? On her instructions?"

"Yes sir. She didn't tell me why, but she DID call in a special team to clean my office."

"The whole suite? Or just your office?"

"I'm not really sure, sir. She shooed me out to go home and change, put my uniform in a special bag she gave me, then ordered me to shower... three times."

Both of Pachis' grizzled eyebrows shot up at that.

"Have you seen her report on the matter?"

"Not yet, sir. I don't think it's anywhere close to finished yet. She pinged me this morning and told me some things were still in work, so..."

"Hm. This shines a completely different light on the matter, then. Captain Rao, you should know that I called you here to issue a formal reprimand. In light of the information you've presented, however, I think perhaps I should put a hold on that and dig a little deeper, because it sounds like your actions may have been fully justified, all things considered. Commander Rosalind Ramirez, you said? In Housekeeping?"

"Yes sir."

"Could you forward me a copy of your release document, there?" He nodded at her electronic display unit.

"Certainly, sir," Rao agreed immediately, and tapped a few places on the screen. "There. That should send it to you through my standard report channel."

A soft chime rose from the VR equipment on the corner of Pachis' desk.

"There it is," he said. "All right. I'll have a look at it shortly. And I think we can do without that reprimand after all... unless I find that you and Ramirez hatched up something between you. But since I've heard her name, and in a good light, I believe you're safe, Captain." Pachis offered her a slight smile, and she returned it. "But I do have instructions for you."

"Yes sir?"

"If this continues, gets worse, or anything else of a harmful nature happens, I want you to report it directly to me immediately, and I want you to go to Intel and demand an investigation. I'll help, if need be, by adding my weight to the request."

"What?!"

"Stop and think, Rao. You are the planetary tactical officer for Jablonka, Captain. And Jablonka is the capital planet of the Commonwealth. As you pointed out, that is an important position. Your job involves planetary safety and security, and by extension, the safety and security of the government of the Commonwealth. I intend to look into this and see what is happening, but had it occurred to you that this might not have been an accident? That you might have been targeted?"

Rao's dark eyes grew wide.

"N-no sir, it... it hadn't," she admitted then.

Pachis nodded to himself, considering.

"Very well, then; please DO consider it. Remember what I said, Captain. Thank you for your stubborn determination. Dismissed."

"Thank you, sir."

And she was gone.

Pachis sat in his luxuriantly padded leather office chair for a long moment, considering the information with which he had just been presented. Then he thumbed the intercom.

"Olivia? Call over to the Housekeeping Department and see if you can hunt up one Commander Rosalind Ramirez. I think I need to talk to her, in person. It can be by comm or visit, whatever is most convenient for her; I gather she may be very busy assisting on an important decontamination."

"Yes sir. And Captain Rao's reprimand? Shall I enter it into the system?"

"Belay that, Olivia. There look to have been some seriously mitigating circumstances."

"Yes sir."

"And so there was a chemical being used that is not approved for use around humans in enclosed spaces?" Pachis noted to the woman who now stood in his office.

"That's what my initial assessment indicated, sir," Ramirez averred. "I can't say for sure until my decon team reports in, and they're still working on it."

"What about the rest of Rao's people?"

"Oh, the contamination appeared fairly localized to the Captain's office, and the decon is being done at night, sir," Ramirez explained. "They may not even realize it's happening. But we always want to ensure that nothing gets stirred up while active-duty personnel are in the area, so we usually do these sorts of decontaminations at night, at least when the facilities in question aren't twenty-five-hour duty stations. Which is also why I insisted on doing the initial investigatory sweep while the rest of her team was at a meeting of some sort; Captain Rao didn't really tell me what, and since I didn't have a need to know in any case, I didn't press, sir."

"Right. And so you have Rao working in the Class 1 secure facility in our basement, here in the Tactical Division headquarters building?"

"Yes sir. Given the nature of her work, it seemed logical. I'm still chasing to see who the regular cleaning team is for her office, though. It seems that about six months ago there was some sort of reorg, and the files got a bit shuffled. So were the teams, for that matter."

"All right, then," Pachis decided. "This sounds... serious."

"Potentially, sir. But I'm on top of it."

"Good to hear. I know I head up a different command chain, but Rao is one of my top people, and I want to see she's looked after properly; keep me posted, Commander, if you wouldn't mind."

"Certainly, sir," Ramirez agreed. "I don't know if she told you, but Captain Rao and I are very old friends; we were childhood playmates, even. She called me because... well, I think initially she just wanted to find out if sick building syndrome was a reasonable consideration, without sounding half-cocked to a complete stranger, and then when I said yes, to find out what to do about it. I was someone she trusted, in a position to give her the answers she needed, without making her look a fool, or worse. More, she trusts me to do right by her through all this, and I will. Not just because she's my friend," Ramirez added, "but because it's my job, and the right thing to do."

"Excellent, excellent. That's what I want to hear," Pachis averred. "Just add me into the loop, and we're good."

"I'll do that right away, sir. I'll even send you my preliminary scanner findings, if you want to see them."

Pachis gnawed on his lip in thought for a long moment, considering.

"No, not right now," he finally decided, "but hang on to 'em, just in case."

"Sir?"

"By the time you get to my position, Commander, you develop certain... instincts," Pachis explained. "And when Captain Rao was explaining matters to me earlier, alarm bells were sounding in the back of my head like a call to general quarters. Something is going on here, something that I don't like, and I want a demonstrable, well-defined paper trail — well, electron trail or whatever — that we can use to prove matters if things go south."

"Um... yes sir," Ramirez agreed, patently not understanding.

'But that's all right,' Pachis decided, watching her. 'She's not Tactical, OR Intel, she's Facilities. She's not going to see the potential ramifications I see. Which is just as well. I believe I need to keep an eye on this situation.'

"...Anything else, sir?" Ramirez was asking.

"No, Commander, that about covers it, I think," Pachis concluded. "Thank you for coming over and filling me in personally."

"Not a problem, sir. Under the circumstances, I think it needed doing. I had planned to do it in any case, but after I had the report ready, so that I could give you actual details." She shrugged. "This way worked just as well, given your concerns. I hope I answered all of your questions."

"For now, inasmuch as they can be answered, at least."

"Good, then."

"Dismissed, Commander. And again, thank you."

"You're welcome, sir."

And she, too, was gone.

Admiral Pachis sat in silence for a long time, just thinking.

The whole time Rao was in the basement secure facility, working on developing new concepts for defending Jablonka from a possible invasion or attack, her team was not only evaluating the plans coming from her, they were submitting their own ideas, and fielding queries from other departments in Tactical, shuffling communiques back and forth from the PTO, as they called the planetary tactical office suite as a whole, and other tacticians in their, and other, buildings.

In general, no one on the PTO staff thought much about it; no one knew about the decontamination work going on at night, because by the time the sampling and general reconstruction of what was happening had finished, Ramirez had met with Admiral Pachis, and kept the decontamination efforts as clandestine as possible.

The PTO staff, however, found the notion that Captain Rao had moved out of her office to work on something classified... exciting. Obviously, in their view, Rao must have had some ideas about how to assemble this or that concept into a larger, and possibly very strategically sensitive, defense plan, and decided that the best place for that work was a Class 1 secure facility.

Not everyone cared for the idea, however.

"I don't know what the hell happened here," a dumbfounded Jim Berg, head of the decontamination team, told Ramirez the next day. "You can't believe the... shit... we're finding, scattered around that office. No wonder your friend Captain Rao was sick! She must have the constitution of a draft horse, to still be going after being around all that crap for nearly two months, and not be in the hospital, let alone the morgue!"

"That bad, huh?" Ramirez wondered, biting her lip in concern.

"Every bit, and then some," Berg averred. "We're gonna have to use hazmat suits to clean some of this shit. And several things are gonna have to just be thrown away."

"Any personal items? 'Cause we'd need to get permission from Captain Rao to trash it..."

"No, not that we've found... yet," Berg decided, after a moment to consider. "But her chair, her desk, several handbooks, the VR unit... it's all contaminated so badly by all this stuff that we're not sure if it CAN be decontaminated, especially the desk, chair, and handbooks. It's all kind of soaked into the wood grain and the paper. Damn, but I hate to throw out old-style books like that."

"Well, take those, and let's see what we can do with 'em," Ramirez decided, "because you've got a point. The rest of it, do what you can, and if it doesn't work, we'll remove 'em, haul 'em to the special incinerator, and have 'em replaced."

"You might want to go ahead and requisition those replacements, then," Berg recommended, "because Sarah actually found a chemical stain on the desktop from where it looks like somebody poured a puddle of the solvent, then spread it out over the desk and worked it in."

"Damn," Ramirez said, in blank shock.

Several days after the meeting with Pachis, Rao came through the PTO office suite around lunchtime to grab a bottle of water out of the community cooling unit, greeted several members of her staff, then headed out to take a walk. She was feeling much better and beginning to get some strength back, now that she was no longer throwing up everything she managed to put in her belly.

"So... yeah, I want to try to speed up that process," she told Lieutenants JoAnn Zinn and David Weiner, as well as her XO, Commander Brian Lee Gnad, as they chatted briefly before Rao headed back out. "And I figure the easiest way to accelerate the process, while not overdoing, is to start adding in a few extra walks. I tend to walk most places anyway, but if I'm not careful, I'll spend the whole work day closeted in the secure facility and not even get any fresh air, let alone sunshine."

"I think that's a good plan, ma'am," Zinn told her. "You've been so pale, we were starting to get worried about you."

"Agreed," Gnad added. "No offense, Mary, but you've looked like hell."

"I know, Brian, but it couldn't be helped," Rao said with a sigh. "At any rate, I'm hoping that's all done with."

"Are you coming back into the office after lunch?" Weiner wondered.

"No, I've got a crap-ton to do down in the basement; I'll be headed back there for the duration," Rao noted. "I know it puts a little bit of a cramp in the usual routine, but believe me — I'm getting a lot done because of it."

"That's great!" Zinn enthused.

"Okay, guys! I'm off for a nice, healthy walk around the base. Catch you on the flop side."

Rao waved, and headed off.

Three hours later, Rao's XO, that same Commander Brian Lee Gnad, received an off-base voice comm on his personal comm unit. He saw the caller ID, and swiftly stepped out of his office, through the side door, and onto the building's patio, easing into the lee of some large shrubs, meanwhile verifying visually that no one was within earshot.

"Gnad."

"It's Marcel," the distorted, genderless voice announced. "Report."

"Oh," Gnad murmured, gnawing his lip as he thought swiftly.

"Well?"

"It's... still in work."

"Still in work? The hell you say. She should be dead by now."

"I know. The bitch won't stay in her office."

"Damn. We're going to have to do something else."

"I'm open to suggestions."

"You keep your nose down. I'll handle this."

And the connection ended.

Gnad sighed and replaced the comm unit in his shirt pocket.

As he came back into the bullpen, Rao was passing through — evidently grabbing yet another water bottle after what he resentfully assumed was her leisurely stroll around the base, which unbeknownst to Gnad, had included departmental errands and needed communiqués with related officers — and noticed the personal comm unit protruding from his shirt pocket. Her face crumpled slightly in concern.

"Is everything okay, Brian?" she wondered. Gnad manufactured a morose expression and sighed, shrugging.

"I suppose," he decided. "Mom just called to let me know that Dad's back in the hospital."

"You really should convince them to emigrate, Brian," Rao pointed out, her face evincing even more worry. "It wouldn't be that hard, given you're a Commonwealth citizen. They don't even have to become citizens themselves, if they don't want to. They can still move here, where there's excellent healthcare."

"I know." Gnad shrugged again. "They're... kinda set in their ways, I guess." Then he added mentally, 'They're also dead for the last ten years, but YOU don't know that, bitch.'

"Well," Rao said with her own sigh, "we are what we are, I suppose. But you know I'm available if you need help, Brian."

"Yes ma'am," Gnad acknowledged, as Rao headed out of the office.

Without missing a beat, he returned to his desk and resumed work.

Three days later, Rao was called to a meeting in the Housekeeping building, she presumed by one of Ramirez' subordinates, though she hadn't recognized the voice on the call. Her pathway from the Tactical Division headquarters building to the Facilities building did not cut through the Mall, but along several side streets, and was made somewhat more convoluted by the need to avoid numerous construction sites of various sizes and extents; Sigurdsen had been built nearly a century and a quarter before, and the historic old buildings were finally getting some remedial attention. As a result, there were refurbishment and renovation projects all over the base.

'Hopefully,' she thought, as she walked across the base, carefully following the sidewalks around all of the renovations being done on the older buildings, 'Rose and her team can finally give me an all-clear and tell me what the hell I'm allergic to, and issue an order NOT to use the shit around ME. At least,' she considered, remembering the meeting with Admiral Pachis, 'I hope that's all it is.' She sighed. 'At least I'm feeling better for working in the secure basement,' she decided. 'And the fresh air on this walk ought to help, too. It's good to finally be able to EAT properly again!'

But despite her improved health, her gut churned at the notion that Pachis had presented, and she glanced about her with concern, on alert.

"Here she comes," a construction worker on the roof of the five-story building near the top of the scaffolding said to his coworker. "You got it set up?"

"Yeah," the other said. "All you gotta do is nudge it. Then we disappear."

"All over it," the first said with a smirk. "And her."

Rao had just rounded the corner of the five-story dormitory being renovated, the brickwork scaffolding barely fitting between the sidewalk and the wall of the building, when she caught a motion out of the corner of her eye, high up along the top of the scaffolding. Instinctively, she shied away, across the grass and toward the street, even as a shout rang out from across that street.

"LOOK OUT!" an ensign shouted, pointing up...

...Just as Rao felt a powerful impact along her leg. This was accompanied by a loud ripping sound and searing pain, and she screamed in instinctive reaction as she fell to the ground.

Running feet sounded all around her, as nearby personnel ran to help. Rao lay on her belly on the ground, panting and trying neither to scream again, nor to cry, nor yet throw up, as intense agony blazed through her left leg.

"Oh damn! Someone call Emergency Services!" someone said. "She's hurt, bad! I can see bone!"

"Yeah, and get the MPs over here!"

"On it!" someone else exclaimed.

"Gimme a handkerchief or something, somebody!"

"A handkerchief? That isn't gonna be near enough for that, Commander."

"Gotta do something to stop the bleeding, ma'am."

With that, Rao rolled over — when she had lunged out of the way, she had landed in the narrow grassy verge between the sidewalk and the street curb — and surveyed the damage.

Her shipsuit trousers leg had been ripped open along the outside of the left calf, leaving a long, narrow, triangular strip flopping loosely at the hem, just above the ankle. The opening gaped from only an inch or two below the knee, exposing the skin of her lower leg, which was likewise sliced open in an irregular fashion, being somewhere between split by blunt force trauma, and gouged by a bluntly-tipped object. Something white and solid, looking suspiciously like bone, was visible at the bottom of the deepest part of the wound. Well more than a dozen bricks, several broken, lay where she had been on the sidewalk; another lay on the grass near her ankle, the blood stains on one corner and adjacent edge mute testament to what had laid open her calf, which was bleeding rather substantially; a small red puddle had already formed on the edge of the sidewalk under her leg, trickling over the side of the pavement into the grass.

Her head spun. 'Don't faint, don't faint,' she told herself firmly.

"Hey, easy, easy; don't pass out on me now. Lie back there and relax; that's it. Easy does it, now. It's gonna be okay," one man, in a commander's uniform, said, in a gentle, soothing tone; having finally collected a wad of clean handkerchiefs from several officers — who were serving as guards over the site, until the MPs could arrive — he folded them into one large compress, and applied it gingerly to the wound in her leg. The contact of the cloth on the raw flesh burned like fury; she hissed despite herself, and he offered her an apologetic glance. "I'm sorry," he murmured. "I know it hurts, but we need to minimize this bleeding, here. You've already good a good little pool going on the sidewalk. I don't THINK it got an artery, by the look... nothing's spurting... but I'm not a doctor, either. No, don't go moving around too much," he said, putting out his other hand. "That damn brick mighta busted something here, and we don't want to turn a nasty wound into a horrible one. You've already got exposed bone as it is."

"N-no," Rao agreed, gritting her teeth against the pain. "Mmmh. Damn, that hurts."

"I bet," the unknown commander noted, offering a slight grin. "Just be glad you got outta the way of that." He jerked the thumb of his free hand at the pile of bricks on the sidewalk. "You wouldn't be feeling ANYthing if THAT had got you."

Rao stared at him, then at the pile of bricks, before looking up at the top of the scaffolding, where roughly half a stack of bricks, intended for the building façade, still remained.

The emergency response team was swift. Within moments, Rao was examined, a special bandage placed on the wound, and she was gently lifted onto a gurney for transport to Sigurdsen Military Hospital on an emergency shuttle. The MPs arrived before the medical responders could depart with their patient, and began cordoning off the site, marking the various fallen bricks, as well as the spot where Rao had landed.

"Ma'am? Uh, Captain?" a dark-haired man, thinning on top, stocky body wearing the uniform of the military police, approached Rao where she lay on the gurney being treated.

"Uhn... yes?" Rao managed to get out. "Rao. Mary Rao."

"Right. Captain Rao, I'm Captain Julian W. Thompson, the military police officer in charge of the investigations unit," the man said, following along as the paramedics headed for the street and the waiting emergency evac shuttle, carrying the gurney over the irregular terrain to avoid bumping their patient. "My people are already handling things. If you don't mind, I'd like to ride in the emergency evac shuttle with you and find out what happened from your point of view. My people can pick me up at the hospital when we're done, and bring me back to the accident site."

"Not... not my call," Rao murmured, waving a hand at the paramedics.

"It's fine, Captain," one of the paramedics replied. "We're used to it, and even have a special seat for the MP investigator."

"Okay," Rao sighed. "I dunno how... mmh... how intelligible I'll be, but I'll try. Damn, this hurts, SO bad."

"As soon as Captain Thompson is done interviewing you, Captain Rao, we have authorization for some pain medication," the paramedic added. "We can't give it to you until he's finished, though, because he needs you coherent and alert."

"Oh, good. Let's hurry, then, please." She leaned back into the pillows and bit her lip, trying to ignore the intense pain that seemed to gouge all the way through her leg... and then explode. Repeatedly.

"Don't worry, ma'am, I'll keep it quick and easy," Thompson told Rao as the paramedics loaded her into the emergency evac shuttle. Once they were inside with their patient, he eased into position beside them, taking the designated seat. "Plus, we'll talk to all the witnesses and get their testimony, and we'll be all over this. Offhand, I'd say someone neglected to secure the bricks, and with that weather system moving in, it's been a bit windy. But we'll double-check everything."

"Thank you," Rao murmured, vaguely wondering what he would find.

"WHAT?!" Admiral Pachis exclaimed, when Thompson reported the incident to him, a little over an hour later. "You had best be joking, Captain. My planetary tactical officer just had a pile of bricks fall on her?"

"No sir, I'm not joking, and yes sir, that's essentially what happened," Thompson averred. "I rode in the emergency evacuation shuttle with her and interviewed her. I don't think she's too badly hurt, though at least one brick appears to have impacted her left leg. She had what looked to be a nasty gash, and I expect she might have a broken leg, but I doubt it will be worse than that. According to her account, corroborated by some half a dozen witnesses, she saw it coming and lunged out of the way, or else she'd be dead. She just didn't quite completely clear the trajectory path, is all."

"Mmm," Pachis murmured; the sound was just shy of being a growl. "Listen to me carefully, son. Go over that scene with a fine-toothed comb. If that was no accident, I want to know about it."

"I can't imagine why it wouldn't be, sir," Thompson noted. "But of course we'll investigate in depth. That said, it was a construction site; you know the major repair work that's been slated for the base over the next year and a half. The workers were repairing the façade on one of the enlisted barracks, and I expect we'll find that they neglected safety regs. That happens a lot — you can lay bricks faster if they're not secured, and then the guys just forget to secure 'em before they leave on break or whatever."

"I understand," Pachis said, refusing to relent his stern demeanor one bit. "But I'm privy to some additional matters, Captain, matters that may end up being classified, and aren't verified yet, in any case. I don't want you to assume this was an accident, and investigate the incident with that as your starting premise. I want you to go in suspicious. Go in looking for who did it, and why."

Thompson's eyebrows went up in surprise. "If you say so, sir."

"I say so. Now go."

Thompson went.

"...And so you say she saw it coming, and dodged?" one of the MP investigators asked an ensign.

"Yes sir," the ensign said, pointing. "She was right there — right where the pile of bricks landed — and just as I saw 'em start to fall, she jerked her head up, sort of... flinched, I guess you could call it... and then lunged toward the street. She almost cleared it, but a brick caught her trailing leg hard in the calf."

"Did you see anything else? Was there anyone on the scaffolding? Anyone on the roof?"

"Not that I saw, sir."

"What do you think made the bricks fall, then?"

"I don't know, sir." The ensign shrugged. "Sometimes, if a stack of... stuff... hasn't been laid properly, the whole pile will get unstable and start to slump. It starts slow, then kind of builds up speed, until all of a sudden, it lets loose. It might have been something like that." He shrugged. "Or it might have been something else. I don't know for certain; I didn't really notice anything until it all went to falling."

"I see. Was the wind up?"

"Not that I noticed, sir. The hag was flanging."

"I beg your pardon?"

"Oh!" the ensign exclaimed, embarrassed and flushing bright red. "I'm sorry, sir. I'm prone to something called spoonerisms. My mom used to say I had dyslexia of the tongue. I was trying to say that the flag," he pointed at the Commonwealth flag on the roof of the barracks, "was hanging down; there was no wind."

"Ah," the MP said, nodding as he took notes. "Anything else you can think of, Ensign?"

"No sir, not offhand. I'm sure glad the Captain didn't get killed."

"So is she, I'm sure." He handed the ensign a card. "Here's my contact information. If anything else comes to mind, let me know, please."

"Of course, sir," the ensign said.

But the MP was already moving on to the next witness.

The site under investigation was not large. It consisted of the sidewalk where the bricks had landed, the adjacent greensward where Rao had fallen, the scaffolding, and the adjacent roof.

Other than noting the locations of the various bricks, as well as Rao's position on the ground, there was little to be determined from the sidewalk and greensward. The bricks had followed Newton's Laws and landed where gravity placed them, with the sole deviation occurring as a result of Rao's leg being in the way.

The scaffolding itself was determined to be solid and secure, properly anchored, and with all stresses taken into effect and countered; there could be no sagging or other such anomaly that would result in destabilizing the stack of bricks on the top level.

The roof showed no special signs of disturbance. There were footprints in the gravel of the tar-and-gravel roofing, but that was not unusual; the construction workers had been up there off and on for several days. The walls had been finished at the top with a kind of mock crenellation, decorative and somewhat reminiscent of a castle; given the height of the lip around the roof, it had proven to be easier to lay these fake battlements from the rooftop rather than the scaffolding. A small stack of bricks for the purpose still remained in the corner of the roof.

True to Captain Thompson's expectations, the stack of bricks on the scaffolding — from which the nearly-deadly missiles fell — had no sign of securing straps, or any other restraint, anywhere on the entire stack, or that level of scaffolding.

Patchwork

The ensuing hours became a blur for Rao, once the pain medications were administered. The paramedics hung a saline IV line while she was en route to the base hospital, aka SMH, and injected the medication through the drip. She never became completely unconscious, but the pain rapidly minimized, and she found she didn't care a great deal when they landed and she arrived at the emergency room... and the doctors began flushing debris out of the hole in her leg — with saline.

"There," the lead surgeon said. "Now let's smooth that bone surface, then trim up the edges of the soft tissue a bit before we hit it all with some medibond, and get this mess closed up."

"On it, sir," one of the nurses responded.

"We're gonna need a lot of medibond," the assisting emergency room physician noted.

"No joke. X-ray said no reconstruction needed, right?"

"No sir. She might have a green break, but the bone is essentially intact and staying put — except for the point of direct impact with the brick, which as you say, needs recontouring. They couldn't guarantee bone fragments... chips, basically... in the surrounding soft tissue, though, so we need to keep an eye out. She's gonna have a helluva scar, though."

"Right. But if that's all? She's awfully damn lucky."

"Oh hell yes! From what I heard, she's lucky to be alive, sir. About a foot or so to the left, and those bricks would have landed on her head."

"Damn. Okay, let's take care of this lucky lady, then. Anesthesia?"

"The Lucky Lady is good to go, sir," the anesthesiologist said, grin audible in his voice. "Awake — barely — but feeling no pain."

"Captain Rao? Are you awake? Oh, there you are. I'm Dr. Kaylle," the surgeon said, bending over her as she slowly opened her eyes. "Can you confirm that for me? Are you good, here? No pain?"

"Nope," Rao declared without regard to military protocol, but with a slight, sheepish grin, as she tried — and failed — to focus on the surgeon's face. "Not hurtin' here! Not any more! Ya gave me th' good shtuff."

Barks of laughter went around the room, and Kaylle grinned.

"You're right, Pete; the Lucky Lady is good to go. Scalpel..."

The hospital kept her overnight, giving her something a good bit stronger for the post-op pain, especially given that bone resurfacing was prone to subsequent pain and swelling, and she slept deeply as a result, only waking late the next morning. When they prepared to release her late that afternoon, her swollen leg was encased in an adjustable splint that ran from ankle to upper thigh, with a special hinge designed to allow the knee to move within a very limited range. She was on crutches, with instructions not to put any weight on the leg until they could verify there were no green breaks.

"Which means you go to your regular physician in about two or three days," Kaylle told her, "for another set of x-rays. That'll tell the tale. If the bones are good, I'd keep the splint on when you're out and about and need to be mobile, for... oh, say another week or so. Easy on the tub soaks for that time, though I sealed up the wound pretty thoroughly; still, we don't want to risk infection. And given the nature and size of the injury... you're going to scar, I'm afraid. There's just no way around that. Once things are healed better, we can look at doing some cosmetic work to minimize its appearance, but for now, let's just get you healed up good, all right?"

"Got it, and yeah," Rao agreed, then winced. "Um. Pain meds?"

"Are you hurting?" Kaylle picked up the chart at the foot of the bed and leafed through it. "Oh, yeah, you're due for another dose; we gave you one last round before we took out the IV early this morning, so that'll be wearing off Real Soon Quick, now. The nurse will be in here in about..." he checked his watch, "about five more minutes with your first dose of the oral meds. Don't worry, I've already got the pharmacy filling your prescription, and I'll send it home with you."

"Oh, good," Rao said with an audible sigh. "I'm not sure HOW I'm getting home, but okay."

"That's taken care of, too," Kaylle noted. "I was told to contact Admiral Pachis' office with the time of your hospital release, and he'd send his personal driver to pick you up and take you home. We'll have to put you in a generic shipsuit; I hope you don't mind. Your uniform was pretty trashed by the time we were done with everything, what with bricks landing on you, and our 'cut it off the emergency patient' protocols. Besides, I think, all things considered, it'll be easier to get onto you than a mess dress uniform." He grinned, offering her a teasing wink.

"Understood," Rao averred, the corner of her mouth quirking despite herself. "I feel damn stiff, though, so I might need help getting into it."

"Oh, that goes without saying. That's why we'll send around a nurse to help you," Kaylle said with a smile. "This ain't my first rodeo, Lucky Lady."

"Huh?"

"Oh, sorry," Kaylle said, flushing. "We heard what almost happened to you, and the ER operating room staff dubbed you the Lucky Lady."

"Oh," Rao said; it was her turn to flush, as she felt her cheeks warm. "Okay, and, well, thank you. All of you."

"Not a problem," Kaylle said, turning for the door. "It's what we're here for."

The nurse did indeed help Rao get into the shipsuit, removing the splint and easing the shipsuit over Rao's stiff, bruised, painful body before slipping the splint back on, over the leg of the shipsuit, and showing her how to do it.

"Mind," she said, "we don't really want you doing a whole lot of taking it off and putting it back on. It needs to stay put to ensure that, if there are any broken bones, they start to knit back. So until we can verify for certain that there AREN'T, I'd recommend doing something like putting on your pajamas when you get home, and easing the splint over 'em, then staying like that."

"Okay," Rao agreed. "Whatever's best."

Rather than the regulation uniform boots normally worn with a shipsuit, however, the nurse slid rubber-soled slip-on shoes onto Rao's sock-clad feet.

"There we go; much easier than having to lean down and zip up, at least for now," the nurse declared, cheerful, as she reached under the bed and produced a small bag. "We don't want you to risk stressing this leg at all, quite yet, and that includes bending it enough to reach boots. Okay! You're all set! And here are your personal effects from your uniform pockets, to include your decorations and insignias, which I rescued off your trashed uniform, and whatever I could find in the pockets." She handed the bag to Rao. "Now let's get you into a wheelchair and downstairs. Your ride should be waiting."

The admiral's personal driver, Chief Petty Officer Ralph Ortiz, awaited in the admiral's own vehicle — in this case, a large, comfortable-bordering-on-luxurious ground car. He came around and helped the nurse put Rao into the back seat, helped her strap in and saw she was comfortable, then returned to the driver's seat.

"And please, call me Ralph, for the duration. It's what the Admiral calls me, anyway, so I'm used to it. Are you good back there, Captain?" he asked, as he strapped himself into the seat behind the controls.

"I'm fine, Ralph," Rao said, mildly abashed. "I feel a little foolish, and kind of like a damsel in distress, which isn't normal for me at all, but I'm comfortable."

"That's good. Um, not that you feel foolish — 'cause you shouldn't — but that you're comfortable. Admiral Pachis has been very worried about you since he got the news yesterday, and I'm to see that along the way, we pick up several boxed meals for you from the Officer's Mess, already prepared on his orders, so you don't have to do a lot today OR tomorrow. And I'll help you get inside and settled once I take you home."

"Oh, but you don't have to..."

"Begging your pardon, Captain, ma'am, but I do," Ortiz said with a friendly grin. "Aside from being the sort to help out a lady OR fellow in distress, Admiral Pachis would have my hide tanned and nailed to his office wall if I didn't. And I rather like my hide where it is, if you don't mind. Oh, and he's sending over a female orderly to help you change, once you're settled in, later this evening; we kind of figured you might need a little help getting into lounge clothes, or pajamas, or whatever you wear around the house and to bed. He also said to tell you that the first place he expects to see you outside your home is at your personal physician's office, a couple of days from now... which means stay home, rest up, and get better. So, if you'll just give me your home address, we'll have you home in a jif."

Rao gave him her home address, and they were off.

Captain Thompson's report on the investigation arrived in Pachis' mail the next morning. Much to the Admiral's annoyance, the conclusion was as Thompson had originally indicated — accidental collapse of the stack of bricks due to failure to properly secure them per regulations.

"Damnation," Pachis grumbled. "Now WHY don't I believe that...?"

Two days later, with the female orderly, Linda Mann, popping in several times a day to help Rao get around, shower, heat meals and whatnot, Ortiz showed back up to take her to see Dr. Rathman. He helped her into the office, where nurses were waiting on Admiral Pachis' heads-up, to see that she got back to the x-ray machine safely.

Half an hour later, Rathman was studying the radiographs.

"Damn, woman," he declared. "Do you eat structural steel for breakfast or something? I heard from Kaylle over in ER, and it's no wonder his team dubbed you the Lucky Lady! From what I gather happened, this should be broken, but it's not. I don't know WHY it's not, but it's not! There's a helluva lot of bruising, I'll admit, including some bone bruising — which means it ALMOST broke — and I can see where they resurfaced it, but that'll heal back nicely. You're good to go... to a point, at least. I'd stay on the crutches until tomorrow morning, though, if you can stand it. Then you can swap to a cane until it doesn't hurt to put weight on it. I'll be prescribing physical therapy once we start to show signs that the tissues are knitting back, so be aware that's coming."

"Right," Rao agreed. "So... when can I report for duty?"

"Does duty require you to be on your feet?"

"No; the current duty station is mostly a desk job."

"Good. Then you can report back for... let's say not more than three or four hours tomorrow, IF you absolutely need to. I'd really like to see you off your feet for another day or two, but the military waits for no one, as I well know."

"Ain't it the truth," Rao said with a grin.

"Yup," Rathman chuckled. "Now... since I don't want you walking far for a few days yet, have you thought about how you're going to get around the base? You usually walk to and from work, don't you?"

"Not... really," Rao admitted. "And yes, I do. Admiral Pachis has been kind enough to send his driver around to take me out and about whenever I needed to leave the house, at least so far. But I can't expect that to continue indefinitely. Probably getting me home today will be the last of that."

"What about your office building?"

"It's... kinda big. It's the headquarters building for the Tactical Division."

"Then let me write out a prescription for a mobility chair," Rathman decided. "You'll only need it for a few days, to get to and from your house and your office areas, and then you should be good to hobble around a bit farther with a cane after that." He put on a VR headset and typed on an invisible keyboard, staring at an invisible screen, for several minutes. "There. It's almost time for lunch. I want you to eat well, lots of dairy and protein, fruits and veggies, for good nutrition — oh. That's what I meant to ask. How are the migraines and nausea coming along?"

"Those seem to have gone," Rao told him. "It suddenly hit me a week ago or so, that it was only happening when I was staying long hours in the office, so I called a friend in Housekeeping, and it seems I was reacting to some cleaning stuff they were using in the office. I've been working in a different part of the building, and it's helped tremendously."

"Excellent," a pleased Rathman said, typing on the invisible keyboard again. "Okay, I just annotated your records; as soon as they tell you what it was, let me know, and I'll add that you have a known allergy to the stuff."

"Wilco," she said with a nod. "So. Good lunch..."

"Right. And then go on home, and by that time, your motorized chair should be there, and a cane already sized to your proportions — I'll send that by your orderly. I want you to use it as much as you can for the first couple days, here — short distances to start, you know, working up to longer and longer distances — then eventually you can begin weaning off it as the pain diminishes in that leg. In about a week or so, they'll come by and get the chair and you'll be on the cane exclusively. That's also when you'll need to come by so I can arrange physical therapy for that leg."

"Okeydoke. Anything else?"

"Not unless you have something."

"No, I'm as good as I'm gonna get until this leg heals up." She patted her thigh.

"All right. Let's get you back outside, and into the Admiral's car."

Once she was settled in the car behind Ortiz, he turned to look over the seat.

"How'd it go?" Ortiz wondered. "Is the leg broken?"

"No, for a wonder it isn't, Ralph, though the whole leg is pretty thoroughly bruised, clear through from side to side, based on what I understood," Rao noted with a smile of gratitude for his concern. "It came CLOSE to breaking, but didn't. That brick really clobbered it. Anyway, I'm supposed to eat well for lunch... you know, healthy... and then, by the time I get home, there'll be a motorized mobility chair waiting. I'll have that for about a week — the doctor doesn't want me on my feet any more than I can help for a few more days yet, even if it isn't broken; something about stress fractures developing in the aftermath, I gathered — and then I'll transition to a cane full-time until it heals. But I'm supposed to stay off it the rest of today, and tomorrow, too, if I can."

"Okay, then let's see about that healthy lunch before we getcha home," Ortiz decreed.

But instead of going to one of the mess halls, or heading off-base to a civilian restaurant, he turned into the rows of flag officers' townhouses. Moments later, he was pulling up in front of Admiral Pachis' home.

"Here we are, ma'am," Ortiz said with a smile. "The Admiral will be waiting for you inside. I'll help you get to the door with those crutches."

"Oh my," Rao murmured, shocked. "I... but I..."

"Won't be nobody but him, ma'am," Ortiz explained, growing serious. "We talk a lot, him and me, when it's just us in the car together. His wife died a couple years back, and... well, you didn't hear it from me, but mealtimes get lonely for him now, I think. Besides, he wants to talk to you in private — he said it was 'damned important' — and this was the best place to do it so nobody else would overhear. So I brought you straight here, on his orders."

"Oh my," Rao repeated, struggling to take it all in.

"Okay, let's go."

The stairs up to the front door proved seriously challenging for Rao on her crutches, and Ortiz offered to carry her up, but Rao refused the offer, determined not to let the Admiral see her being carried. Nevertheless, the solicitous chauffeur trailed her closely the whole way, ready to assist — or catch — in case something went amiss.

She was glad to finally reach the top, but hadn't the energy left to even ring the doorbell; Ortiz handled that matter, while she stood there and panted.

"There you are, Captain," Admiral Pachis said a few minutes later, standing from his favorite armchair by the empty fireplace, as Ortiz and the major domo, Chief Petty Officer Edwin Tomlinson, jointly escorted the hobbling woman into his study, practically shadowing her lest she trip on an area rug or otherwise lose her balance. "How are things?"

"Urf," was all Rao got out, as she attempted to negotiate her way to the Admiral on two crutches and evidently only one leg allowed; the admiral strongly suspected that today was the first day she had made much use of them, other than perhaps going to and from the necessary in her quarters, and she was rapidly and obviously wearing out as a consequence. Pachis raised a grizzled eyebrow in concern.

"Ralph, Ed, let's get her seated as fast as we can, before she falls over," Pachis decided, moving to assist. "She's still a bit weak from a, uh, a recent illness, and I'm betting she's not much used to crutches..."

Panting too much to speak, Rao shook her head in the negative, as all three men moved in. Pachis took her crutches as Ortiz stabilized her, then Ortiz and Tomlinson together formed a seat carry, moving her to the other armchair and easing her down into it. She groaned in relief, and sank back into the overstuffed leather with a sigh.

"Well, that's better," Pachis noted. "Somehow I don't expect you'll be back at the office tomorrow..."

"That... that remains... to be seen... sir," Rao said, still a little breathless from the effort at negotiating the distance from the street on the crutches, especially given the front stairs; the townhouse had no street-level entrance except the servant's entrance, and no one had thought to bring her in that way.

"Whoa, whoa, sit back there and catch your breath, Rao," Pachis ordered. "Just relax. We're not standing on ceremony, here. I thought this might be a pleasant change of pace for you, from staring at the four walls for a couple of days, and I needed to discuss some matters with you in private, regarding this whole pile of... excrement." He quirked his lips in annoyance. "I didn't consider that it might be too difficult for you to even get in here, with that bum leg."

"I probably should have carried her up the steps, sir, or else... well, hindsight being 20/20, I should have brought her in the servants' entrance, but that seemed... inappropriate," Ortiz admitted. "But she insisted she could make it. And I didn't want to disobey the Captain."

"I'm... okay," Rao insisted, still somewhat out of breath. "Just... not used to... the damn crutches. Like you said, sir."

"And still a little weak from the, ah, 'intestinal virus,' eh?" Pachis wondered.

"Probably, sir, now that you mention it," Rao said, beginning to settle.

"Ed, perhaps a glass of ice water or lemonade might be good? It's been a hot day," Pachis suggested, and Tomlinson nodded.

"Indeed, sir; I expect the Captain could use a bit of cold refreshment after all that exertion. I'll bring a pitcher of each, and glasses, right away. Begging your pardon, sir," Tomlinson interjected, "I know you had planned on dining in the private family dining room as it's smaller than the formal one, but perhaps it would be better to simply bring a cart and trays in here? That way, the Captain can sit in this nice soft chair and rest, and not have to go anywhere else, for the time."

"That's not a bad idea, Ed," Pachis considered. "Yes, let's do that. I don't need the formality, and I'm sure Captain Rao just wants to relax for a few minutes."

"I should have saluted," Rao blurted in chagrin, just then.

"Nonsense," Pachis soothed. "You rather had your hands full."

"Still."

Ortiz touched Tomlinson's shoulder and gestured toward the door, and the two non-coms slipped out, leaving the two officers to converse in private.

"There, that's better," Pachis murmured. "Now. For the time being, Captain, and while we are in my home, I think it would be good if we went on a less-formal footing. You're worn out and stressed, you've been ill, you've been injured, and I'm willing to lay a great deal of money on the likelihood that none of that happened by accident. And yet you're still trying to fight your way through doing your job, and according me the respect you feel my rank requires. And for that, all of that, you are to be commended, and I personally thank you for your efforts at respect."

"Thank you, sir," Rao said, trying to sit at attention in a chair that would barely allow her to sit upright. Pachis smiled.

"At ease, Captain. Lean back there and try to relax as much as you can. I swear, I will not bite! May I call you Mary for the time?"

"Of course, sir."

"Then, Mary, I want you to sit there and rest for a bit, while Ed fetches us some nice cool drinks, and then you can tell me how your doctor's appointment went, and we'll discuss why I asked you here, over lunch," Pachis said, giving her a smile.

A tired, sweaty Rao smiled back, then drew a deep, relieved breath, and settled back into cushioned comfort with a deep sigh.

"...And it's absolute nonsense, Mary," Pachis said over a delicious and healthy three-course luncheon, after telling her about the military police report of the brick-fall incident. "Especially given the timing. You find out that there's something in your office that isn't supposed to be there, something capable of killing you, which has made you sicker than twelve dogs according to a couple of your staff, and you move OUT of your office into the Class 1 facility, then within days of escaping that danger, a wheelbarrow-load of bricks nearly lands on your head?! Coincidence? The hell you say!"

"Well, it certainly seemed odd, sir," Rao agreed. "To be honest, if it hadn't been for you, I'd probably be dead."

"What?! How did I have anything to do with it?"

"You warned me, that day I was in your office when you almost reprimanded me," she reminded him, "that you thought it might not be an accident, the cleaning fluid in my office. And you told me to watch my back, and be wary of something else happening. And so I was."

"You saw it?"

"Pretty much," Rao averred. "I was on alert because of that, because of your warning. Out of the corner of my eye, I saw movement up at... mm, say roof level... there was someone there, because I saw him. And then the bricks fell, and I dodged. I just wasn't quite fast enough."

"You saw someone?! Was he the one who pushed the bricks...?"

"I'm... not sure, sir. Maybe. It all happened really damn fast."

"Well, it doesn't take a brick long to fall only five stories," Pachis noted, dry. "But I'm glad you took my warning seriously, and that it prevented your being killed outright."

"Me too," Rao agreed. "But... if the MPs decided it was an accident..."

Pachis shook his head.

"No. It won't do," he decreed. "Mary, as soon as you're able to do so, I want you to go over to the Intelligence Division headquarters and find Commander Ryan Byrne. He's the assistant head for Counter-Intelligence on Sigurdsen. And you tell him that he needs to investigate all this, because it's no accident. There's coincidence, and there's outrageous probabilities, and then there's deliberation. And in my estimation, this is NOT either of the former."

"But what if he doesn't believe me?"

"Ping me," Pachis declared. "I'll throw as much weight around as it takes to ensure that my planetary tactical officer is safe." He shook his head. "I only wish it didn't have to wait until you can get mobile again."

"I will be, by tonight," Rao noted. "Dr. Rathman ordered a mobility chair thing, and said it would be delivered by the time I got home from lunch."

"Really? That IS good news. When Ralph takes you home, I'll have him check it out — the reason he's my driver is because he's part of my bodyguard contingent, so he'll know what to do — to make sure the damn thing's not booby-trapped or some such shit," Pachis grumbled, staring at the empty fireplace. "Because at this rate, I wouldn't put it past whoever's doing this, if they can get their hands on it."

Rao stifled a giggle, and Pachis looked up, saw her expression, and grinned.

"Well, but it's true," he averred. "But you're right, that sounded funny as hell. A booby-trapped scooter."

They laughed together, just as Tomlinson brought in a luscious strawberry shortcake decadently piled with whipped cream.

"Ooo, my favorite!" Rao exclaimed, and Pachis smiled.

"Good," he said. "My own intelligence network still functions."

On the way out, Pachis personally escorted Rao down the service elevator and out the service entrance in the rear of the townhouse, with Tomlinson assisting as needed. Ortiz waited at the lower level with the car to take Rao home. Pachis stood in the drive and waved until they turned the corner, then went back into the service entrance, where Tomlinson awaited.

"You like her, don't you, sir?" Tomlinson wondered quietly. Pachis drew a deep breath.

"What I know of her, yes," he admitted. "But not the way you might be thinking. You're far too young to have known her, but Mary Rao reminds me a lot of my daughter Karen, who was an ensign in that Outer Colonies attack on Parchman about twenty years back..."

"Oh," Tomlinson murmured, surprised. "I knew you had a daughter, and that she died... but I didn't realize she was in the service at the time."

"She wanted to follow in her Da's footsteps," Pachis said with a sigh. "Except she didn't make it far. I sometimes feel responsible for letting her do it... but I'm responsible for a lot of young people's deaths, in the end. That's what the stars on my shoulders are about, I suppose. It just hits harder when it's the child of your own loins, I guess."

"And Captain Rao reminds you of her, you said?"

"Yes, perhaps a bit too much. I'll need to be careful not to get too involved here, but I'll be damned if I'm going to let her die like Karen did," Pachis said in a fierce almost-growl. "It's getting close to time for me to retire, Ed, and my reaction to this situation tells me it's probably the right thing... and sooner rather than later."

"But sir, you live and breathe this job," Tomlinson protested. "You love it. What will you do if you retire?"

"Oh, there's plenty to keep me busy, Ed," Pachis noted with a shrug and a wry smile. "I could go into politics and run for the Council; I could become a consultant for a corporation, or even an officer in a corporation. Start my own business. Or... I could just retire to the family farm and go fishing every day."

Tomlinson laid a light hand on the older man's arm.

"Sir, please don't be one of those officers who retires and then dies inside six months because they have nothing left to keep them going."

"Better that than wasting away as a useless hulk," Pachis pointed out. "But if I can keep this woman alive as my last act in this position, then maybe when Karen and Laura meet me in the hereafter, I can hold my head a little higher."

An exhausted Rao got a late start the next day, but Linda Mann, the orderly assigned to help her, arrived and helped her get up and properly dressed to go in to the office. Soon Rao was tooling down the sidewalk at a fair clip on her mobility chair, grinning and honking the horn as she approached any pedestrians along the way, who generally stepped aside and grinned back.

Upon arriving in the Class 2 workspace assigned to her in the basement secure facility — effectively adjacent to the Class 1 rooms, on a different corridor — she found a reminder in her messages from Admiral Pachis:

FROM: TD104669B1206548734
TO: PTO05231523598439084T8Y
SUBJECT: Reminder
Don't forget to contact CDR Ryan Byrne.
~HJP

So she contacted Byrne's secretary, Lieutenant Sofia Falk, and arranged a meeting for an hour and a half later.

Then she spent the next hour clearing her inbox before heading across the Mall, over to the Intelligence Division headquarters building.

"...No, Captain Rao, there's no need," Byrne, a handsome man with cinnamon-toned skin and riveting mahogany eyes, shook his head. "I understand that you're relatively new to the job and anxious about it, but you're being a little bit paranoid here, if you'll pardon my saying so. You've had some serious allergies, by the sound of it, of course. And being the victim of a nearly-tragic accident had to have been upsetting, and not a little frightening. But you have brought me NO evidence that anything untoward is going on, when I have in hand the military police report defining your construction-site incident as a simple accident resulting from failure to follow base regs."

"Commander Byrne, I can promise you it was no accident," Rao declared, squaring her shoulders. "There was someone on the rooftop, someone who pushed that stack of bricks to make them fall. Someone who then vanished by the time the MPs could investigate. I SAW him."

"Someone who bumped the stack and, upon seeing them topple, fled the scene to avoid getting into trouble," Byrne redefined the incident.

"If you'd seen the smirk I saw, you'd think different, Commander. I really must insist that your group investigate the circumstances that have been happening around me."

"Captain Rao, I realize you outrank me, and you may think that gives you the right to order me to do your bidding," Byrne said, calm. "But I'm in a different chain of command, we are NOT in an emergency situation, and let me suggest in the strongest possible terms that you return to your office, have a cup of chamomile, and settle down, before you do something that you may regret later... such as when you come up for your next promotion." He turned to his VR station. "This meeting is at an end, Captain."

A fuming Rao drove her scooter out of the office...

...And straight to the top floor of the Tactical Division headquarters building.

"Oh HELL no," Admiral Pachis cursed, in high dudgeon. "He may be in a different Division, but that does NOT give a commander the right to completely blow off the concerns of a captain. Hang on, Mary; let me place a few calls. Would you wait in the outer office with Olivia?"

"Certainly, sir," Rao agreed, thankful the scooter was zero-turning-radius; she spun the little vehicle and puttered quietly into the outer office, where she chatted with Lieutenant Commander Andre while waiting for Pachis' summons.

"Jake Durand," came the voice on the other end of the private line.

"Jake! Haden Pachis," the Tactical Division chief said. "Listen, I've got a bit of a situation here, and I thought maybe I needed to discuss it with you in private. My planetary tactical officer just got nowhere with your planetary assistant chief of Counter-Intelligence, and in fact, from what she tells me, he pretty much blew her off. And I'm the one that sent her to him, Jake. I think we might have a serious situation on our hands, and I'd really like your people to have a look into it before somebody actually DOES get killed."

"Damnation, Haden," Durand's surprised voice said on the connection. "Tell me what the hell's going on."

"It apparently goes back a couple of months, Jake..." Pachis began.

"Oh shit," Durand said, a few moments after Pachis had finished, allowing himself time to absorb it. "You're right; this is potentially serious. That's some helluva big coincidences to be going down, especially in such close succession. And you say she'd only been in the secure facility a few days when the bricks fell?"

"That's right, Jake," Pachis verified. "More, I double-checked, and she's not gotten any more attempts at contact from her friend over in Housekeeping, which makes me personally suspicious whether it was her friend, or anyone on her friend's staff, at all."

"I can see that," Durand decided. "Okay, Haden. Give me a little bit to look into this, and I'll see what I can do, then get back with you. After that last little reorg we got over here, Counter-Intel is, but isn't, under me any more, if you understand me, so I might have to tap-dance a little, to avoid stepping on any toes, or getting noses out of joint as to jurisdiction..."

"Understood," Pachis agreed. "Be aware that I have Rao in my outer office right now, but it's her first day back since having her leg split wide open, and I know for a fact that yesterday, her stamina wasn't up to snuff with all of the health issues and near-death shit she's been put through. AND her doctor didn't want her here more than a few hours. So I can't keep her here indefinitely."

"Got it," Durand said. "I'll work fast. If I can't get something worked in the next hour, I'll ping you a text and tell you to send her on home, and maybe I can get something planned for tomorrow."

"That'll work. Thanks, Jake."

"No problem, Haden. Wait to hear."

"Wilco."

"Later."

"Later."

Pachis rose and headed for the outer office.

"So I'm in waiting mode for right now?" Rao wondered.

"You are, but not indefinitely," Pachis said. "I know you're tired, and I know you're on light duty per doctor's orders, so if it takes too long, we'll send you home, and try to schedule something for tomorrow."

"I'm better today," Rao vouched, squaring her shoulders. "You fed me great at lunch yesterday, and Ms. Mann brought me a damn big boxed dinner from the mess last night, AND I slept like a rock. Plus, I got the scooter now. I feel a lot better."

"That's all good, but I'm still not going to push our luck," Pachis told her. "So sit here and try to rest as much as you can, and I'll let you know how this is going to go down as soon as I hear back from Intel. And if the answer is still 'No,' I have a few more aces up my sleeve I can pull, if I need to."

"Admiral, maybe it IS just all a big coincidence," Rao murmured.

"Maybe. But the probabilities are vastly against it, Captain," Pachis pointed out. "I'm not going to let this go until we have definitive proof, one way or another. I really don't want to have to bring in a newbie planetary tac officer to train," he added, giving her a slight grin. "It can be a royal pain in the ass to get you lot up to speed, you know."

Rao saw the expression, realized the great admiral was actually teasing her, and tucked her head slightly, partly disguising her own grin.

Lieutenant Commander Andre watched the byplay and smiled.

"Admiral Birken's office."

"Ken? Kennedy Fierro? That you?"

"This is Captain Kennedy Fierro. Admiral Durand?"

"Yes, it's Durand. Is Pavel in right now?"

"He's in, but he's on some paperwork."

"Tell him we might have a situation over in Tactical, and I need to talk to him as soon as he comes up for air. I'd rather not bump it to Admiral Adeler if I can help it..."

"Oh! No sir," Fierro agreed. "All right, let me see what I can do. Stand by one."

Durand waited on the line for a couple of minutes before Birken came on the line.

"Admiral Birken here. Jake? That you?"

"It's me, Pavel."

"What's this about a situation, then?"

"Well, I got a call from Haden Pachis just now," Durand explained. "He thinks he's got a situation, potentially serious, and he wants us to look into it. The tac officer in question already approached Byrne, but he blew her off, and Pachis isn't happy about it. Given that recent reorg, I can't entirely go ordering Byrne around, because counter-intel isn't fully under investigations any more, so I thought about it and decided to call you. I'd rather not bother Dagny if we can avoid it; she won't admit to it, but I don't think her health is great, if her temperament in the last year or so is any indication..."

"No," Birken murmured. "Secure line."

A series of beeps sounded, and Durand realized that he was about to be privy to a classified conversation.

"No," Birken repeated. "You're right. She's got pancreatic cancer, and the doctors can't quite get control over it."

"Oh damn," Durand murmured. "So she's hanging on until she can get to retirement?"

"Exactly. Her husband is disabled — he was involved in that mining accident in the Bliss system about ten or twelve years back, while she was stationed there — and she's trying to maximize the resources to see he's properly taken care of, when she's gone."

"Gone? You mean it's incurable?"

"That's what I gathered from her conversations, but you did NOT hear it, Jake," Birken sighed. "Not from me, anyway. Pancreatic cancer is apparently rather... persnickety and, and difficult. Modern medicine has slowed its progress a lot in the last few centuries, or she'd have been dead long since. And usually, they can knock it out. But not this time. They're not sure why."

"Well, that explains a lot," Durand decided. "I'd be in a bad mood ALL the damn time, if I was in that sitch. Never mind I'm sure she feels like shit, what with the pain and all. So... no. Let's keep Dagny out of this and you and me handle it, if we can. No reason to dump more stress on her that she doesn't need, just for the sake of protocol."

"I can get behind that." Birken gave another sigh. "She's been a great boss and a good friend, Jake. I hate like hell to see this, to watch her deteriorate like she's doing. And know she's only going to auger in, and there's nothing anybody can do."

"I understand, Pavel. Chin up, ol' buddy."

"Yeah. Let's change the subject. About this thing you got..."

"All right. So. Anyway, what I got here might be something, or it might be nothing, but it never pays to leave Tactical Division with an itch they can't scratch," Durand pointed out. "And when Iron Spine Pachis calls and asks you to start an investigation, well..."

"Mm. Yeah, good point. Okay, what are you doing in the next, oh, hour?"

"Coming to your office, it sounds like."

"Good man. I'll ping Byrne and have him up here by the time you can get here."

"On my way."

Conclaves

"Yes sirs, I understand, but seriously, she must have Admiral Pachis' ear or something, because there's nothing THERE," Commander Byrne explained. "She had some ongoing allergies to some cleaning product that was being used in the office — or, by the sound of it, she might have just had a rip-roaring case of the flu — so she started working in the Class 1 facility as she got better. After a few days of that, she was walking between buildings, got too close to a scaffold, and some unsecured bricks fell, bumping her in the leg. It's a non-issue. Even the MP investigatory report says it was an accident due to failure to follow base regs on the part of the construction firm."

He gave them printouts of the report. Both admirals studied the report in silence for long moments.

"Mm," Durand hummed.

"Exactly," Birken agreed. "It does look pretty straightforward."

"Well, not necessarily," Durand disagreed. "I could see where there might be more going on than meets the eye, here..."

"Sir, with all due respect, Captain Rao is a newbie, several times over," Byrne attested. "She was promoted to captain right at a year ago, and has only been in her current position for about seven or eight months. We're just placating an anxious officer, here."

"Is that how you see it, Commander?" Durand wondered, voice firm. "Because that 'anxious officer' happens to be the planetary tactical officer for Sigurdsen Fleet Base, and by extension, all of Jablonka — the capitol of the Commonwealth. There's a damn lot of responsibility on those shoulders, and she must be capable, or she's unlikely to have made it into that position."

"Point," Birken decided. "Still, Jake, I'm not seeing anything here to support her position, other than Iron Spine Pachis."

"Who has, by his record, excellent instincts for this sort of shit," Durand pointed out. "Frankly, as head of the Investigations Section, I think we might want to put someone on this, just to verify matters. Better to do it and not need it, than need it and not do it... and live to regret it."

"Who have we got available, then?" Birken asked Byrne, who studied the roster on his electronic display unit.

"Um, let me see," he murmured. "No, she's assigned; he's busy... those two are off-world... huh." He looked up. "There are no experienced investigators available, sirs," he said. "They're all already working other cases, and have been for at least a week, now. Of the rookie investigators, the one at the top of the roster is Ensign William Campbell. However, given this is just a babysitting mission, it should be within his abilities."

"Oh really?" Durand said, perking up. "Perfect."

"You're kidding," Birken demanded. "You're going to assign a rookie fresh out of the Academy to investigate a series of incidents for Haden Pachis?"

"He's not fresh out of the Academy, Pavel," Durand countered. "Bill Campbell graduated from the Academy three or four years ago, and frankly, he's probably in the zone for a promotion. He's the analyst who determined the aggressor in the Battle of Saarestik in that recent report."

"Then why hasn't he got some case experience under his belt?!"

"Because most of the personnel who come to us with cases don't want to be assigned an ensign. And nobody's gotten around to giving him that promotion yet, so..."

"So you're going to give Pachis and his lap dog an ensign? You're slitting your own throat, Jake."

"No, I'm not, Pavel. The Durands and the Campbells have known each other since Jablonka was first settled. We came out on the colony ship together, our ancestors. I knew Campbell's parents, and I watched him grow up when I was able, when I was around."

"But so then—"

"No," Durand denied. "I've never done anything to affect his career. He wouldn't want that, anyway. He'll rise or fall on his own. But let me tell you this, Bill Campbell is nobody's fool. If we put this in his hands, he'll go after it like a bulldog. But he's got sense; if he gets out of his depth, he'll be the first one to come to us and admit it, and ask for help. It's all about the mission, for him."

"Mm," Birken considered.

"I'd have to agree, sir," Byrne told Birken. "More, when he digs in and finds out there's nothing there, he won't try to make a mountain out of an anthill; he'll come back to us and report in, explaining that it's all in Rao's head, and there's an end of the matter."

"You're convinced it's nothing, then?" Birken verified.

"Yes sir," Byrne insisted.

"But if it isn't, and something goes down, Captain Rao is toast," Birken said.

"Not with Bill Campbell on the job," Durand declared, confident. "Trust me on that."

"So if there IS something wrong, she's safe with him?"

"Oh yeah, or I wouldn't even consider it," Durand averred. "Mark my words, Pavel, Campbell is gonna go places. Which is good, in this case; Rao IS the planetary tactical officer, after all. She might or might not be a hypochondriac, and maybe paranoid to boot, but we still have to keep her safe."

"Damn, Jake! Shouldn't we REALLY put a senior investigator on this, then?"

"Nah. At this point, it's unverified, as Commander Byrne points out. I'm gonna ride this one closely, though. If Campbell finds something, then we can bring in someone more senior... if we need to. Look, Pavel. It satisfies Rao by giving her an intelligence investigator, we can tell Pachis we have someone on it, yet we aren't calling our senior people off a known case to send 'em chasing what could be nothing. This. Works."

"I really must agree, sir," Byrne added.

Birken leaned back in his chair, throwing up his hands.

"Call Campbell in," he ordered. "And Jake, you damn well better know what you're doing."

Durand sat back with a smile.

By the time the trio had worked matters out, it was nearing the end of the normal business day, and Durand realized that the ill and injured Rao would long since have gone home, per Admiral Pachis' direction. So he messaged Pachis and Rao to let them know that matters had been worked, and if Captain Rao would come to Durand's office the next morning at 10:00 hours, he would introduce her to the investigator assigned to her case.

Both officers in the Tactical Division responded with thanks.

"All right," Commander Byrne said, once Ensign Campbell had arrived in his office at 09:00 the next morning, saluting and remaining at attention. "At ease, Campbell. Rejoice. You're getting your first case, Ensign, though it's really more a case of hand-holding than anything serious. Still, we had a request from higher-ups in the Tactical Division to handle this, so... we're handling this."

"Very good, sir," Campbell said, shifting to a slightly more relaxed stance appropriate to the situation. "I had the dossier you sent me, and reviewed it thoroughly. What's the problem?"

"We have a recently-promoted captain who's been given a very important job that she's only been in a few months," Byrne explained. "She has severe allergies but is, unfortunately, decidedly paranoid and imagines it's something dangerous. More unfortunate still, she appears to have convinced Admiral Pachis of her delusions, and he is insisting on an Intel presence in her life until matters resolve. Your mission: go calm her down."

"Is there any evidence that anything potentially serious has happened?" Campbell wondered, puzzled.

"Precious little," Byrne sniffed. "According to her, Housekeeping indicated there were known allergens in her office, but I have yet to see a report out of Housekeeping, and she couldn't produce one. But she moved out of her office and started working in the secure facility downstairs in her building, and of course got better, because she wasn't in contact with the allergens any more. A few days after that, she cut too close beside a building whose façade was being refurbished, and some unsecured bricks were accidentally knocked off the scaffolding. She avoided more serious injury, but her leg took a hit. She's tooling around on some sort of motorized chair." He shrugged. "Probably just to get sympathy. She didn't look like she was in too much pain to me."

"Mm," Campbell said, noncommittal. "Sir, is it desired that I check things out, or...?"

"Do whatever you have to do to convince Captain Rao that everything is all right, Ensign," Byrne said, waving an aggravated hand in the air. "As long as you do that, we'll be good."

"Understood, sir."

"Now, if you have no other questions, we need to get over to Admiral Durand's office, to introduce you to your new charge. Take good care of her; we don't need the head of the Tactical Division coming down on us like the wrath of God."

"Yes sir. No questions, sir."

"Let's go, then."

It didn't take long; Captain Mary Rao was already waiting on her scooter in Admiral Durand's office when they arrived.

"Oh!" Byrne said, glancing at his chronometer. "I'm sorry we're late, sir."

"No, no, not a problem, Commander, Ensign," Durand observed. "You're NOT late; Captain Rao, here, was a bit early, owing to not knowing how long it would take her to motor over here on her doctor-mandated mobility chair."

"I'm sorry," Rao apologized. "This is really only my second day out on this thing, and I'm still getting the hang of it. Too fast, the power pack dies halfway through my day; too slow, and I'm late everywhere..."

Durand held up a hand.

"It's quite all right, Captain," he said. "When one has one's leg laid open to the bone, the rest of us have to expect an adjustment period." He delivered a direct glance at Byrne, and Campbell realized that Byrne must have said something to the Admiral about the possibility of a faked injury, as he had to Campbell, moments before.

'Which means that something serious really DID happen, whether it was an accident or not,' Campbell thought. 'Hm. Now why are my instincts getting all in a knot...?'

"So," Durand continued, "Captain Rao, may I present Ensign William Campbell? Ensign Campbell, this is Captain Mary Rao, Tactical Division headquarters. Captain, Ensign Campbell is the investigator assigned to your case."

Rao blinked.

"An... ensign?"

"All of the more experienced investigators are already away on assignment," Byrne interjected smoothly. "Campbell, here, was at the top of our roster."

"But... an ensign?"

"Oh, don't let that bother you," Durand soothed, as Campbell flushed. "Campbell, here, is one of our up-and-comers; he's been out of the Academy several years, and is coming into the zone for promotion, so he won't STAY an ensign long. You're in good hands, I promise. You heard from Admiral Pachis about this, didn't you? About the communiqué I sent him?"

"Oh," Rao said, seeming to remember. "Yes, I did. All right, then. Ensign Campbell," she said, offering him a hand, "I'm very pleased to meet you, and even gladder you're on my case."

"Yes, ma'am," he said. "Likewise. I swear I'll do right by you, to the best of my ability, Captain Rao."

"That'll work," Rao said with a smile.

"Okay, let's get started, I suppose," Campbell decided, as they left the Intelligence Division headquarters building, the ensign automatically matching pace with the captain, who was motoring about on her scooter.

"Where do you want to start?" Rao wondered.

"Let's head over to your office and take a quick look," Campbell decided. "Have you gotten a report back from Housekeeping about what was wrong with it?"

"Not yet, no," Rao said, rueful. "That's one reason why I had to get Admiral Pachis to back me up to your superiors, to even get the ball rolling on this."

"Yeah, and then they assign you an ensign as an intelligence investigator," Campbell noted, more than a hint of glumness in his tone, though he tried to keep it from his face. "I'm the excuse investigator, somebody to farm off on you so they can claim they're acceding to your request, if Pachis asks. I swear, I know my stuff, Captain," he added, "I just haven't had time... nor much in the way of opportunity... to make it known, that's all. And all the rest of the experienced investigators are already out on cases, like Commander Byrne said."

"It's okay," Rao said with a placating smile. "Admiral Durand evidently pinged Admiral Pachis and told him I was in good hands. I gathered that the Durands are old family friends of the Campbells?"

"Something like that, yeah," Campbell confirmed. "He knew my parents, and I remember seeing him around when I was a kid, though I can't say as I really know him much. I guess he sorta watched me grow up, and, well, he knows I have a definite bent for this kinda stuff. It's not nepotism; he's never done anything to smooth the way for me, or anything remotely like that — and I wouldn't WANT that. It's just... he knows me. He trusts me to watch out for the situation, and know when I'm getting in over my head, so they can call someone else in. That, more than anything else, is why you got ME, and not another ensign, I think."

"That's fine. If I can't have experience, sometimes skill, talent, and determination work better anyway."

"I sure intend to try. So, about that Housekeeping report," Campbell readjusted the track of the conversation. "Do you know what the hold-up is?"

"No, I have no clue; my friend Rose-ah, Commander Rosalind Ramirez is on it, so I know there's a reason, but I haven't been able to catch up to her to find out what that reason is. Especially after this." Rao waved at her swollen leg.

"Are you sure you're going to be able to get around the base like this?" Campbell wondered, concerned. "I mean, is the battery on the chair up to that much travel?"

"Not a problem," Rao averred, "if you don't mind going a little slow. I found out yesterday that if I go too fast, I drain the power pack faster, so turtle mode seems to be better than rabbit! I know it still looks like I have an entire small building frame attached to my ass... and sometimes it feels like it!... but I can manage with the cane now, at least for short distances," she slowed the scooter's progress long enough to tap the cane set in a holder-slot. "I'm just not used to hiking around very far quite yet; it takes a surprising amount of coordination, and I'm supposed to mostly stay off the leg another day or so anyhow, so I use the scooter, as Admiral Pachis calls it. Oh, and be prepared to catch me when I get out of the thing; I tripped on the damn cane twice yesterday when I tried to get around on my own. See 'surprising amount of coordination.'"

"Oh damn! Not with the bad leg, I hope," Campbell exclaimed, worried.

"No, no. I keep it on the opposite side now," Rao said, giving him a wry grin. "The first day I was on it, though — which was the evening after the follow-up doctor's appointment, and DAMN, was I glad to get home and ditch the crutches — but that night, I didn't; I used it on the bad side, like they told me to do. Except inside five minutes, I'd whacked my calf with it, RIGHT on the medibond seam, and howled like a banshee. I expect all the neighbors heard! The next-door-right-hand neighbor, Captain Morgan, even came over to see about me! I know they say I should use the damn cane on the bad side, but shit. Lesson learned. I ain't doing THAT again!"

They laughed.

"So when does the brace come off?" Campbell wondered.

"Mm, tomorrow, maybe the day after," Rao considered. "My doctor said to keep it on as long as it hurt a lot — and I hate to admit it, but it's still pretty sore — but that as things healed, I could leave it off longer and longer. Which is kind of the same with the scooter, too. I'm hoping it heals up fast; this is already getting old."

"I can understand that. Um, change of subject. Listen, when we get to your office, kinda follow my lead, even if it seems embarrassing," Campbell told her then.

"Why?"

"Because, if this IS something bad going on, something deliberate, like you and Admiral Pachis suspect, then there's no telling where they're watching or listening, or who might be involved," Campbell explained. "I know we're in the clear so far, because Byrne is a stickler, and so is Durand; they both personally sweep their offices for bugs every day at least once, and sometimes several times, depending on what's going down, intel-wise. But if you're the target, chances are, SOMEbody is watching you. And that somebody is who we want to catch, among others. So I'm gonna analyze the situation really fast, and then go into some kinda cover, so hopefully they don't realize I'm an Intelligence investigator. Um, how do you feel about younger men?"

"What?!"

"I don't mean that as a come-on," Campbell added hastily. "I'm looking at it as a possible cover. I'd suggest a distant cousin or other relative, but that gets tricky; I don't yet know your background, and it could trip us up. We want to give anybody watching ANY other reason for my visit than 'He's investigating this shit.' You're a captain, but I'm just an ensign. If I was a little older, a potential new boyfriend would become an option. If you're personally open to dating younger men, it's still an option. I think the old-Earth term was 'cougar.' It isn't fraternization because we're not in the same chain of command. Besides, as an ensign, I'm a junior officer, not enlisted."

Rao stopped dead on the sidewalk and stared at him; fortunately, the foot traffic was low in that area at that time of day, so not only did no one run into her or fall over the scooter, nobody was around to pay any attention at all. Uncertain of her reaction, Campbell stopped also, and turned toward her. She was scanning him up and down with a coy expression, and he realized she was considering possibilities.

"Oh, I think that might work," she decided. "You're handsome, you're built; I could get into that. And now that you mention it, I'm better than 99% certain I've seen you at Don's Bar — several times. Haven't I?"

"Yes, probably; I'm a fairly regular customer there..."

"Okay. This could work. How much experience do you have?"

"I beg your pardon?" Campbell said then, feeling his face flushing. "What?"

"You KNOW what I mean, Ensign. I don't think I need to spell it out for you. I need to know how to play to your... skills."

"Um... some," Campbell finally admitted, his face feeling red-hot by this point; her coy smile became a grin, and he grasped she was joking with him. "Several. I can hold my own in a cover story like that, so watch out how you tease me now, Captain! And I'm a damn good actor, if it comes to it. Not, um, that... shit," he grumbled, breaking off what he had been about to say. "Any way I go with that is apt to get me in trouble. What I'm trying to say is that you're an attractive woman, ma'am, so it wouldn't be hard. Please don't take offense."

"Heh. None taken," Rao said, chuckling. "And thank you."

"Good," Campbell breathed, careful to ensure she couldn't hear. "One disaster averted. Bill, son, you are SO wet behind the ears at this case shit."

"Mm. How far might we have to take it?" Rao wondered then, sobering. Campbell's eyebrows shot up.

"How far...? Wait. How serious do you think this is?" he countered. "I mean, have you got an ex after you, or did you piss someone off, or...?"

"Pachis thinks it's an attack on the planetary tactical officer... me."

"Shit. Damn serious, then," Campbell decided, thinking fast. "I knew you were the tactical officer, but I didn't realize that was actually a part of this; nobody told me that when they briefed me."

"What DID they tell you, then?"

Campbell stared at her, pondering how much to tell her of Byrne's disparaging remarks. Just then, she sighed and answered her own question.

"I get that. 'Recently-promoted captain given important job that she's only been in a few months, has severe allergies but is paranoid and imagines it's something dangerous; go calm her down' or the like, right?"

"Um," Campbell said, realizing she had very nearly nailed the actual wording. He rapidly concluded that that was as much confirmation as he dared, while seeing her understanding of his response... or lack thereof... in her eyes. "Look. I've never been keen on that whole 'sleeping with somebody because it's your job' concept, and I hope I never have to go there... though I guess I would if I absolutely HAD to, to keep the Commonwealth safe, maybe, or possibly to save my own skin... though I doubt it. But this could get messy and, um, well, we might need to make it LOOK like it..."

"Fair enough," Rao agreed, "if you know how to make it look like it without it actually happening. No offense intended, because I agree with you, and with your philosophy on the subject." She paused. "I guess maybe I need to have my home scanned for, I dunno, bugs?"

"That might not be a bad idea," he allowed. "And I can have that done, or do it myself. But in the meantime, we can always go over to my place if we need it to look... seductive."

"You aren't in barracks?" Rao asked, eyebrow shooting up. "Single ensign...?"

"Single ensign in INTELLIGENCE," Campbell pointed out, "with a certain amount of 'he's got promise' behind him. I have an apartment in base housing."

"OOOooohhhh," she said in sudden understanding. "I see now. So that way, you have the privacy to do what needs doing, if something just like this situation ever comes up. And I bet the building is controlled by the Intelligence Division."

"Right on all points," Campbell confirmed, nodding. "That said, it IS a flat in base housing. Just not barracks. It's not fancy, but it's nice, and it's comfortable. And I know it's clear, because I make sure it is. Every day."

"Hm. Okay, that might work and still meet the proprieties," Rao decided. "So... your answer is, 'Yes, I'm open to the concept, at least, provided there are limits to how far this charade has to go.'"

"Got it," Campbell said with another nod. "And I'll see to it that Admiral Pachis knows this is a cover, so you don't get in trouble. But be prepared: when we get to your office, I'll assess FAST, and you need to be ready in case I plant one on you."

"Uh," Rao grunted, discomfited. "Um, okay. I suppose it's better to fake an affair and survive, than die a gruesome death. Which I almost already did. A couple times over, if Pachis is right. So I guess I'm a cougar now. Rawr."

Campbell snorted, and Rao grinned.

"Okay, let's go."

When they arrived at the building where the Tactical Division was housed, Campbell took her near hand; the controls of the mobility chair were such that she could, and usually did, 'drive' with only one hand. They headed inside, aimed for the suite of rooms housing the Planetary Tactical Office.

On arrival, Campbell slapped a shit-eating grin on his face, and followed Rao into her office, closing the door behind them.

"Finally! Out of sight! C'mere, baby," he said in a normal voice, leaning over her and planting a big, but completely chaste, kiss on her mouth. "There. Now, what did you need outta here?"

"Um," she murmured, apparently taken off-guard. "I, uh, lessee... oh!" she exclaimed then. "I needed to transfer some files to the Class 2 workspace downstairs." She paused, then her jaw dropped. "Where's my VR set? It's gone! What the hell happened to my damn VR set?!"

"Hold on, honey," Campbell said, reaching into a pocket of his shipsuit. "I got my portables, right here." He pulled out the small device, and hooked it into the plug on her desk — certain linkages were hard, to provide for a certain increased security — then handed it to her. "Here you go."

Rao donned the small set, typed on an invisible keyboard, then thought for a moment before swiping her fingers across an invisible screen, then typing again. Finally she removed the device, decoupled the link and removed the plug, then handed it back to Campbell.

"Thanks," she murmured. "I guess Rose is cleaning mine."

"Prob'ly," Campbell agreed, maintaining what he was starting to think of as his 'dumb boy toy' character. "You done with the work stuff now, baby?"

"Yes, I think so."

"Good. How 'bout you introduce me to some of your people?" Campbell said, opening the door for her scooter. "I mean, it looks like they may be seeing a lot of me now, so..."

"Heh. Good point, sweetie," Rao noted with a mischievous grin; it seemed she had finally settled into the cover story, and was up for playing the game. She trundled the scooter into the main bullpen. "All right. Hey, everybody, when you get a chance to come up for air for a few, I have someone I'd like you to meet."

Absent responses met her call, and within a few minutes some half-dozen people clustered around.

"Okay, guys, this is a, um, a new friend of mine," Rao said, blushing slightly. "I ran into him at Don's a few nights ago, and we, uh, hit it off. He's been, well, helping me after the accident with the bricks..." she tried, and Campbell realized that she had decided to use the MP report when referencing the brick-fall incident, at least for purposes of a cover story. "Anyway, this is Bill Campbell. We're kind of, well..."

"If things keep on like they're going, we might file as companions," Campbell noted, allowing another of his patented shit-eating grins to spread across his face. "Mary's something special."

"So like I said, this is Bill," Rao said. "Bill, this is my team." She gestured at each person in turn. "My number two, Commander Brian Lee Gnad; his assistant, Lieutenant Commander Robert Glaub; Lieutenant Jeffery Kooistra; Lieutenant Susan Powers; Lieutenant David Weiner; Lieutenant James Burk, and Lieutenant JoAnn Zinn."

As Rao introduced them, Campbell stepped forward and shook their hands, smiling that same nigh-idiotic grin.

"Pleased to meet you, er..." Gnad began, then glanced at the rank pips on Campbell's shoulders. "Ensign?"

"Yup," Campbell said, grin getting wider. "Older women are just SO sexy, don't you think, Commander?" He shot Rao an amorous glance, and she blushed.

"I have heard so, yes," Gnad noted, somewhat prim; Campbell suddenly realized he was desperately stifling a smirk. "I can't say that I've had personal experience, though."

"Oh, well, you should try it sometime," Campbell declared. "You'd be amazed what you can learn, that way." He winked at the other man, even as Rao flushed even deeper. "Anyway, you can figure on seeing a bit more of me in future. I'm completely smitten with your boss, here, and I hope she feels the same."

"It's a wonderful relationship so far," Rao admitted. "And yes, I do hope it continues, and goes well." Only Campbell knew what she was really referencing.

"That sounds awfully sweet," Lieutenant Zinn noted with a friendly smile. "I'm glad for you, Captain Rao. And you too, Ensign Campbell."

"He's on the brink of coming into his promotion window," Rao pointed out, "so we have hopes he'll be a lieutenant soon, too."

"Even better," Kooistra declared. "Come by any time, Ensign; we'll be glad to see you."

"Thanks ever so," Campbell said, offering another smile. "I'll probably be with this lovely lady whenever my supervisor lets me off my leash."

"Or whenever you can slip that leash, eh, Bill?" Rao riposted.

"You bet, babe." Campbell blew her an air-kiss, then added, "Ready to grab some lunch?"

"I could be talked into it," Rao decided. "Ever since I got dropped on by a ton o' bricks, I've been starved."

"I suppose healing up will do that to a body," Powers commented.

"I suppose," Rao agreed. "Mess hall, or off-base?"

"I dunno," Campbell said, as they turned for the door. "What do you feel like? Oh!" He turned and waved at the group of officers. "Nice to meet you all! Be seeing you!"

A chorus of "Back atcha! Good to meet you too!" floated back to him as he and Rao exited the office suite.

"Well? What did you think?" Rao wondered, as they headed down the sidewalk outside the Tactical building. Campbell had held her hand until they got to the corner, when she needed both hands on the scooter controls to navigate the turn, so he let go. "Did you pick up anything?"

"I'm not sure yet," Campbell said. "Give me some time to mull over the interaction, first."

˙"Okay. Were you serious about lunch?"

"Yeah, I was. I figure, if the hole in your leg was as bad as it sounded, you probably need to keep up regular meals, and I need to help you with that whenever possible."

"Oh. Well, yeah. It went to the bone, and then some. They had to resurface the bone and smooth it out. Why it didn't break outright, I don't know, and apparently neither do the doctors. Maybe the angle was just lucky for me or something." She shook her head. "Unless I have some serious cosmetic work done, I'm gonna have a nasty-bad scar. And even then, I'll still have a bad scar, they said. Just not AS bad."

"Why so bad? I'd have thought a brick would be a blunt-force type injury."

"The corner of the brick gouged down almost the whole length of my calf," Rao explained. "It was a very ragged kind of... I guess you could call it a cut, only with a big flap of flesh dangling at the bottom. They had to kind of trim everything up, lay it all back in place a little at a time, and medibond it back together, from what the doctors told me... and what it looks like. And right now, it's every shade of the rainbow," she added.

"Ow." Campbell winced in sympathy. "All right, let's hit the mess, but let's use the one over near the Intelligence Division; it's always swarming with intel people, and it should be safe. Plus, whoever seems to be after you won't expect it."

"This works."

So they headed out for lunch.

Over lunch, they carried on a quiet discussion of what to do next, and Campbell decided he needed to see the construction site where the bricks had fallen.

"And I want to see exactly where it happened," Campbell declared. "I might be able to pick up a few things from it."

"Okay," Rao agreed. "It isn't that far away, anyway."

"Good," he said, picking up her empty tray along with his own. "Let me dump these and we'll head out."

At the site of the construction accident, Rao showed Campbell where it happened. Once the military police had finished their investigation, they had removed their markers and opened the site back up for construction, so she had to point out specifics, such as where she had fallen, and where the brick had ended up that injured her leg. The blood stain on the sidewalk where her leg had bled rather profusely was still fairly conspicuous; it had not been washed and the weather had remained clear, so there were still clots and blobs of dried blood on the pavement, in addition to the stain.

"But the place where the main pile landed is pretty obvious, too, even after clearing the site," Campbell noted, pointing out the red brick dust all over the pitted slab of sidewalk. Then he looked up, craning his neck and shading his eyes with one hand, trying to judge where the stack would have been, where the fallen bricks had originated.

"Yes, it is, isn't it?" Rao agreed, pointing. "It was right up there; see the new bricks in the façade? They weren't there when the bricks fell on me, but the stack was to the immediate left of that. And the guy that I think pushed 'em was on the roof directly over that, though I can't say for sure, it all happened so fast. I guess I'm damn lucky not to be dead."

"What caused you to notice it in time to dodge?" Campbell wondered. "It doesn't take a brick long to fall five stories, after all; only, mm, a second, second and a half, maybe. Plenty high enough to kill, not high enough to really see it coming..."

"Because of Admiral Pachis' warning, I was sort of on alert, I suppose you could say," Rao admitted. "I saw the motion out of the corner of my eye and instinctively lunged away. See, I'd gotten a call from Housekeeping to come over — I assumed my friend Rose had finally completed HER investigation on my office—"

"Wait. You 'assumed'?" Campbell followed up. "You don't know? It wasn't her that called?"

"No, I didn't recognize the voice, though he said he was Jim, and I know Jim was the guy she called to come decontaminate my office," Rao said, then stopped, her jaw going slack as comprehension hit. "Oh shit. Someone set me up, didn't they?"

"That sounds like a definite possibility," Campbell said, quickly double-checking the roof and the scaffolding — which had been moved — but seeing nothing of substance that could be dropped on them. "Okay, we're clear today, it looks like. Unless someone leans over the top and drops a hammer or something."

Rao's eyes widened in concern, but the workers had moved on and started repairing the brick façade around the corner from where the pair now stood, so even had such a thing occurred, the perpetrator would have had no cover for his act. Just then, one of the workers looked up and saw the pair, and his eyes widened. He leaned over and said something to his coworker, then laid down his tools and made a beeline for Rao and Campbell.

"Heads up," Campbell murmured, *sotto voce*. "Here comes a construction worker."

"Oh shit," Rao breathed...

...And then the brick mason was there.

"Wow, oh wow," the man said, anxious and concerned. "Ma'am, forgive me for not bein' able to tell your rank; my name's Peters, an' I'm a civilian contractor hired to help; I di'n't serve, so I don't have no experience readin' th' insignia..."

"She's a captain," Campbell filled in for the man. "Captain Rao."

"Okay, but... she's the lady that the bricks fell on, right?" Peters wondered. "She's inna scooter, an' got th' bad leg an' all, where they hit 'er..."

"I am," Rao said, a bit prim in her manner.

"Oh shit, pardon my language! Ma'am, my deepest apologies," Peters exclaimed. "I dunno what th' hell happened, but I swear to you on everything I find holy, I put in those restraints afore I headed out for lunch! In fact, I work with 'em in, 'cause I had a friend got kilt 'bout three year ago, when a stack what wadn't secured proper fell on 'im, an' it wadn't pretty. Way I figger, better t' be a little slower an' safe, than ta go fast an' somebody get kilt."

"But the Military Police investigative report said there was no sign of restraint on the stack," Campbell noted.

"I know — my supervisor 'uz very upset over that, an' he and I both swore up an' down to Captain Thompson 'at they were on there when we left," Peters averred, upset. "He 'uz a little curt, Captain Thompson, and I could tell he didn't believe me..." He paused, and glanced between Rao and Campbell, his expression sober. "They's gonna fine th' company f'r not followin' regs, but I swear, sir, ma'am, the restraints were on there. You can put me through some sort o' lie test if you want to."

"Tell me what happened from your point of view, if you would," Campbell said, as he recorded the man's testimony on his small electronic display unit, which he'd just produced from a pocket of his shipsuit. Rao nodded in approval and confirmation; Peters nodded agreement.

"Well, we've been workin' on the base refurbishment contract for 'bout six months now," Peters explained. "We started on the barracks, here, 'bout two weeks ago, and since we're only responsible for th' external masonry, it's moved pretty fast. We work on one wall at a time; we put up th' scaffolding an' survey the entire wall for what needs t' be popped off an' replaced, then we bring in cubes o' brick an' a scissors lift, and offload what's needed to each level of the scaffold, in turn, as we move up — ya don't want all th' levels workin' at once, on accounta if somebody slips an' drops a brick, it'd land on somebody under ya. An' as ya know by now, that ain't good." He gave a wry excuse for a grin to Rao, waving a hand at her braced leg. "In between transferrin' bricks from the scissors lift, whatever's left o' the cube gets secured on top o' the lift, accordin' to base regulations — with our own best practices added on top of. Then the lift gets cranked back down t' the ground an' th' whole thing secured, in case the wind gets up or somethin', ya know." He shrugged. "Ord'nary wind won't affect it, o' course, but if we get a nasty storm or somethin', well, that can be a whole 'nother story, dependin' on how severe it is."

"Okay, go on," Campbell said, nodding.

"Um, okay. So we'd finished th' lower levels an' were finishin' off th' top courses, while our foremen were surveyin' th' next wall — the one we're workin' on now — to determine th' best places t' affix an' anchor the scaffolding," Peters continued. "It was comin' up on lunch, an' I was gonna be gone an extra-long time; th' master mason,

Jimmy, knew 'bout it, 'cause I threw out my back last weekend — I got a little boy, an' he likes ta play cowboy, with me on all-fours as his horse..." Peters flushed; Rao offered him a soft smile, and Campbell gave the other man a friendly, understanding grin. Encouraged, and his embarrassment lessened by their sympathetic responses, Peters went on with his tale. "So anyways, I 'uz goin' to the doctor f'r my back right after I grabbed a bite, so's I made especial sure to secure the stack b'fore I left. An' Jimmy, he SAW me do it."

"Is this Jimmy handy to confirm that?" Rao wondered.

"Yassum." Peters turned and waved at the coworker to whom he'd spoken before coming to apologize, and the man, who had been watching with a worried expression, immediately headed over. "Captain Rao an'... um, friend," Peters tried, as the other man reached them.

"Friend, yes; I'm Ensign Campbell," Campbell said, proffering a hand to shake, as did Rao; all four shook hands. "Mary, here, was just showing me how she got hurt, and your man Mr. Peters, here, has been trying to explain that you don't know HOW the bricks got loose."

"Yeah, Jimmy, what he said," Peters averred. "Ennyhow, this is our foreman an' master mason, Jimmy Adams, sir, ma'am."

"Pleased to meet you both," Adams said. "So what do you need from me?"

"Oh, nothing, sir," Rao said with a smile. "Mr. Peters was just saying that you could confirm that the bricks were restrained, because you saw him do it."

"Not only saw, lent a hand," Adams insisted. "To do it right, the way my construction firm prefers — which, let me note, somewhat exceeds base regulations — you really need four hands. And I knew Dan, here, was going to be gone a good while, 'cause of the doctor appointment for his back. He was hurtin', and everybody here could see it, so I was glad he was getting it looked at. Given he's just shy of hitting master mason himself, he's one of my best people, and I like him to be in top form. Never mind seeing a friend freed of pain."

"So you can both vouch for the fact that when you broke off for lunch, the bricks were secured?" Campbell confirmed.

"Yes sir," Adams maintained. "I'd swear to that on a stack of Bibles."

"That," Peters affirmed.

"But somehow, those restraints disappeared..." Campbell murmured, thoughtful.

"Good way of putting it," Adams observed, scratching his head, "since we haven't found the restraints yet. It's like they just vanished into thin air."

"And nobody saw anything unusual, no strange or unfamiliar workers?" Campbell pressed.

"No sir. There WAS some scuttlebutt about a couple of the guys coming back and moving some bricks to the roof, 'cause it's easier to do those decorative crenelations from there than from the scaffolding, but it wasn't done at the time under consideration, and none of my guys claimed to have been involved," Adams informed them. "So I figured it was just some talk that nobody followed through on. You think somebody's tryin' to sabotage my site?"

"I think the two of you need to be very quiet about it," Campbell warned, dropping his voice, "don't talk to anyone else except a proper, identified investigator, and be prepared to testify about it, if it comes to that."

Rao shot him a surreptitious glance, and the two masons stared at each other in concern.

As the two masons returned to the job, Campbell absently watched them go, deep in thought, as Rao, in her turn, watched him.

'Hm,' he thought, mulling over the information to which he was now privy. 'Two major safety reg violations negatively affecting the same officer — and only that officer — in a matter of weeks. Violations such that either of them could have resulted in her death. More, that officer is the planetary tactical officer for Sigurdsen, and therefore for essentially all of Jablonka, the Commonwealth capital. This isn't good. More and more it's looking to me like Admiral Pachis is right, and this is a targeted attack. I can see several possible reasons, though: one, throw the planetary tactical defense into confusion, while someone — whoever's behind this — seizes the opportunity to attack the heart of the Commonwealth; or two, eliminate the loyal tactical officer, supplanting her with someone loyal to another officer; or three, eliminate the loyal tactical officer, supplanting her with someone loyal to an outside agency, most likely an enemy of the Commonwealth. And I get to decide if, and which. What fun.'

Just then, a young man wearing the silver bar of a lieutenant walked by, staring at the pair. 'But more at ME than Rao,' Campbell decided, as he absently watched the other man. 'Almost a glare, even. And his face... he's familiar. I know this guy. Who... aw, shit. Was that Marc Huber? I'm better than ninety percent certain it was. I thought I'd shaken that guy years ago, when he got out of OCS. Didn't he get assigned...? Well, by now, though, he's probably back. Might be in between assignments, I suppose. But given the chip on his shoulder where I'm concerned — and I never did figure out why — I sure as hell don't need him nosing around, throwing a monkey wrench into my first real investigation.' He stifled a sigh. Then a recollection hit him. 'Oh shit. Waitaminit. Wasn't he from...? Yeah, he was an import. From an Outer Colony, if memory serves. Becker, wasn't it? I need to check. 'Cause that is one damn interesting coincidence, if he happens to just be walking by here, watching us, as Rao is showing me the site of what's looking more and more like attempted murder. And I don't believe in coincidences.'

Campbell watched until Lieutenant Huber turned the corner and disappeared behind a building down the street, pondering whether or not the apparent chance encounter truly did have anything to do with what had happened here only days earlier, or if the word had already gotten around and he was being watched as much as Rao.

After a few moments, he shook himself out of his reverie, privately determining to look up Huber later, and see if he couldn't compile a dossier on him, just to check things out. Then he turned to Captain Rao.

"Okay, now we need to go talk to your friend Commander Ramirez right away," Campbell decreed. "You know where her office is?"

"Of course," Rao declared. "Down the street three blocks, and around the corner."

"Let's go. I have a shit-ton of questions for her and her team now."

CAMPBELL: THE SIGURDSEN INCIDENT

They headed down the street.

Confirmation

"WHAT?! Oh damn! No, I most certainly did NOT order that summons!" Commander Ramirez declared in her office. "And I know none of my people did, either, because I expressly told them to tell no one until the report was ready to be issued. And then verified it with each of them only yesterday in our staff meeting! Either somebody lied, or somebody... ¡condenación!" she cursed, briefly dropping into her grandfather's linguistics.

The three — Ramirez, Rao, and Campbell — sat in Ramirez' office in the Facilities building, door closed. Ramirez had come out from behind her desk to sit with the other two in a small but comfortable conclave area shoehorned into the corner of her not-overlarge office. Now she sat forward, eyes wide.

"Do you mean to tell me that I was the carrot used to lure Mar' into position to kill?" she demanded to know.

"It's looking more and more like that's what happened, yes," Campbell admitted, as Rao leaned over and put a calming hand on Ramirez' shoulder.

"Oh damnation cubed," Ramirez cursed, furious. "That confirms it, then. We have a traitor on staff here, somewhere."

"That's likely," Campbell agreed. "Can you tell us where this 'Jim' was, at the time the call was made?" He handed her his electronic display unit, which displayed a copy of Captain Thompson's investigative report.

"Mm. Let's see," she murmured, scrolling through the report. "Late last week... Thursday, about... mm. Yes, as a matter of fact, I can," she determined. "He was in the lab, with me, working out details of exactly what the shit is that was in Captain Rao's office."

"You're sure?"

"Positive. We've been working on this, he and I, all day, every day, since Mar' called me about it. Some days, we don't even take a lunch break. And to tell the truth, we haven't taken our days off, either. It's that bad."

"I thought you were decontaminating at night."

"His team is. He started with 'em, but once the worst of it was cleared, he left Robert in charge of finishing the job and started popping back and forth, beginning the lab work. Once her office was largely cleared — which happened the day AFTER the incident with the bricks — he transitioned to full-time with me, doing the lab work. I haven't told Mar' to move back in, because until we figure out how it got there in the first place, I can't say it wouldn't happen again."

"Is that what happened to my VR set and my chair?" Rao wondered. "Were they contaminated?"

"To the hilt," Ramirez confirmed. "And yes, it was too bad to clean; we had to have them destroyed. I guess the replacements haven't arrived yet."

"All right; I understand," Campbell decided. "Do you have a report on the contaminants in Captain Rao's office ready for us, or is that still in work?"

"I had just been about to send it to her, Vice Admiral Takala over in Tactical, and Rear Admiral Westerfield, my superior, the head of the entire Housekeeping department."

Campbell and Rao exchanged glances; he raised a querying eyebrow, and she nodded.

"Might I modify that distribution a bit, Commander Ramirez?" Campbell asked.

"I think not, ENSIGN Campbell. Why are you even here?" Ramirez responded, reserved, cool, and mildly offended.

"Rose, he's INTEL," Rao breathed, leaning forward to murmur into Ramirez' ear. "He's investigating what happened. So don't tell anybody."

"They gave you an ENSIGN as an...?" Ramirez began, incensed. "Honestly!"

Campbell sighed to himself.

"He's good, hon," Rao told her. "He only got assigned the case this morning, and he's already surveyed my office suite and staff, studied the brick-fall site, interviewed two of the brick masons, and headed straight here... AND determined there definitely IS something to worry about."

"Not one hundred percent definitely, not yet," Campbell corrected. "The likelihood is high, in my estimation, but I need to get this all together, then go back to my office and check on a few things first. But if I find what I think I'm gonna find, then... yeah. I'll be reporting straight to Commander Byrne and Rear Admiral Durand, who will, in turn, most likely notify Admiral Pachis."

Ramirez' eyebrows shot up.

"Hm. Well, all right, Ensign. What's your proposed distribution?"

"I'd like you to send it, under SECURE cover, to Captain Rao, here," Campbell ticked off fingers, "myself, and the aforementioned Commander Ryan Byrne, assistant Counter-Intelligence chief; Rear Admiral Jacob Durand, head of the Investigations Section of Intelligence Division; and Admiral Haden J. Pachis, the head of Tactical Division. And ONLY those five people, for now."

"Because they're the only ones who know Intel is investigating this," Ramirez suggested. "You, specifically."

"Exactly. And right now, that's ALL we want knowing," Campbell pointed out. "We don't know who is doing this, or who is involved. And as you suggested, you certainly have at least one mole in your organization, possibly — I'd say probably — more. Some of whom may even be on your decontamination team. And now you know it. Which puts you in danger now, too. So I'm going to go to Admiral Durand and have him arrange with Admiral Westerfield for you to go on a temporary leave... effective immediately. So when we leave here, I want you to go home and pack a bug-out bag with whatever you need to spend a few weeks to months away... and then go. And don't tell anyone where you're going, except maybe me or Admiral Durand."

"Whoa," Ramirez mumbled, sitting back. "This IS serious."

"Deadly serious," Campbell pronounced. "Emphasis on deadly."

"But... why?" Ramirez wanted to know. "Mary doesn't have an enemy in the world..."

"Hold up, Rose," Rao murmured. "Think about my job."

"You mean... oh hell," Ramirez whispered. "It isn't YOU, it's the POSITION..."

"You didn't hear that," Campbell noted, keeping his voice as low as the women's had been. "Now, is there any chance I could get an advance look at your results?"

"Yeah, hang on a moment while I pull it up," Ramirez said, rising and going to her desk.

"...It appears to be a cleaning compound that might possibly be used for industrial cleaning of heavy equipment," Ramirez said, showing them the display of ingredients on her electronic display unit. "As nearly as we can tell, it seems to be composed of four chemicals, all of which can be inhaled, inadvertently consumed through deposition, and even absorbed through the skin... which means lots of routes to enter the body and cause plenty of problems."

"Shit," Rao grumbled.

"Go on," Campbell said.

"All right. The first is toluene, otherwise known as methyl benzene. In low doses, it can cause skin and eye irritation, dizziness, nausea, loss of appetite, vomiting, tiredness, confusion, and in higher concentrations, unconsciousness and death. The symptoms typically disappear in time, when exposure is removed."

"Which would explain why I got better when I was off-duty," Rao realized. "And the low-dose symptoms are all me. I had all of those."

"Yes, but I'm not nearly done yet," Ramirez noted. "The second chemical is benzene itself. It can also cause skin and eye irritation, drowsiness, tiredness, dizziness, nausea, vomiting, confusion and headaches in low doses, and in higher doses, unconsciousness and death, but it's also a definite carcinogen, and is considered unsafe to handle in any amount without significant protective measures... which, of course, Mar' didn't have. We'll need to have Mary checked out thoroughly by her physician, and any preventative measures she needs taken right away, to clear her systems of the toxins, and counter the long-term damage. Because there WILL be some, if we don't."

Rao paled.

"The third chemical is called cellosolve in the trade, or butyl cellosolve, known chemically as 2-butoxyethanol," Ramirez continued. "It can cause skin and eye irritation, nausea, vomiting, and headache, at low doses or concentrations. In higher concentrations, it can cause respiratory difficulty, low blood pressure, damage to red blood cells, subsequent weakness corresponding to same, and it is considered a teratogen."

"What's a teratogen?" Rao wondered.

"It can cause birth defects," Ramirez elaborated, but gently, even as Rao paled again. "So all the more reason why we need to get you in to see Dr. Rathman as soon as we can. I mean, I know you're not expectant, but I don't know if it can affect the eggs or not, 'cause I'm not a physician. So we need a physician to verify that there's no long-term damage."

"That's three," Campbell noted. "You said four components."

"Yes. The fourth is called MEK."

"Methyl ethyl ketone, or butanone," Campbell said, recognizing the chemical. "I remember it from my chemistry studies at the Academy."

"Right," Ramirez confirmed. "Now, it has similar nasty side effects relative to the other chemicals, but there is also evidence that it actually potentiates — amplifies — the effects of other chemicals."

"Meaning," Campbell extrapolated, as he raised a comprehending eyebrow, "that whoever used that mix could use less of the other shit, because the MEK would bump up the effects."

Ramirez stared at him.

"I... hadn't thought of it like that," she finally admitted. "But yes, it would have that effect. I was by way of, 'This is a really damn bad combo,' not, 'somebody did it deliberately.' But... hell." She shook herself, then continued. "More, this is NOT a commercially-available blend of cleaners... for ANYthing, that we could find. It's a unique blend, and would have had to be custom-mixed."

Campbell nodded.

"Yes. I'm not surprised. I fully expected that, after you explained about the MEK," he said. "This was a mixture deliberately concocted, then applied to Captain Rao's office with the intent to cause her harm, and over time, to kill her."

Rao went nearly white.

"Were the proportions consistent over time, or could you tell, given that most of those are volatiles?" Campbell wondered.

"We were able to determine a little of the time distribution," Ramirez said. "It took a bit of doing, but I called in our special chem-lab team — they have certain forensics skills, for situations... well, not LIKE this, but like this, if you understand me."

"I do. And?"

"The proportions of most of the chemicals were consistent over time," Ramirez noted, "but evidently the amount of benzene in the mix was being gradually increased."

"And it's the most toxic," Campbell observed.

"Yes."

"Commander Ramirez, let me ask you one more thing."

"Of course, Ensign Campbell; ask me anything. You just demonstrated to me that you DO need to be here, and to have this information. And that you may be capable of sorting this out, and protecting Mar'. Any info I have, or knowledge I can impart, to help protect my childhood playmate from whoever these bastards are is at your disposal."

"Is it normal for the inner office of a suite, such as that for the Planetary Tactical Officer, to have a negative atmospheric pressure differential?"

"Wha-I beg your pardon? To have a what?"

Campbell gave a wry laugh, even as Rao and Ramirez both stared at him in confusion.

"I noticed that this morning, when she took me there. Captain Rao's office is set up to have negative pressure, relative to the outside office," he pointed out. "The air flows INTO her office, not out from it. The main air intake and filter for the entire suite is in the corner of her office, not in the bullpen outside... but the outflow vents are all in the external office. The air is drawn in... and thus, the chemicals within can't escape to contaminate the bullpen."

The other two stared at him in horror. Finally Rao regained the capacity for speech.

"You think it's one of my own people...?"

"Not necessarily," Campbell said, keeping his voice low and soothing, as he held up a staying hand. "None of your staff may even know this is happening. It may simply be that whoever wants you dead has someone in your office in mind to take your place, someone he deems more suited to his eventual intent, possibly because of, say, an inherent docility, bias, bent, or the like."

"And therefore is protecting his desired candidate for the position," Ramirez grasped.

"Exactly, Commander." Campbell sighed. "After your little chemistry lesson, I think it's confirmed, though — somebody IS trying to kill Captain Rao."

"...But yes, I can confirm that," Ramirez said, accessing files from her VR. "The base-wide retrofit and refurbishing reached and completed Mar's building about two and a half, maybe three months ago. Does that sound right, Mary?"

"Yeah, Rose, that's when they finished," Rao averred. "About two and a half months ago, or roughly two to three weeks before I started getting sick."

"And the air vents were re-routed at that time, supposedly to provide for a more even distribution of air flow, and better efficiency," Ramirez said, her voice growing caustic. "So something changed about three to six months ago, when this was being planned in Facilities — because this reroute would be Facilities, not the Housekeeping department WITHIN Facilities."

"Mm," Campbell hummed. "That's good information. So this has been in planning maybe as long as six months, but the actual activity occurred — and was completed — not longer than about two or three months back."

"Correct."

"All right, then," Campbell said. "Commander Ramirez, please finish anything urgent you have in hand right away, send the report to that limited distribution we decided upon, making sure it is under classified header, and then leave at once, like we discussed earlier. I'll see to it that your ass is covered for the matter. I understand that you're responsible for sending Captain Rao to work in the Class 1 secure facility in the Tactical Division headquarters building, which is where I've gathered she's been working?"

"Yes," Ramirez agreed, quickly donning a VR set and typing on an invisible keyboard as she apparently prepared matters for her extended departure. "Given her work, and the situation, I thought that was the best place for her to set up a kind of remote shop. Not that I expected this to be deliberate, but I thought we might have to re-train an idiot for another line of work."

"That was excellently thought out, though," Campbell agreed. "Now, you finish and then GO. I'll escort your friend Mary back to Tactical, to the secure facility."

"Right," Ramirez said, coming around the desk. "I'll be out of here in five. Mar', you be careful, okay? I want you around when I come back."

"I will, Rose," Rao asserted, as the two old friends hugged. "You be careful too. Don't get yourself offed before you can get out of harm's way."

"I planned on calling Ted," Ramirez said with a grin.

"Ooo, the fiancé of long standing." Rao returned the grin. "Will he go with?"

"I hope so."

"Long standing?" Campbell caught the term.

"Another childhood friend," Rao explained. "We three all hung out together. We were inseparable. There's no way Ted would ever hurt either of us, and he'd fight to the death to protect Rose, now that they're about to file as permanent companions."

"Good plan, then," Campbell decided. "Captain, shall we go?"

"Let's," Rao agreed.

Holding her hand as befitted a smitten new boyfriend, Campbell escorted Rao back to the basement secure facility in Tactical, then, after a couple of brief detours, he headed for his own 'office' in Intel — a desk in one of the bullpen areas, given his junior status.

He logged into his VR system and pulled up some basic info — org charts, personnel files, and the like.

"Mm, that's interesting," he decided. "Huber and his mother ARE from Becker. And she married the chief of staff to the ambassador to the CFP from Stadt. That throws suspicion on expats from Becker and Stadt, notably the chief of staff from Stadt; the kid probably isn't old enough to run an operation of this magnitude, but he IS plenty old enough to participate."

Then he pulled up Rao's org chart and looked at her personnel.

"Well, damn," he grumbled. "Two staffers are imported from Seacrest, a third from Drake, a fourth from Stadt, and her organizational second, that Gnad guy — who would replace her if anything happened — is from Guernsey. So I got five people out of seven in her org chart that need investigating, though all of 'em look to have good reps. They may BE good people, but whoever wants Captain Rao dead is sure trying to protect one or more of 'em. Meanwhile," he added, pulling up another Division's org chart, "over in the Housekeeping department, we have two with Outer Colonies affiliations that, per Ramirez' last communique before departing, had

had access to Rao's office. And of COURSE, one is from Becker, and one is from Stadt. THERE'S a huge coincidence." He shook his head. 'It may be something, or it may be nothing,' he considered, pondering the matter. 'Just because they're not originally from the Commonwealth doesn't mean they're not loyal. But it's interesting, and warrants looking into a little more, maybe.'

Just then, a mail notification came in, and he opened the utility and checked on it. It was a final message from Ramirez. It read,

> **TO: ID1654651111561651684641**
> **FROM: HK14852115461235522172**
> **SUBJECT: (none)**
> **Ted is here; heading out in two.**
> **Managed to put this attachment together for you while I was getting things together to leave; I thought it might help. It's a roster of the construction and design people involved in the restoration/remodeling of Mar's office suite.**
> **I'm depending on you to take care of her, okay? Thanks.**
> **~Rosalind Ramirez, CDR**
> **Facilities**

Another alert came in through the mail utility, hard on the heels of Ramirez's communiqué, this one with a bit more urgency behind it. He opened it, and gaped.

"Aw damn," he cursed. "THAT can't be coincidence."

It was a notification of unauthorized access to the Saarestik space battle case history file.

"I think I might've been made," he considered, grimacing.

He gave some consideration to the matter, and finally decided that continuing to work with Rao was unlikely to put her in any more danger than she was already in, though it might not be so healthy for him. 'Still,' he considered, 'I think I probably have a little more knowledge of what to look out for than she does.' He was thankful he'd worked with some of the most experienced investigators in Intel in the last few years; he stood a chance of living through it.

'All the same, I think it's time I reported in to Byrne and Durand about the whole mess,' he concluded. 'Even if I did just start this case today.'

Campbell closed out his files and utilities, then rose and headed for the door.

Campbell strode up to Lieutenant Sofia Falk's desk and snapped off a salute.

"Ensign William Campbell to see Commander Byrne on the Rao case, ma'am."

Falk glanced up.

"Oh. Is Commander Byrne expecting you?"

"No ma'am, not as such; but he's not NOT expecting me, either. He told me to report in as soon as I had anything of import."

"All right. Hold one." Falk tapped the intercom toggle. "Commander, Ensign Campbell is here to see you."

"Oh really? Does he have anything?"

"Quite a bit, sir," Campbell said, loud enough for the intercom to pick up the statement.

"Send him in then, please, Sofia," Byrne's voice ordered.

"Please go on in," Falk said, gesturing Campbell at the inner door.

Campbell snapped off another salute by way of thanks, and headed for Byrne's office.

"...Wait, wait, wait. You CONFIRMED it?" Byrne demanded to know.

"I still need to verify a few things, sir, but yes. The verbal report I had out of Housekeeping via Commander Ramirez was very nearly the nail in the coffin, so to speak. The formal report will be out soon, likely within the hour. I ensured you and Admiral Durand and myself would be on the distribution, along with Captain Rao and Admiral Pachis... but no one else."

Byrne gaped at him.

"Shall I report, sir?"

"Stand by, Ensign," Byrne ordered. "I think we might need a couple more people in this meeting, first." He hit the intercom. "Sofia? Ping Admirals Durand and Birken, and see if they have time to meet with me and Ensign Campbell for a few. Tell them it's about that concern we had brought to us recently, and it's apparently damn important, after all. Ensign Campbell and I can meet them at their convenience, here or at either of their offices, but preferably as soon as possible or practical. Mm... consider it a semi-emergency situation."

"Yes sir."

"So we do, in fact, have an ongoing attempt to take out our planetary tactical officer," Birken pondered, as he sat back in the 'conversation corner' of Durand's comfortably-sized office.

"Multiple attempts, it sounds like," Durand offered. "Campbell?"

"Yes sir, at least two, one apparently ongoing," Campbell verified. "The restructuring of the air vents in the overall office suite, which was completed some two or three months back, is what enabled the subsequent contamination of her office, and ONLY her office, by a specially-compounded cocktail of toxic chemicals. This was the first — and ongoing — attempt, and was without doubt premeditated. When this failed due to her realization of a problem with the office itself, and she moved to the Class 1 facility in the basement, a more direct attempt was made, via removing the securing straps on a stack of bricks on the top level of construction scaffolding — straps that at least two witnesses are willing to swear were originally there. I did a little digging this afternoon, just after I escorted Captain Rao to her Class 2 workspace in the basement, while en route to my own desk, and uncovered a few other eyewitnesses among nearby construction crews who swear there were workers on the ROOF of the building with the bricks, mere moments before Rao's incident, though they were gone immediately after. This, despite the construction crew being on their lunch break. Let me also add that their disappearance immediately after lent suspicion in the other workers' minds that they had caused the 'accident,'" he quirked his fingers in air-quotes about the word, "and knew it; they figured the two workers on the roof cleared out to avoid trouble. Yet there was NO work done on the crenellations capping that side of the wall until well AFTER the regular workers returned from their lunch break. Not even to the removing of the old, damaged brick."

"Wait. The what?" Byrne wondered. "What's a crenellation?"

"Oh," Durand interjected. "You know how one of the old, old castles on Earth, the oldest ones, have those battlements with the square gaps in the top wall? Notches, where projectiles could be fired? Those are formally called 'crenellations' in architecture circles."

"Oh," Byrne said, raising an eyebrow. "You learn something new every day. Sorry, Mr. Campbell; please continue."

"Um, okay," Campbell said. "So there was no work done on the top of the wall at ALL that day; it wound up being another day or two before they got to the point of being able to do that."

"Interesting," Durand murmured.

"Yes sir. Combine that with the previous witnesses, comprising no less than two of the brick masons, one of whom is the foreman, BOTH of whom personally and together secured that same stack of bricks and are willing to swear to the fact while under truth testing, as well as to the completely missing securing straps — they've had to acquire new ones — and we have deliberate sabotage."

"Shit," Byrne breathed. "So it wasn't a hyper, anxious new officer in a new position, after all."

"No sir," Campbell averred, refraining from adding, "not at all," with an effort.

"Were you able to pick up anything from or about her office workers?" Birken wondered.

"Well, I had to play it close to the vest," Campbell explained. "The way I figured it, there were several possibilities, one of which involved someone on her team, and all of which left SOMEone on her team as the new tac officer..."

"So everyone is a suspect until proven otherwise, eh?" Durand wondered, with a slight smile.

"Yes sir, absolutely. Especially in a case like this. So I gave Captain Rao a heads-up before we went to her office, did a quick assessment of the situation, and went into one of several possible planned cover stories," Campbell explained. "In this case, and given our respective ages, I'm a not-too-bright pretty-boy that Captain Rao picked up at a bar. A 'boy toy,' if you will. If one of you would please make sure that her chain of command, or at least Admiral Pachis, is aware of this, it might be helpful to avert possible misunderstandings."

"Of course," Birken said, nodding. "Perfectly reasonable request, that. So you wanted them to underestimate you."

"Very much so, sir. In fact, when they see me, I want them to think of anything but the idea that I'm investigating matters."

"Smart man. And?" Durand pressed.

"Nothing in particular," Campbell decided, becoming slightly abstracted as he pondered the interactions in more detail. "But there are at least two, and possibly four, members of her support staff of seven who don't like her nearly as much as they would like her to think."

All three senior officers sat back, wide-eyed.

"Body language?" Durand wondered after a moment to consider.

"Exactly, sir. They closed off when she came around or directed her attention at them, or otherwise addressed them. Whereas the rest of the team remained open."

"Who are they?" Byrne asked.

"I'd rather not say until I've had time to dig deeper into their backgrounds, Commander," Campbell dodged the question. "It might be something as insignificant as them having had a disagreement with her at some point, or possibly a general personality clash. In which case, I'd be maligning the character of an innocent, useful officer, simply for not having the greatest chemistry with his or her C.O."

"Point, and fair enough," Durand agreed, cutting off a comment that a scowling Byrne had been about to make. "And so you intend to go digging deeper into the files next?"

"Yes sir."

"No," Byrne countered. "Ensign Campbell, you are now officially relieved of this case. You will prepare to hand it off to a more senior investigator which Admiral Durand will specify."

"Hold up," Birken said. "Campbell has done well by Captain Rao to this point, and it sounds like he and she have worked out a cover for him, AND initiated it. You go yanking things around now, you could screw everything up, and give away the whole intel investigation. And then we could end up with a dead tactical officer, despite our best efforts. And maybe a dead up-and-coming intelligence investigator, as well."

"Yes," Durand agreed. "I think, if nothing else, we need to ask Captain Rao's opinion on the matter. And inform Admiral Pachis, as well."

"But..." Byrne began.

"Commander Byrne, if you would be so kind as to contact Captain Rao and Admiral Pachis, and inform them that we intensely desire that they attend this conclave if at all convenient?" Birken ordered, couching it as a request... that dare not be protested.

"Yes sir," a docile Byrne said, rising and exiting the office, to work with Durand's assistant, Commander Jones, in bringing the desired parties into the meeting.

Ensign Campbell sat silently, watching the two admirals watch him, the barest hint of pleased smirks on their faces.

While Byrne was gone, Campbell decided to broach the other matter.

"Sirs," he said, "it may be a moot point, in any case. My cover may already have been blown."

"Oh? How so?" Durand wondered.

"Just before I went to Commander Byrne to report, I got a notification of unauthorized access of a report I wrote a while back," Campbell explained. "The analysis on the Saarestik battle."

"But that's a classified report," Birken observed.

"Just so, sir," Campbell agreed, "and I had all the appropriate covers and secure entries placed on it. Still, someone hacked it. I find it an odd coincidence that this happened on the very day that I begin looking into Captain' Rao's case. AFTER I've made contact with quite a few people who may or may not be involved, including her staff," he pointed out. 'Not to mention the guy who had it in for me in my Academy days,' he added to himself, before continuing aloud. "And frankly, sirs, I don't much believe in coincidences. Oh, the occasional outlier probability event happens, but in general? No, things like this have too many possible connections. It doesn't do to ignore them."

"Do you think you're in danger?" Durand wondered.

"If they want Captain Rao dead, then anyone investigating their attempts is in danger, Admiral," Campbell noted. "So... yes."

"Do you want off the case?"

"No sir. I'm not asking for that at all. Frankly, my teeth are in this one, and I hope that neither Captain Rao nor Admiral Pachis wants me off the case. I simply wanted to make you aware of the incident, and its potential tie to the case."

"Told you," Durand murmured to Birken, smirking.

"You did," Birken agreed, a slight grin on his own face. "Bulldog, this one. But we need to do something to give him the ability to defend himself if he should need it. Including, I think, the ability to pack."

"Let's wait and see what falls out from Pachis and Rao," Durand decided. "As for that, I have some ideas already. Just roll with what I suggest."

"I can do that," Birken agreed.

"But why?" Rao wondered. "I understand the protocol, but Ensign Campbell has done a fantastic job so far. I feel much safer with him on the case. I don't especially WANT another investigator."

"Captain Rao," Commander Byrne explained, his tone straying a wee bit into the patronizing, "surely you understand that this case has progressed beyond the ability of a mere ensign to prosecute. If the planetary tactical officer is threatened by an outside agency, we MUST go to all lengths necessary to ensure your safety, and the apprehension of the parties responsible."

"Might I note, COMMANDER," Pachis murmured, his tone pointed, if subdued, "that, according to my understanding, it was your call to assign an ensign to the investigation in the first place, and that only after I personally requested an investigator be assigned? You turned down Captain Rao flat." He paused. "That could be viewed as brushing off, or even making light of, the request of the head of the Tactical Division. Never mind a failure to adequately protect the planetary tactical officer."

Byrne paled to an ashy gray. Given his darker ethnic skin, this was a bit of a feat. He also shut up.

"Now, Haden," Durand chided in a gentle tone, "I don't think there's any call to go pulling rank here, over a simple mis-read of the situation. Besides, as the commander and I pointed out yesterday, our rosters are full to bursting with case loads at the moment; Campbell's name came up because it was his turn. It looks to me like Lieutena-er, excuse me, Ensign Campbell is doing a fine job. If Captain Rao wants him to remain the investigator on the case, I think we can arrange for that — provide him with higher-level equipment, some upgraded software, perhaps a Class 2 workspace in the secure facility in our own building, and access to a senior investigations officer in the Intel chain to mentor him, that he can go to for advice if he needs it. Even authority to carry and utilize a personal sidearm if needed, on-and off-base. That sort of thing. If, that is, Captain Rao wants him to remain on her case." He glanced at Rao.

"I do," Rao declared, expression determined. "He grasped the situation essentially immediately, and he's done great, and that on the first day!" She looked around at the officers in the room. "Believe me when I say that Ensign Campbell has talent, skill, and smarts, gentlemen, and he knows how to use them. Even when it's only to play like he's dense." She shot Campbell a grin, and he returned it. "There's no ego there that I can see; nothing but a sincere desire to find out what the hell is going on, stop it from happening, and protect me — and, by extension, Sigurdsen and Jablonka — in the process."

"But protocol," Byrne finally dared interject.

"Is easily rectified," Birken noted, following Durand's lead. "Especially after I reread that white paper he wrote on the Battle of Saarestik earlier this afternoon, AND double-checked his personnel file, I think it's high time. He's almost in the zone, anyway. Jake?"

"My pleasure, Pavel," Durand said, standing and fiddling in one uniform pocket. "Ensign Campbell, please stand at attention."

Campbell stood as requested, shoulders squared.

"Lieutenant William Campbell," Durand intoned, "you are now the official investigator on Captain Rao's case. More, you are hereby given the position of inspector for the duration. This is a permanent increase in rank, but a temporary position upgrade to inspector, so it will enable us to provide you with some more sophisticated tools than you would otherwise have available, as well as giving you certain permissions and accesses. If you do well, you might get this back, one of these days. In the circumstances, use it with discretion." He produced an inspector's badge from his pocket, and handed it to Campbell. "Go get your silver bar."

Campbell accepted the badge with some surprise, and beside Durand, Byrne gaped. Birken grinned, Rao beamed, and Pachis looked satisfied.

"That'll work," Pachis decided.

"So Lieutenant Campbell wrote a paper on the Battle of Saarestik?" Pachis wondered a bit later, when Byrne stepped out to ensure the promotion and formal assignment was duly entered into the section rosters.

"He did," Durand noted. "We needed an analysis of the incident with an eye toward who might have been the aggressor. Since all five of the attacking ships were destroyed, we had no direct evidence on whodunit. And he has a known bent for those sorts of tactical analyses, so..."

"Right," Pachis said, comprehending. "And Campbell worked it out?"

"The Intelligence Division believes so," Birken observed. "Lieutenant Campbell is nothing if not thorough, and not only did he pick up on some signature maneuver attempts, he was able to determine ship make based on explosion signatures, cross-correlated that information with relative mining data, THEN verified that the planetary system in question was missing that specific number and class of ships based on the merchant-ship sensor database."

Pachis raised an eyebrow, watching Campbell, who flushed slightly.

"Well, sir," Campbell murmured, "I'm told I have an eye for details like that."

"It sounds like it," Pachis replied, apparently impressed. "Pavel, is there any chance I can get a copy of that white paper? I can argue a need-to-know based on Tactical Division's need to prepare for future aggressions by the system in question..."

"I think we can do that, Haden," Birken agreed, as Byrne re-entered the office. "I'll see to it personally once we're finished here." He paused, then added, "Unfortunately, it seems those of us here in this room may not be the only ones interested in it."

"What do you mean?" Pachis wondered. Birken waved permission at Campbell.

"Um, someone hacked through the security on the file late this afternoon, sir," Campbell explained. "AFTER I'd gone around and investigated the various scenes of interest with Captain Rao."

"Damnation," Pachis grumbled. "So you think they're onto you?"

"Maybe, sir. It COULD be just coincidence, but the probabilities are against it. That said, I know it, so I can watch my back."

"And we're already all over patching the security system," Birken informed them. "I got that in work immediately Lieutenant Campbell, here, told us about it, earlier today."

"Good man."

"We try, Haden."

"I know. Lieutenant Campbell?"

"Yes sir?"

"Are you sure you want to stay on the case, if you've been identified as the clandestine investigator?"

"Yes sir, I do," Campbell said, earnest. "It's like I was telling Admirals Birken and Durand earlier: I've already sunk my teeth into this. I'd like to see it through, if it's all right with you and Captain Rao."

"Good. And it sounds to me like we have exactly the right investigator. Captain Rao?"

"I definitely want him on my case, sir," Rao agreed. Then she cast him a worried glance and added, "But I want him to be careful."

"I will be," Campbell averred. "If we play our cards right, like you and I discussed this afternoon, we might actually be able to fool them into thinking I'm a desk jockey, first, last, and only, and I really AM your 'boy toy,' I think."

"Okay, so you'll be over to my place to sweep it later, under the guise of a date?"

"Just like we discussed."

"Okay." Rao nodded. "I'm tired of being a target! Let's nail these sons of bitches to the wall, Lieutenant!"

"Let's," Campbell said, offering her a smile. The admirals watched, pleased at the interaction.

"Well, then," Pachis said, "if there's nothing further?"

"No, I think that has it, Haden," Durand decided.

"Good. Rao?"

"Sir?"

"Are you ready to head back?"

"If the other Admirals have nothing more for me, I am, sir," Rao agreed. "Lieutenant Campbell, I will expect you about an hour after my shift ends?"

"Yes," Campbell agreed. "I'll swing by your place at that time and sweep it, then initiate the plan we developed to keep whoever's doing this guessing."

"Then you're free to go, I think," Durand concluded.

"Thank you, sirs," Rao said, switching on her scooter as Pachis rose to depart.

After Pachis, Birken, and Rao left— with Pachis and his bodyguard escort personally escorting Rao back to the Tactical Division headquarters building, even as they'd arrived — the newly-minted lieutenant addressed his two immediate superiors.

"Sirs," he said, "I wonder if you might help me with a... more personal matter."

Before Byrne could say anything, Durand wondered, "What's up, Campbell?"

"Well, sir, this current situation could have some negative repercussions with my girlfriend," Campbell admitted, wincing.

"Oh, damnation," Durand murmured, understanding. "Yes, I can definitely see that."

"What is it you're wanting, Ensi-uh, Lieutenant?" Byrne asked.

"I'm not completely sure; that's why I'm asking," Campbell said. "Since this IS my first real case, I don't entirely know how it's generally handled."

"Is she trustworthy? Your girlfriend?" Durand queried. "CAN we work with this?"

"Yes sir. She's trustworthy," Campbell said, flushing slightly. "This might sound cold-blooded, but ever since I realized I was going to go into Intel, I realized I didn't need that kind of complication in my life. So I started checking out my potential girlfriends as soon as I recognized there might be a relationship there; if I had any indication there might be a problem, I simply eased out before things got too serious — before I could get attached. She's Ensign Lily Martell, over in Maintenance Division. Brilliant when it comes to repairs, and rapidly becoming the go-to person for shuttle fix-its. Not particularly savvy as regards intelligence and investigation, but not stupid, and not a security risk."

"No, not if she's working on shuttle guts," Byrne decided. "What did you have in mind to do? Let's start there, and maybe we can help advise you."

"Good idea," Durand agreed.

"All right. I plan on meeting her shortly and explaining the cover story concept to her in just enough detail that she understands that it IS a cover story and nothing she needs to worry about, but also tell her that, if she hears scuttlebutt, she needs to react as if it's real... without going into more detail with her except to explain I'm helping to protect someone in potential danger," Campbell noted. "She doesn't have a need to know the details of the case, and I don't need her accidentally saying something in a fit of jealousy, or worry, or something, that would give things away. But..."

"But?" Durand prodded.

"It wouldn't surprise me if I have to go under cover for a couple of days to check out a few things," Campbell admitted. "Especially if I get targeted on account of the Saarestik paper. I've already worked out how to do that, long since. But if I'm gone for a few days, she might get worried, might even think I'm dead. And, well..."

Byrne and Durand looked at each other, and nodded.

"We're all over this one, son," Durand told him. "Intelligence staffers aren't expected to be celibate for the entire duration of their careers, and so there are always spouses and children and significant others to be taken care of. Hell, we've actually got instructions on how to handle it; there's a protocol, and my office is the point of contact, because I'm head of the Investigations department for all of the Intelligence Division. So in the event something like that happens, she'd be expected to come here, to this office, present proof of ID, and then I'd personally meet with her and give her a basic status on your condition."

"Okay, that makes sense," Campbell decided.

"Before you leave here," Durand added, "I'll have Jany dig up a couple copies of the instructions. Keep one for your own reference — you do have permission to copy it, if need be — and give the other to your lady friend at the same time you explain about your current cover story. Make sure she understands she should follow it to the letter, and we'll be good."

"Oh good," Campbell said in relief. "I figured you might have a protocol, but it never occurred to me that it would be a frequent enough occurrence to have instructions laid out!" He laughed. "I guess I AM pretty green about some of this!"

"Well," Byrne began, thoughtful, "there's green, and there's green. It's one thing to be green about peripheral matters like you're asking about, simply because you've never had call to deal with it — or even ask about it — before, but it's another thing entirely to be green about the actual investigation... which it sounds like you're NOT green about."

"I'm green, but I'm not," Campbell pointed out. "It may be my first official case, but I had good schooling, good teachers — Admiral Durand was one of the instructors for a specialized course sequence — and plenty of in-class simulations and live exercises."

"And Bill was good at them," Durand observed. "If memory serves, he finished at the top of my course sequence... the entire sequence."

"Yes sir, I did," Campbell confirmed. "Not meaning to sound too juvenile, but I had a blast in that course! And while I've been out of the Academy for several years now, I haven't wasted my time. I've studied case histories and planned pretty thoroughly, gathering what tools I could for when I'd need to use 'em. And I've worked as an assistant to a couple of the more experienced investigators on around, oh, a dozen or so different cases."

"This sounds much more promising than I'd originally thought," Byrne concluded. "We need to set you up with an assigned Class 2 workspace in the secure facility downstairs, and provide you with a few more, and more sophisticated, tools than you currently have. I'll get the tools shortly, and have a room assigned for you in the secure area by tomorrow morning. What are your plans for the next step in the investigation?"

"Well, like I told her earlier, I need to find out if Rao's home is bugged or otherwise compromised," Campbell declared. "I already verified with Commander Ramirez that it hasn't yet been tainted with any sort of chemical compound as of, oh, say yesterday, but that doesn't mean she isn't being watched... or that an attempt won't be made to contaminate it. So we'll go on a 'date' later tonight," he quirked his fingers around the word, "then I'll check out her place while she grabs an overnight kit to 'spend the night' with me at my place, which I know is secure, because Intel, and because I scan the apartment at least once a day, and usually twice. I know she'll be safe there. And she'll take the bed, and I'll take the couch, and keep an eye out while she gets some rest."

"Good man," Durand murmured. "You're on top of things. And a gentleman, to boot."

"I do my best, sir, at all of that," Campbell replied, the ghost of a smile gracing his face. "Anyway, while I'm at Rao's home, I'll plant a few devices of my own, with her permission, intended to allow me to keep a remote eye on things and ensure it isn't compromised in any fashion from this point onward. And tomorrow I'll start digging into the backgrounds of the people in her office, looking for any sort of links to something they shouldn't be linked to. I'll also do the same with the personnel from Facilities that Commander Ramirez suggested in her mail to me, just before she bugged out, on my instructions."

"Pavel's already taken care of that with her Division head, by the way," Durand informed him. "And let Admiral Cho, who heads the Facilities Division, know that she has at least one mole, and probably several operatives, embedded in her staff — and it looks like that includes Housekeeping AND Renovations. From what Pavel told me, Cho was not at all happy to find out about that, and I can't blame her. But she immediately understood the need for secrecy, and for getting Ramirez the hell away from danger. More, she's calling in the decontamination team — it seems the decon is done, they're just not sure how to keep it from recurring — and putting them in seclusion in a safehouse off the base, as well."

"That's good, then," Campbell decided. "So I'll start digging deeper." He shrugged. "Then I'll collate what I find, and go from there."

"Good. So let's get you the promotion orders, the significant other instructions, and some upgraded tools in hand, so you can run by the commissary, get that lieutenant's bar, and set to," Durand decreed.

Commander Byrne headed out to fetch several small items that would constitute Campbell's tools upgrade. Commander Jones, Durand's executive assistant, dug out what she called, "The Companion Instructions, basic, two copies," and delivered them into Campbell's hands. Meanwhile, at his desk, Durand dictated the orders concerning Campbell's promotion into the VR set, and moments later, they spat out on the printer beside Jones' desk.

"There we are," Durand said, coming out of his office as Jones handed the printout to Campbell. "Now you can run down to the commissary and swap out that gold bar for a silver one, Lieutenant."

"Thank you, sir."

"Not a problem, Campbell. Meanwhile, we still need to set you a mentor, but I think I know who will work quite well for that, especially given your current case."

"Who, sir?"

"Me. I came up through these same ranks, doing the same job you're doing now, so I know the ropes pretty thoroughly. And I want to make sure you live through this," Durand said, earnest. "Your parents would never forgive me if I let you get killed on your first case. And I'd like to meet them on friendly terms in the hereafter. So I'm going to do this personally."

"Oh! I don't — I mean, I..."

"Enough of that, Campbell. I can make it an order if I need to."

"He's done it before, Lieutenant," Jones noted, "for other new investigators. Not all — he tends to mentor only the ones he thinks show REAL promise — but a few. It's definitely a compliment, but it isn't unusual. Not for Admiral Durand. Just say thank you and run with it."

"Um, yes ma'am," Campbell said with a sheepish grin. "Thank you, sir."

"You're welcome, son," Durand said, returning the grin. "Now, we just need to get Byrne back here with your tool kit, and you're on your way."

Moments later, Byrne had returned with a small pack of items which he went over and explained. Campbell listened carefully, unassumingly tucked the pack into a pocket, then he was off.

But instead of heading straight for the commissary to acquire the silver bar and epaulet of a lieutenant, Campbell headed for Lily Martell's quarters, in the Maintenance Base Housing building; he knew that she had the evening shift this week, so she'd have only risen within the hour and would be getting ready to go to work; he wanted to catch her before she left, just in case scuttlebutt got back to her before he could. 'And if I wait until after I go to the commissary, this time of day, she could be gone before I even get checked out at the cashier,' he realized.

So when she opened the door to him, he slipped inside and closed it before accepting her welcoming kiss.

"Hey, hot stuff," she murmured with a smile. "What brings you by here?"

"We need to talk, and you need to know about some things going down, Lily," he said, then held up a hand. "I know, you're leaving for work in half an hour; I'll make it fast. But you HAVE to know this, honey. Right now."

Martell stared at him, then gestured to the little sofa, sitting down on one end and facing him as he sat.

"Okay, so I've gotten my first case assignment," he said, then held up another stilling hand as she made to exclaim in happiness. "It's a serious one, Lil'. Someone's life is at stake, maybe more than one. But the lady whose life is at stake most immediately is who I've gotta protect. Now, I scoped out everything, and I decided that the easiest way to ease me into the picture without the as-yet-unknown bad guys figuring out I'm investigating, is to pretend to be her lover."

He broke off, waiting to see how she would react. Martell gazed at him in surprise, which gradually morphed to concern, then to a worried frown.

"Are you gonna have to, you know, do any Hata Mari stuff?" she wondered, and bit her lip.

"No, honey," he said, desperately stifling a laugh; she always seemed to invert the initials of the historical spy's name without ever realizing she was doing it; it was cute, and it amused him no end. But, he realized, now was not the time to laugh, or upset her. "You know me better than that. But I'm gonna have to make it LOOK like I'm sleeping with her, so people won't really notice me being around her all the time, and so I can escort her here and there without anybody realizing it's for her protection."

"Oh! I get it," she said then, face lightening. "A boyfriend can go anywhere with her, and nobody's gonna think twice about it. But if you just start showing up, taking her everywhere, and she's never 'met' you before..."

"Yes," Campbell confirmed. "Whoever is behind the murder attempts is going to realize that I'm there for a reason. And then she and I could BOTH be in trouble."

"No, no, stay safe, Bill," she murmured, leaning forward to hug him, before depositing a quick kiss on his lips. "That's okay. I'll just ignore any gossip I hear."

"No, you can't do that, either; people know that you and I have dated some, Lil'," he told her. "We need to work out how you're going to react, because you HAVE to react. Either you're hurt and jealous, or you and I broke up and you're angry and all, 'I don't CARE!' kinda thing. But you have to react."

"Oh. Because if I don't react, if any bad guys are watching, they'll know you're faking it? Because I'm not bothered by it?"

"Right."

Martell chewed on her knuckle for a moment, thinking. Then she sighed.

"I really wish they taught more about this whole spy thing in the other divisions," she grumbled. "I feel so stupid about this, when you start explaining it. And it's your job; it's easy for you."

"Well, look," he said, wanting to make her feel better. "Can you take apart a shuttle engine and put it back together?"

"Sure," she said with a shrug. "It would take a few days, each way, but that's what I'm trained to do."

"And from what I've heard, you're damn good at it," Campbell said earnestly, and she gave him a shy, pleased smile. "But I couldn't begin to do it. Because I'm not trained in it, and that's not the way I think. THIS... is."

"Oh," she said then, seeming to grasp what he was getting at. "Okay, I see. I'm good at that, and you're good at this. And it doesn't make either of us stupid that we can't do the other."

"Exactly."

"All right; I guess that works. I'll try to remember to not feel so bad about it, then. So, back to your case. You need me to figure out how I'm gonna act, if I hear gossip about you and this other woman?"

"Right. And just so you know, she outranks us, so the gossip might get kind of... nasty. But she's in a different division, so it should be okay. My superiors are going to try to ensure it's okay, and so are hers."

"Got it. So, um, lemme think," she said, considering. "I think... I think I would first be confused, then hurt, then angry... if it was real, I mean."

"Then that's how you need to act if you hear something," Campbell told her. "Like, the first time or two that you hear something, you're confused. 'Oh, Bill would never do that.' Then the next couple-three times, you're hurt. 'How could Bill do this to me?!' You know what I mean. Then you're angry — 'Wait'll I get my hands on him, that two-timing bastard!' How does that sound?"

"Like me," she giggled. "Okay. I can do that. Is that all?"

"No, not quite," he said, pulling one of the 'companion instructions' from a pocket in his shipsuit and handing it to her. "You need to put this someplace safe, out of sight, and hang onto it. If I had to go undercover or something, pull it out and follow it. It tells you how to get some basic information about me from Admiral Durand's office, so you could make sure I was okay... though you couldn't tell anybody else."

"Oh. So they'd tell me about your case, and where you were? So I could come see you?"

"No, no. That could put me in danger of being discovered, and you in danger of being caught and used as a bargaining chip against me," Campbell explained. "No, you wouldn't have a need to know about the case; this is just to get basic status information on me. You know — alive, dead, in the hospital, mildly injured but still on the case; I think those are the basic status categories. So if something unexpected happens — I disappear, or someone claims I'm dead, or whatever — this gives YOU 'special status' information."

"Oh," Martell murmured. "I hope that doesn't happen, Bill. But... but, okay, I get it." She accepted the printout, folding it and going to her desk in the corner. There, she opened the bottom drawer, pulled out a stack of folders, and tucked the folded paper in the bottom, before putting the folders on top of it. "There. Is that a good hiding place?"

"That'll do, honey," he said with a smile. "I don't expect anybody's gonna come over here hunting for it; it only needs to be out of sight. Just don't forget where you put it."

"I won't."

"All right. Then I need to go; I have a buncha stuff to do tonight, and my 'new girlfriend' is going out with me..."

Martell pouted. "I wish I could go, instead," she said.

"I do too, Lil'. But then an innocent woman with an important job might die."

"Oh! I don't want that! Go protect her, Bill!"

"I'm gone," he said with a smile, leaning forward and giving her a thorough kiss before rising and heading for the door. "Have fun at the garage."

Cat And Mouse

Two hours later, as he'd arranged earlier in the day, Bill arrived at Captain Rao's residence in his dress blues, the ensign's single-stripe epaulets having been swapped out for the double stripe of a lieutenant. He knocked on the door in the special signal they'd arranged, then called "Mar'? It's me, Bill."

"Coming!" came the response, muffled by the door.

Seconds later, the door was opened a crack, then opened all the way, as Rao smiled at Campbell, her cane in one hand.

"There you are, Bill!" she exclaimed. "I'm almost ready. C'mon in."

But instead of coming in, Campbell stepped forward, took Rao in his arms, and planted a long kiss on her. It was open-mouthed, and gave the appearance of being passionate, while being nothing more than a stage kiss. After a few moments, he broke the kiss and raised his head, smiling down at her.

"That's better," he declared in a low, throaty voice. "Now I'll come in."

Once the door was closed, Rao snorted and glanced down, blushing.

"Wasn't expecting that, huh?" Campbell said, a mischievous grin spreading across his face.

"No, I wasn't," Rao confessed. "And, uh, I hope you don't take offense, but damn, part of me kinda wishes that had been—"

"Stop," he ordered, holding up a hand. Her face blanked in surprise, and Campbell gave the room a careful once-over. He pulled out what looked like a comm unit and tapped several places on the screen, then turned around as if trying to get a signal, before walking deeper into her apartment. He wandered through every room, closet, and alcove of the flat, before turning back to her.

"Okay, that's done," he said in a low voice. "Your apartment is clear. No observation devices that I can find, and that with some new gadgetry I just got this afternoon."

"So that's what you were doing," Rao murmured. "I wondered..."

"Commander Ramirez' appraisal of no chemical contaminants appears to also be holding," he added, checking the readout on the 'comm unit's' screen. "So the apartment is safe. That doesn't mean it will STAY safe, though."

"Good point. Oh, and congratulations on the promotion. You deserve it."

"Thanks. It was useful, in the circumstances, I guess," Campbell decided. "Oh, and thanks for the compliment I had to abort a couple minutes ago, too."

"Eh. Sorry about that," Rao apologized. "I wasn't thinking. But I did mean it. So now what?"

"Now we go out to dinner," he said. "It won't be fancy, because my salary doesn't cover that, but it's my favorite restaurant, it's off-base so it'll be a little harder for somebody to start something, and it'll look like what we want it to look like. And don't worry; I'll avoid the red-light district off-base. That'd make us too prime a target anyway. It'd be WAY the hell too easy for somebody to start something THERE."

"Good point."

"Yeah. I'm looking for a relatively quiet night for both of us."

"And frankly, I like that idea; I've had more than enough excitement lately. But I got a question."

"What?"

"If I'm 'cougaring,' shouldn't I pay?"

"I've been debating that," Campbell admitted. "I think, if we have to keep this up for more than a day or two, then yes, but we'll work out how to submit it as an expense, if we do. See, right now, I can toss it onto an expense account through the Intelligence Division, but I think Tactical might have a cow or three if YOU tried that."

"Admiral Pachis would approve it."

"Yes, but it has to REACH Admiral Pachis, first. And there's a few tiers between you and him."

"Mm. Good point."

"But if, as I said, this keeps up for a while — which it might, if these guys are burrowed in — we can probably rig something up through my expense account," Campbell added. "And to that end, we need to leave in the next few minutes, or it'll look odd to anybody watching us... and I expect, on some level, we ARE being watched. Once we eat, though, we'll come back here so you can grab your overnight kit and come to my place, while I set up my own observing devices in your apartment."

"Why?"

"Because, with you working in the Class 1 facility, it's the next logical place for them to try to set something up. Don't worry, Captain; I'm on this."

"Go ahead and call me Mary, if you would. May I call you Bill? Because if I'm swapping back and forth between military protocol and cover story first-name intimacy, I'm gonna screw up sooner or later."

"Good point. Sure. Call me Bill."

"Okay, Bill. I trust you, so let's get this show on the road."

"Let's go eat, then."

"I'll get my scooter."

Campbell's favorite restaurant turned out to be a mom-and-pop type of establishment, a bit more than a simple diner, but not quite as fancy as a prime sit-down restaurant. The food was plentiful and excellent, and the proprietors, on a subtle signal from Campbell, seated them in a secluded corner booth. Three courses later, a hungry Rao was stuffed to the eyeballs, and Campbell, who was bigger and more active, was duly sated.

More, Campbell had quietly and subtly outlined his plan for outfitting her apartment with his own bugs, enabling him to hear and see and record any unauthorized activity, while still protecting Rao's privacy.

"So you don't have to worry about that," he explained. "I'm not gonna, I dunno, see you nude or in the necessary, or anything like that."

"Okay," she agreed, then her expression became sultry. "But I'm not sure I'd mind, at this point. I rather like the attention, I think."

"I appreciate the compliment, but..." he dropped his voice lower, "not only would that be... unethical, in the circumstances, not to mention very unwise, I don't think my girlfriend would care for it much."

"Oh," Rao said, surprised, face falling. "Oh. You're taken. Well then. Never mind, I guess."

"I'm sorry," Campbell offered. "And I'm not offended. It has nothing to do with you personally, Mary. But I think you'd much rather have me maintain my objectivity and see anything coming at you, than spend a few nights with you as a lover and end up getting you killed — maybe getting us both killed — because I couldn't see past my own hormones."

"Mmph," Rao grunted. "You have a point. I'm sorry. I was out of line."

"Don't worry about it," Campbell soothed. "You've had some bad health, some bad scares, and you're under a lot of stress. Let's just let it go."

"...Okay."

"Now, what would be entirely acceptable, even to my girlfriend," Campbell suggested, "would be a good friend..."

Rao eyed him, considering. Then she smiled.

"I think you're right."

After dinner, they returned to Rao's apartment, and she went into the bedroom to pack an overnight kit — Campbell reminded her to pack the scooter charger — while Campbell delved deeper into the package Byrne had brought him that afternoon, as well as a special kit of his own that he'd tucked into a hidden cargo pocket of his dress uniform once he'd gotten home from the commissary. This resulted in a series of strategically-placed monitors throughout her flat, all set to provide him access from his Class 2 workspace in the Intelligence Division headquarters building's secure facility.

Then they headed out the door and down the street, toward the building that housed Campbell's quarters, she in the scooter, him walking beside, hand in hand, with Campbell carrying her travel kit for her, slung over his shoulder.

"...It's a little smaller than yours, but it's comfortable, and my mom taught me to be a good housekeeper, so I pick up after myself," Campbell said with a grin, as they entered his flat. Then he lowered his voice. "Are you ready to play cougar again?"

"Huh?"

"We were followed," Campbell murmured. "Stocky male, medium height, brown hair, in a shipsuit. Couldn't see the details; he stayed far enough off that I couldn't catch his rank, for instance. He was also wearing shaded glasses to obscure the upper part of his face."

"Well, the setting sun was a bit bright, I suppose," Rao decided. "So he could get away with it."

"Yup. So ease out of the scooter and come over here into the den, and let's give the guy a show, shall we? He's across the street; I saw him duck down behind the trash disposal bins just as we came in the door."

"Right. Well, my reputation as a lover ought to go up some after this. Not that it was bad before, mind," she added with a rueful chuckle, but flirtatious body language. "I just tend to stay too busy with work, I suppose."

And with that, he wrapped his arms around her and kissed her again. She slid her hands up his arms and around his neck, lacing the fingers of one hand in his short, dark hair, and turning slightly to press close.

But this kiss, like the previous, was staged; it looked intensely passionate and erotic, but their lips were barely touching.

It went on for nearly five minutes. Finally Campbell broke the embrace, and in full view of the window, gave her a seductive smirk.

"Let's close the curtains and dim the lights, shall we?" he said, going to the window and suiting action to statement. "There's a dimmer switch on the lamp over there; take it down to the lowest level, would you?"

Rao did as he asked, and the room grew shadowy.

"There we go," he murmured, after turning his back to the window. "These are blackout curtains, expressly designed to ensure that light of virtually any frequency does not get in or out if I don't want it to. I keep the sides sealed, so we're good at the moment."

"But they're not all the way closed, Bill," Rao pointed out. "There's about an inch gap between them."

"I know," Campbell said with a smirk. "We want him to get the wrong idea. So let's sit over here on the couch... which, you'll note, is NOT in line with the window... and chat for a bit, and then we'll get you set up in the bedroom."

Some forty-five minutes later, they rose, turned off the lights in the den, and repeated the process in the bedroom, stage kissing, before pulling the curtains almost closed.

"Okay, leave it like that for a bit, and help me strip the bed and put fresh sheets on it," Campbell told her. "Sorry you're having to help, but I haven't hardly been back here long enough to do it since I had your case dropped in my lap this morning. Besides, any movement or change in lighting he sees from across the street, he'll interpret as us getting it on, and it'll enhance our charade, here."

"All right," Rao agreed, hobbling around the room and helping her protector as he suggested. "But it's still kind of early... I mean, I'm not really sleepy yet..."

"That's okay," Campbell grinned. "Sit right there on the bed a sec."

She parked herself on the side of the freshly-made bed, and he disappeared out the door, returning moments later.

"All right, done," he said. "I completely closed the curtains in the den, fastening them closed. Now we can turn on the lights in there and he won't be able to tell a thing."

"Oh."

"Right. So. See that mobile sculpture over there by the lamp on the side table?" He pointed to the object on the nightstand.

"Yeah?"

"There's a switch on the base. Turn it on."

Rao leaned over and toggled the switch. Immediately the sculpture began to move slowly, gyrating in front of the lamp, casting soft, sensual, almost-erotic shadows on the walls... which included the curtained window. She clapped her hand over her mouth to muffle the sound, and began to giggle.

"Right," Campbell said with a devilish grin. "And it goes into a kind of standby mode on roughly forty-five-minute intervals, though I tweaked the timer on it so it's a little irregular. When we get ready to finally crash for the night, we'll turn it off, and I'll fasten the bedroom curtains, then we'll hook the charger cord to your scooter, so it will be ready to go tomorrow."

"Wait a minute — we?" Rao began. "There's only one bed..."

"Yes. And you'll have it," Campbell promised. "Alone. I have two options for where I spend the night, and it depends on YOUR call, Captain... er, Mary. I can either spend the night on the couch, which is pretty comfortable AND happens to be directly in front of the bedroom door, or I can set up a pallet on the floor in here, against the bedroom door. Either way, I'll be armed, and nobody will come in here that I don't personally allow to be here." He shrugged. "But the snoop across the way won't know that, and will think you and I are lovers, which is what we want him to think, rather than deciding I'm investigating the situation."

"And tomorrow morning?"

"Tomorrow morning we take turns in the necessary getting ready, I feed you cold cereal for breakfast, then we hold hands while I walk you over to the basement of the Tactical Division headquarters building," Campbell explained. "And then I'll head for the Intelligence Division headquarters building to see what other juicy information I can dig out about what we learned today."

"Ah," Rao said with a grin. "If I wasn't so worried about who's trying to kill me, this cat-and-mouse game might almost be fun."

"She gets it," Campbell declared to the air, matching her grin. "But yes, it's deadly serious, too. So. Am I on the couch or on the floor?"

"I think couch for tonight, if you don't mind, good sirrah," Rao said in a mock-courtly fashion. "If this needs must go on longer, or if things get more serious so there's reason for you to stay closer, we will consider the second option."

"The 'imperial we,' huh?" Campbell said with an amused snort.

"Pretty much," Rao said with a smirk. "Effectively, I have a bodyguard. Might as well enjoy it, I thought."

"You do, and you might as well," Campbell agreed. "Now c'mon, let's go into the den and watch some VR shows or something. I've got a pretty good setup."

"Okay."

About an hour after Rao went to bed and turned out the lights, Campbell tiptoed into the bedroom, unfastened the curtains and snuck a cautious peep out the bedroom window, careful to don a special cowl to obscure his IR image, only to find that the spy across the street was no longer there. A quick perusal with his own brand-new multi-spectral goggles depicted no one hiding anywhere in the street visible from the line of sight of the window.

He fastened the bedroom curtains closed once more, and moved to the den, where he repeated the process, since the lines of sight were slightly different for each window.

Still seeing nothing, he sealed the curtains and ensured the security system on the apartment was active and all possible entries were locked. Then he stretched out on the couch, plumping the spare pillows, before burrowing into the extra blankets... but he made sure his concealed weapons were to hand.

Campbell sighed, tired, and allowed himself to drift into a restful — if subconsciously-alert — sleep.

The next morning, Rao and Campbell managed to coordinate getting ready for work without anyone becoming embarrassed, though it took a bit of effort; the necessary wasn't that big. As promised, Campbell offered a bowl of cold cereal to the woman now under his protection; she accepted, and they ate breakfast together in a comradely fashion.

Then they headed out, hand in hand, and walked across the Mall to the Tactical Division headquarters building.

When they arrived, instead of going straight to the Class 1 facility in the basement, Campbell murmured, "Let's run by your office suite for a sec. Can you come up with something you need to do in there?"

"Um, probably," Rao decided. "What's up?"

"I have some ideas about how to ward off any 'bad publicity' from that white paper being hacked."

"Oh. Okay."

While Rao went into her office, Campbell remained in the outer office and bullpen area, moving to the nearest window — which did NOT overlook any of the work spaces — to look out, and positioning himself in the sunbeam in such a way that the light caught the bars on his shoulders.

"Oh hey," Lieutenant Zinn said then, and the others glanced up, "I thought you were an ensign, Campbell."

"Ah! I was — yesterday," Campbell said with a grin, turning. "Brand-new promotion."

The room rang with congratulations.

"Why so sudden?" Gnad wondered. "You didn't know it was coming?"

"Oh, it was high time," Campbell said with an ingenuous smile and shrug. "I was 'in the zone,' as they say, and I knock out some pretty good desktop analyses. Nobody else in my group is interested in doing shit like that, so I get 'em, and I've learned to bullshit with the best. It's a damn sight easier than having to go out in the field on some silly investigation."

"What do you mean?" Lieutenant Commander Robert Glaub, Commander Gnad's assistant, wondered.

"Aw, it isn't hard to impress the brass, is all I'm saying," Campbell said, shrugging again. "It's a lot like when a teacher assigns an essay in school, you know? You figure out what they want or expect to see, then check A and B and C, look for anything that matches what they want, then string it together and turn it in." He tapped the bar on his right shoulder with his left hand. "And this is the result."

"But... so are you in Tactical Division?" Lieutenant Kooistra asked.

"Nah. If I was in Tactical, they might actually put me on a ship," Campbell said, laconic. "And that's the last thing I want! I'm in Intel, so it sounds cool — you know, like spies an' shit. But I prefer riding my desk to going out and actually risking my neck."

"You're a desk jockey," Lieutenant Powers said, with a patronizing smirk.

"I've been called that by my colleagues, yeah," Campbell averred with a grin. "Nobody bothers me much, though. I'm an analyst *par excellence*. I go to the office every day, I get off duty and hit the pub for some brews, stagger back to my quarters, and fall into bed. Get up the next day an' do it all again. Lather, rinse, repeat. I got no complaints."

"Sonuvabitch," a disgusted Lieutenant Weiner muttered under his breath. "What a..."

"I been called that, too," Campbell said, grin growing wider. "I don't care. I like my life as it is. No pain, no problem."

Just then, Rao came out of her office.

"Bill," she called, "are you ready to go?"

"You got your shit taken care of, baby?"

"Yes, honey, I did," she said, but to Campbell's ear, she sounded slightly hoarse.

"Well, let's go, then," he said, sketching a rudimentary salute to the others, and making a beeline for her. "I gotta get you downstairs, then get my ass across the Mall to the Intel building before somebody notices I'm not at my desk yet."

They headed out, as her staff stared after them in dumbfoundment.

"That... was not what I expected," Zinn noted, after the pair had departed.

"No shit," Burk agreed. "I suppose 'Saint Rao' has a naughty side, if she likes THAT."

"It certainly gives... food for thought," Gnad agreed. "Well, back at it, everybody. WE have important work to do, at any rate. Even if some people we could name... don't."

The little gathering broke up as they all got back to work.

As soon as they were in the closed elevator — which was empty at that time of day — Campbell turned to her.

"Are you okay?"

"No," Rao averred. "I think they've managed to contaminate my office again. My eyes are stinging like fury, and my hands and face feel like a whole swarm of ants is running over 'em."

"Damn," Campbell murmured. "Did you touch anything?"

"No," Rao said again. "I was careful. I used your portable VR unit — here it is, by the way," she handed it back to him, carefully sealed in its case, and he made a mental note to decontaminate it, "and didn't touch anything. I didn't even sit down. It was just the damn air in the room!"

"I'll see this gets passed to the right people. Once you get yourself set up in the Class 1, run to the necessary and wash your face and hands really good. Like, three times, at least."

"Yeah, I figured that, too. And I already notified Admiral Pachis; when I felt the irritation coming on, I used your VR connection to pop him a message."

"That's good, then," Campbell decided. "I'll ping Durand and see that he knows, too — assuming Pachis hasn't already told him — and

I'll make sure the head of the Facilities Division knows, as well. Maybe she can get it re-decontaminated. If that's even a word."

"Okay."

Campbell escorted her all the way to the basement secure facility, where she delivered a chaste peck to his cheek, and disappeared into the room assigned to her. He waved, then turned and headed across the Mall, en route to the Intelligence Division headquarters building.

"Ah, there you are," Byrne said, waiting for him at his desk in the bullpen. "I assume the captain is well?"

"More or less, I guess," Campbell said, thoughtful. "We swung by her office on the pretext of her getting something, so I could 'run into' her staffers and try to counter any damage that might have gotten done with the white paper hack. But when she came out of her office, she said her eyes and skin were badly irritated... which means her office has been contaminated again. She was going to wash her hands and face in the necessary in the Class 1 Tac center downstairs."

"Right. I'll see that Admiral Durand knows this immediately, so he can notify Admiral Cho," Byrne offered, then frowned in consideration. "Damn, if this keeps up, that office may have to be stripped down to bare studs and completely rebuilt."

"I'd thought about that," Campbell agreed, rueful. "Unfortunately, I don't know that I'm in position yet to stop THAT. But I think my stratagem worked, at least. They now think I'm an analyst, first, last, and only, and a suck-up, at that. Worse, they think I'm a LAZY-ASS, GOLDBRICK suck-up analyst, whose analyses aren't worth the paper they're printed on. More, they probably think that's how I got the promotion yesterday. Because they did notice. Of course, I intended for 'em to notice." He chuckled. Byrne grinned.

"Well, from what I've seen of you over the last few years, 'lazy-ass goldbrick' is about as far from the truth as it could get, never mind 'suck-up,'" the commander offered. "Now, let's head to the Class 1 downstairs; I'm here to get you set up there. We already have an assigned room for you."

"Great!" Campbell declared, as they headed for the elevator bank.

"Now, while I'm here, let me show you one or two techniques you can use to try to spot links while you're in the fully-immersive VR," Byrne noted, once they were in the Class 2 room assigned to Campbell. "Park your ass in that chair, while I use this one, and we'll do this."

Campbell obeyed, and within moments he was all but goggling over the display Byrne was showing him.

"This is a beta-test software module," Byrne explained. "I'm one of the beta testers, so don't let on I showed it to you yet. But it looks promising, and I thought it might help you out here, under the circumstances. If they can get the resource utilization down a bit more — this version fairly chews through the computational resources, so I try to use it during off-peak hours — it'll be released for general use in the Intelligence Division."

"What's it called?" Campbell wondered.

"Right now it's just called Correlation 0.1A." He brought up a full display.

"Holy shit," Campbell murmured, studying the spaghetti imagery and gradually sorting through it. "Oh, this is damn cool, Commander."

"You already get it?"

"I sure do. Yeah, I wanna play in this sandbox."

"I'll submit you as another beta tester, then," Byrne decided. "You'll probably be approved and added to distribution by tomorrow morning, at the latest. Any questions?"

"No sir, I don't think so."

"I'll get out of here and let you have at it, then."

"Yes sir."

Campbell took to the beta-test software's use like the proverbial fish to water, and in a couple of hours he had it set to check out his case suspects. Byrne had also set him up with software to tap into mail and voice calls. Soon he was studying what he could access, though he quickly noted the fact that the correlation package would take a while to complete its work.

Still, he was beginning to see patterns. Most notably, he was seeing links between the Planetary Tactical Office staff and some Facilities staff.

CAMPBELL: THE SIGURDSEN INCIDENT

Several hours later, while he continued to study the data he'd already gathered, an alert interrupted his ponderings, and he realized that the correlation software had finished earlier than he had expected, apparently given his relatively small cast of characters. He pulled it up and studied it for a long moment.

"Aw shit," he grumbled, spotting one link that he had hoped he wouldn't see. "There's a link to Lieutenant Marc Huber through the Stadt embassy, on damn near every one of 'em."

He stayed in the immersive VR until it was time to go meet Rao. They had another 'date,' but he was debating about whether or not to spend the night at her home rather than his, in order to make it look more realistic, especially since her quarters were larger. So he linked his VR to the feed from the bugs he had planted the day before, and quickly reviewed what they'd picked up.

When they depicted a Housekeeping staffer coming in to clean, he studied the woman in detail. "Image tag," he murmured. "Cross-correlate with known staff from Housekeeping department."

It took a few seconds, but a label finally popped up: it was no less a person than Commander Nancy Adamson, chief of staff for Rear Admiral William J. Westerfield, head of the Housekeeping department. And she had no connections that he could find with any of his suspects.

'Wow,' he thought. 'Westerfield and Adamson must really want Rao to stay safe. Pity that didn't work with her office.' Then again, he decided, it was one thing for a ranking officer to show up at a private residence in janitorial garb and clean in relative obscurity, another entirely to show up during business hours at a busy office complex. 'And that wouldn't look good,' he concluded. 'For anybody.'

Campbell had swung by his apartment at lunch, while the various software modules cranked, and packed an overnight duffle... complete with a few extra items, such as the special 'bedroom' light. So when he and Rao finished dinner at another little retired-CSF-owned diner he knew, they headed for her house.

"But how do we know that it's safe?" she wondered in a very low tone, intended for his ears only, as she tooled down the sidewalk at his side.

"I checked my feeds this afternoon," he told her, matching her tone and volume. "It's safe."

"Same song, second verse?"

"Pretty much, yeah. I, uh, I brought the special light you liked so much."

She grinned.

After a relatively peaceful night, she in her bed, he on the sofa he'd dragged up to her bedroom door, the following morning Campbell again escorted Rao to her Class 2 facility in the Tactical building basement, where they exchanged a chaste kiss before he headed for the Intelligence building and his own Class 2 workspace. He spent the morning studying the links highlighted by the correlation software, looking for common elements. There were two, as far as he could see — all were nominal citizens from the Outer Colonies, and all had some sort of connection, communication, or relay from Marc Huber or the Stadt embassy, he couldn't be sure which as yet.

'Huber's stepfather is running an intel ring, I'd lay odds,' he decided, 'and Huber himself is the go-between. And if the next Planetary Tactical Officer winds up being loyal to Stadt and its allies in the Outer Colonies, Jablonka and the Commonwealth are in deep shit.'

Hardball

Just then, a maximum-priority call from a private comm unit came in from the Tactical building. He stared at the alert, and the ID for the incoming call, for a split-second before answering through the VR, maximizing security on the call as best he knew how... which was quite a bit.

"Campbell."

"Bill, it's Mar'. I need your help, Bill. Ugh! I-I'm in the necessary right outside my Class 2 workspace, and I'm... urgh... barfing my f-fool head off."

"Have you been to your regular office at all?"

"I haven't been anywhere except the basement facility, Bill," came the response. "I stayed right where you put me. Until I had to run in here and throw up."

"Aw shit," Campbell grumbled.

"Don't even go there."

"Um, right," Campbell replied, feeling sheepish. "All right, Mary, is it any better in the necessary?"

"No, it isn't."

"Can you navigate on your own?"

"I can, but I can't get far enough away from the toilet because of the vomiting."

Campbell opened up a second communications line in addition to the one with Rao. This one was a classified priority mail to both Byrne and Durand. It read,

FROM: ID5577AS525755875444
TO: ID03A526853225360685, ID05Q3365462324SD36
SUBJECT: Assistance needed
Bird sick. Gilded cage needs cleaning. Need help in freeing bird from cage. Suggestions appreciated.
~Lt.WC

A few moments later, a reply came in.

FROM: ID03A526853225360685
TO: ID5577AS525755875444, ID05Q3365462324SD36
SUBJECT: Re: Assistance needed
Lt.WC,
On it. Tell me exactly where the bird is.
~JD

Campbell responded.

FROM: ID5577AS525755875444
TO: ID03A526853225360685, ID05Q3365462324SD36
SUBJECT: Re:Re: Assistance needed
JD,
Soiling papers on bottom of cage.
~Lt.WC

Durand replied, succinct.

FROM: ID03A526853225360685
TO: ID5577AS525755875444, ID05Q3365462324SD36
SUBJECT: Re:Re:Re: Assistance needed
Gotcha. Done.
~JD

"Mary, honey, try to stay calm," Campbell said then. "Somebody's on the way to get you out and tend to things."

"You... how... urgh... soh-sorry..."

"Shh. It's okay," he murmured, listening to the sound of vomitus splattering in the toilet bowl. "I have connections, remember. Just hang in here with me. Help is on the way. I'll stay on the line until they arrive."

"O-oka-blarrgh!"

Admiral Durand remote-locked his office door, sending Commander Jany Jones a coded message that he would be unavailable until further notice at the highest possible classifications, then entered immersive VR. Seconds later he was notifying Admiral Pachis of the security breach.

"Damnation," came Pachis' response. "What do I need to do?"

"Go hit the nearest fire alarm," Durand instructed. "I'm on this."

"Done," Pachis agreed.

Lieutenant Commander Andre watched in shock as Pachis — nearing retirement age, and no longer remotely considered a young man — sprinted from his office at a speed that might be expected of a freshly-graduated cadet executing a drill. He pounded through the outer office and into the corridor outside. She leaped up to follow him, just in time to see him slam his hand down on the nearest fire alarm trigger. He spun to face her.

"Secure your office, Liv," he told her, not remotely out of breath, "then evacuate."

"What?!"

"Do it. NOW."

As soon as Pachis broke the comm, Durand contacted a clandestine subordinate.

"Endurance to Rover," he murmured. "Do you copy?"

"Rover here, Endurance," came the response. "What's the word?"

"Phase One is culminating the way I expected, if a bit sooner," Durand replied. "Execute the plan immediately. Fetch the handler, then free the bird. This is not a drill. Repeat, this is not a drill."

"Copy; plan live. Gone," Rover replied, and severed the communication.

"Godspeed," Durand whispered.

Within minutes, the Tactical building had evacuated... except for one ill captain in the secure basement's necessary.

Only a handful of people knew that, however; that handful mostly comprised three people in the Intelligence building, the head of the Tactical Division... and the squad in a firefighting shuttle that landed and set up its base along the loading dock for the building, then sent a team wearing full heavy gear into the side entrance.

It only took a scant fifteen minutes of waiting with Rao on the call before Campbell heard another voice, though it was muffled and somewhat distant.

"Captain? Captain Rao? This is Commander Adamson. I'm Admiral Westerfield's chief of staff. I'm here with a team from Intel to fetch you out of here and get you some help."

"She's clear, Mary," Campbell murmured into the voice connection. "I've already checked her out. Go with her."

"O-okay," Rao managed to respond. "I'll... I'll talk to you later, Bill."

"Go get out of there and feel better, honey."

"Gone."

And she hung up.

Five minutes after they had entered, the same firefighting team came out the side entrance; the shuttle's commander reported a negative result to the fire captain, about the time several other teams made the same report. The fire captain declared the incident a false alarm and the building cleared, and all fire response teams returned to their stations as the Tactical Division returned to their offices.

Had anyone bothered to count, they would have noticed that one more person exited via the loading dock than entered.

But everyone was too agitated to notice.

Durand, Byrne, and Campbell 'met' in VR forty-five minutes later.

"I just got notice," Durand told the other two. "Our people extracted her — with a little assistance by Admiral Pachis in giving us a cover excuse — and got her away and everybody decontaminated, with a little help from a trusted friend out of Housekeeping. Rao is lying down in a safehouse now, resting and recovering, while the extraction team's medic cares for her. I've notified Pachis, and he's... relieved."

"Good," Campbell asserted. "Thanks, Admiral. What are we going to do about the contaminated secure room?"

"Haven't decided yet," Durand said. "I want to discuss that one with Haden and Melinda, and see what we can come up with that'll keep people safe without tipping off our perps. Don't worry about that one, Lieutenant; we'll handle it, and I swear it won't interfere with your investigation."

"Right. Thank you, sir."

"This won't do," Byrne said. "At this rate, the woman is going to experience permanent health repercussions! I think maybe we need to get Captain Rao off the base altogether, and into complete seclusion, while we investigate this."

"With all due respect, Commander Byrne, that plays right into their hands," Campbell pointed out. "It takes her out of the loop, and since it's most likely her second that the sabotage ring seems to want in play — whether he's one of them or not — it puts their preferred officer in charge."

"Mm. He's right, Commander," Durand agreed. "After all, if she's too ill to work, or if we whisk her into hiding, it has the same effect as if they'd killed her. It gives them exactly what they want. It's already given them far too much access in recent weeks as it is."

"Then what do you suggest, sir?" Byrne wondered.

"I'm still thinking on that one," Durand admitted.

"What we need," Campbell brainstormed, "is some way to allow her to stay in the loop, but simultaneously keeping her hidden and under secure guard, while we work out what's really going on..."

"How far have you gotten on that, Campbell?" Durand wondered. "On what's really going on?"

"I've ascertained that all of my suspects, in the PTO and in Facilities, do have a common link, and that common link is in a particular embassy, Stadt, to be specific," Campbell informed them. "I still need to figure out who the contact focal point is in that embassy, though."

"Mm. Interesting," Durand murmured, thoughtful. "So there's no doubt we have something here, and it's offworld."

"None at all, sir."

"Is Earth behind it, or is it all Outer Colonies?"

"Oh, Outer Colonies, definitely, sir. I see no sign of Earth involvement at all, but there are Outer Colonies imprints all over it."

"We still have no plan to move forward with Captain Rao," Byrne pointed out.

"Stand by, Byrne," Durand remarked, a hint of annoyance in his tone, "I have an inquiry out on that. I multitask pretty damn well in full VR, after all."

"Ah. Standing by, sir," Byrne said, quiet. "Sorry to annoy. I'm just... concerned for Captain Rao."

"After not believing her?"

"...Yes sir. That's why I'm most concerned," Byrne confessed. "I... misjudged that situation, largely on account of the military police investigation report, and now I want to make sure she's properly taken care of."

"Do you have a problem with how Lieutenant Campbell has been handling the case?"

"No sir, not now. Campbell seems to be doing an excellent job," Byrne pointed out, "but he's just one man, and he can't be everywhere at once. I'm trying to back him up, support him as best I can." Byrne paused. "I'm glad you had a plan ready, Admiral, to extract Rao without Campbell having to risk contamination himself. He shows a great deal of promise, and I don't want to lose him to this case."

"You were worried?"

"I was, sir."

"Good, then; I'm pleased with responses and reactions all around," Durand declared. "I — stand by..."

"Standing by," Campbell and Byrne both murmured.

Five minutes later, Durand once more became VR-active to the waiting pair.

"Well, it looks like that'll work out nicely," he said to Campbell and Byrne. "We all get our wish. The safehouse where she's currently resting has a Class 1/Class 2 toggle facility with VR equivalent to what we have here, gentlemen, because it's where an off-site clandestine Intelligence team makes its headquarters. I've discussed it with the team's commander, and they have the capability to sequester her from the rest of the safehouse — so she doesn't see too much of their work — because of planning for just such situations as this. So she can stay there, off-base and safe, while still performing her work... once she recovers a bit more from this latest chemical attack."

"Terrific!" Campbell exclaimed.

"Perfect," Byrne declared. "We got this."

By the time the emergency situation with Rao was resolved, it was past midafternoon, getting late in the day. More, Campbell found himself restless, unable to focus on the vast database he'd created in the immersive VR.

'Mm,' he considered, 'maybe I need to get out and about and take a walk, move around a little and get some fresh air. I hadn't planned to do this quite yet, but maybe it's time to go scope out the Stadt embassy.'

He pulled out of the VR, shut down what needed closing for the sake of security, and headed out.

Campbell wasn't looking for anything in particular; he simply wanted to familiarize himself with what the base inhabitants called 'Embassy Row.' He had never had any particular reason or occasion to go down there until now, and he suspected that at least knowing his way around the area might come in handy. And sooner rather than later.

So he hiked off-base into the edge of Jezgra, where 'Embassy Row' — really called Westlake Conference Drive, except no one but the top brass ever called it that — lay, complete with Commonwealth planet, Earth, and Outer Colonies embassies. Not that any but the other Commonwealth planets were especially friendly, but still. And strictly speaking, the other Commonwealth planets' embassies weren't so much embassies as simply additional means to support the Representatives in Council Tower, several blocks north. But the Commonwealth Founders had chosen to arrange it like that, and no one had seen fit, in the intervening time, to change it.

So Campbell spent the rest of the afternoon strolling down Westlake Conference Drive, looking at the various structures. He found the architecture interesting, as each embassy had chosen to construct a complex based on their own planet's culture, and some were relatively ordinary, but some were striking. And a few were just... odd. At least, in Campbell's opinion. But it made for an excellent cover, as he had considered the matter and swung by the commissary to pick up a booklet on the architecture of various parts of Jezgra on his way there; from time to time, he pulled out the booklet and consulted it, in case anyone was watching.

The street was a long one, with many compounds and even more structures, and was, like the rest of Jezgra's layout, broken into blocks. Campbell took his time, exploring the side streets as well as the main street, and learning his way around the diplomatic environ.

He also discovered that some of the embassies offered tours, for a small fee; nothing of any significance was on the tours, but if the Stadt embassy had one, it might be a way for one of his alter-egos to slip inside and scope the place out. Often the best way of hiding a thing was in plain sight, so there was not much telling what his trained eye might catch, that an untrained civilian would walk right past.

The Commonwealth embassies were on the east side of the street, arranged in alphabetical order, and the Outer Colonies on the west side, likewise alphabetical, with the Earth embassy on the south end of the street, nearest the base, and looking across at the Commonwealth Center complex, in the near distance. Campbell wondered if that positioning had been intended as a reminder of history.

It took a while to reach the Stadt embassy; it was near the north end of the street, twenty-second out of twenty-five embassies, all of whose grounds were slightly staggered in order to allow for the same area for each embassy on the street, given the Outer Colonies did not have the same number of planets as the Commonwealth. But at least layout-wise, it worked.

Campbell slowed down as he neared the Stadt embassy, and looked carefully about him without appearing to do so. The Stadt embassy structure was a multi-story structure, at least three floors above ground and one or two — it was difficult to tell from the outside — underground; since it sat on a rise, evidently the architects had decided to make use of the fact. It had no especial distinguishing architecture, safe for a slight hint of what might have been Bavarian in its façade; the roof was a classic gable, with a few gable windows here and there protruding from it at right angles to the ridgeline, and the structural support was all visible externally. The grounds were well-manicured, with clumps of brightly-flowering shrubs here and there, and a formal hedge garden in the back.

A narrow side street, almost an alley, ran along one side of the compound, down to the next street to the west; it was lined with numerous outbuildings and support structures, as well as a ground car driveway that led to the embassy's underground garage, and an adjacent servant's entrance.

Campbell looped the block on which the Stadt embassy sat a couple of times, to make sure he got a good feel for the overall layout of the compound. Fortunately, the next street west had no structures on the east side; this had been to provide sufficient security for... and against... the embassies.

Having finally gotten the view of the Stadt embassy he wanted — at least from outside — and ending up one street over from 'Embassy Row,' Campbell decided to cut through the little side street hard by the embassy and head back to the base. There, he intended to see about wangling a way to look inside the embassy and try to get a feel for its layout and personnel.

'Though,' he realized, 'I'll probably have to come as somebody else. I don't think it would be good to show up as me. Especially not after walking around the neighborhood.'

He began to ponder which disguise might work well for the purpose.

In the servants' quarters of the Stadt embassy, downstairs, D. R. Zinn, one of the bodyguards, was reading on his personal electronic display unit when an encrypted message came in on that device. Zinn tapped a specific sequence on the screen, then pulled down a suddenly-unlocked overlay that translated the message.

CAMPBELL OUTSIDE ON SIDE STREET. "MUG" HIM. END IT. NOW.

Zinn shoved the electronic display unit into a pocket and ran for the side servants' entrance.

Campbell heard the soft patter of running feet somewhere behind him, and instantly went on alert. He had been wary from the moment he reached 'Embassy Row,' especially once nearing the Stadt compound, but this sound ramped up his vigilance from *Pay attention,* to *Battle stations* — whoever was behind him was in a hurry, but was also trying hard to be as quiet as possible. And that meant an attempt at swift stealth... which in turn meant danger.

'Somebody not only saw me from inside the embassy, they recognized me,' he realized. 'He doesn't have a gun, or he'd have used it by now,' Campbell rapidly analyzed. 'Which means, given my location in a little-used side street with plenty of alleys and outbuildings, they want it to look like a mugging gone wrong. Knife at best; bare hands possible. I'd prefer a knife, though; if the killer comes at me with bare hands, this could take a while, because it means he's good.'

He listened carefully, gauging the closing distance by the sound; he'd have to time this one just right, or he could be badly injured... and that was the BEST outcome for such a circumstance. Dead was definitely an option.

When the sound was less than six feet away, Campbell spun, dropping into a shallow horse stance, his hands already in motion even as his brain took stock.

The assailant was indeed armed with a knife in his right hand; his build indicated he was most likely a bodyguard from the embassy, but that was neither here nor there, since he was not dressed in any sort of livery or uniform. More, that knife hand was raised to strike. The assailant had just time to snarl at Campbell when he acted.

Campbell caught the assailant's right wrist in his left hand, holding it up and well away from his own body. A swift palm heel strike to the nose with Campbell's right hand broke it, temporarily blinding him and sending a spray of blood across the man's shirt, even as he grunted with unexpected pain. The young lieutenant followed through by hooking his right forearm behind the assailant's, then vigorously pulled it toward him while forcing the wrist back with the other hand; at least one bone broke with a grisly snap, and the man gasped, reflex action causing him to release the knife, which clattered to the pavement.

Scant seconds later, the would-be assailant was lying on the sidewalk, neck broken and temple stoven inward, dead.

Campbell glanced around; no one else was within sight, and he'd slowed down to ensure the encounter occurred behind a rise of ground, preventing anyone inside the embassy building from seeing the fight. Spotting a shaded alcove between buildings nearby, he dragged the body into the alcove, then returned for the knife, extracting a polymer glove to pick it up. He moved it back to the body of his former assailant, placing it back in the body's right hand and wrapping the fingers around the hilt, then using his own hand to squeeze the dead fingers around it, forming them into a fist; once rigor set in, the knife would be held firmly. Given the nature of rigor, it wouldn't stay that way long, but most likely it would do until the body was found.

Then he gave another glance around; still no one in the area. Campbell smirked to himself, then extracted a small vial with a viscous red liquid inside from a pocket; he'd started carrying it with him as soon as he'd realized his role in the current case might have been exposed.

'I had a feeling I'd better start keeping this on me, just in case,' he thought, as he opened the container of his own blood and, using the gloved hand, ensured the tip and edges of the blade were thoroughly coated in same. He removed the glove, turning it wrong-side-out, tucked the empty vial inside, and the whole went into the zip-closure polymer bag out of which the glove had come, and that went into a pocket of his shipsuit.

After dragging the body deeper into a niche where it would remain out of sight for some time, and setting the scene so that it would look as he wished it to look, Campbell searched the would-be assassin with swift care; by his reckoning, he didn't have long to do so. He ascertained that the dead man was indeed a bodyguard for the Stadt compound, one D. R. Zinn, according to his identification, which Campbell quickly tucked back into Zinn's pocket. After several anxious moments of additional searching, Campbell finally came up with an electronic display unit. When activated, a cryptic message displayed onscreen.

XX0vi12#$88P10e7a46545WRR@
@#$Gawe#**&*azsd$

It was apparently an encrypted code, but it had been careless — or rushed — on the part of the assassin to leave it onscreen. 'Most likely rushed, given the timetable of my walk,' Campbell decided.

Campbell shoved the device into one of the more capacious pockets of his shipsuit. Then he slipped inside an outbuilding nearby. It was late in the afternoon, nearing sunset, and he wanted it to be solidly dark before he made his next move. Because his next move was to disappear. For all intents and purposes, and until further notice, Lieutenant William Campbell... was dead.

Once the sun set, but before the street lights had turned on, he slipped out of the outbuilding...

...Headed for a bolt-hole he'd loosely planned for months.

Given the need to remain unseen, it took him several hours. The fact that the bolt-hole was some distance away, and in the opposite direction from the base, did not help that situation; he made a mental note to see about developing a couple more, in different parts of the city... provided he could find a way to afford it. Granted, he had been the sole inheritor for his family, but they hadn't been rich and that only went so far, so he didn't want to waste it on something that he wouldn't use most of the time.

As soon as he was safely ensconced in his secret lair, Campbell contacted Durand on a ciphered line from his personal device, despite the lateness of the hour. As Durand was an old friend of Campbell's parents, and had always played straight with the young lieutenant, Campbell trusted him. Never mind the fact that Durand had voluntarily and insistently assigned himself the role of mentor.

"Durand," came the voice on the other end of the communiqué.

"Jake, it's Bill from Stabljika," Campbell said, hoping the admiral would not mind the less-than-formal mode of address, once he understood the circumstances. "I've got a little situation, and I was hoping you could help."

In his office late that day, given what had gone down earlier, Durand now sat up straight in his desk chair, recognizing the voice and instantly understanding the reason for the mode of address.

"Tell me," he barked. "No, wait — let me set the line..."

CAMPBELL: THE SIGURDSEN INCIDENT

Once Admiral Durand had applied a special cipher to his end of the conversation, Campbell filled in the admiral on what had just gone down.

"...So I think it's time I disappeared for a bit," Campbell explained. "A... friend... of mine will be taking my place."

"Right," Durand agreed immediately, fully comprehending the cryptic statement. "Do you have this 'friend's' personnel file?"

"As it happens, I do," Campbell said with a wry chuckle, "and I'll send it to you about a minute after we end this call."

"Good. I'll handle it from there, don't worry," Durand confirmed. "If your friend waits until in the morning to come on the base, he'll find everything smoothed out for him. I'll also handle any problems that may arise from the Jablonka police force, once that body gets discovered."

"Much appreciated, sir. How do you intend to handle it?"

"Are you open to being 'dead' for a while?"

"If that's what it takes."

"Good. Then you were badly wounded in the altercation, and you made it back to your quarters on base, but collapsed and died once you got inside."

"That works."

As promised, Campbell immediately sent Durand the personnel file on one Petty Officer First Class Philip Samples. Moments later, a notification came back that Samples had been designated a 'fixer,' a direct-action operative, with an annotation that "a deceased former associate" had also been given the designation.

'Well,' Campbell thought, 'that proves useful, in the circumstances. Now let's see about breaking this code and responding.'

It took the software that Byrne had given him on the special chip all of about twenty minutes to break the encryption and decipher the code. And it was indeed as Campbell had suspected: it was the order instruction to kill Campbell, sent from one codename, 'Marcel.' More, it had arrived within moments of the attack, so the assassin had not had time to do anything but go after Campbell.

'Which means,' he decided, 'someone was in the embassy, watching, and saw AND RECOGNIZED me.' He shook his head. 'That sure sounds like Lieutenant Huber. I don't know anybody else who would be in the embassy, let alone who would recognize me.'

Quickly inserting a reverse-encryption code into the electronic display unit, he replied to 'Marcel' in a kind of broken type.

Asssignment vcompleted. Target not dead yeeet but will be soon.am injurrred. Headded out of site need hhelp

Then he sent the message.
Moments later, a response came back. It was cold and merciless.

You know the rules. You're on your own.

Campbell shook his head.
Then he turned to his next task.

His bolt-hole wasn't large; it was an old, somewhat ramshackle basement apartment with access down an old back alley, and little more than a studio apartment — one room containing a bed, a cramped desk/dining table combo, a tiny kitchenette, and an even tinier necessary. But it had what he needed, and after a few clandestine trips a few weeks earlier, the kitchenette was well stocked with nonperishables that he could use to fuel himself as required.

Likewise, the necessary had a few special things in it, intended for the times when William Campbell needed to disappear.

He ducked into the necessary and began his transformation.

Petty Officer First Class Phil Samples was about 36 years old, balding, with what hair he still had starting to gray at the temples, and clean-shaven, if scruffy. More, that hair was black.

This meant that 24-year-old Campbell had to dye his light brown hair black, shave the crown of his head — he'd have to shave all of it when he came back, to allow it to grow in the proper color, but that would be easier to explain away than coming back from the dead — get rid of his beard, and apply a bit of white to the hair remaining at his temples. Then he had to add a few crow's-feet around his eyes, and some lines to his forehead. As an afterthought, he deepened the naso-labial folds around his nose, then carefully applied a latex scar across his left jawline. A bit of discreet makeup, applied with a very light hand and then thoroughly set, caused it to blend into his skin rather nicely.

More, he had to swap out the various insignia on his shipsuit. But one of the experienced investigators with whom he'd worked a few months earlier had helped him acquire the replacements when he had created the character, modifying and upgrading it from the original, which was an idea he'd successfully tried in his Academy days, in the theatrical makeup course.

At the same time, he had worked out the details of the 'Samples' character in terms of what would constitute a reasonable and believable personnel file, and prepared it in the proper format, keeping it in a hidden, encrypted file on both his comm unit and his electronic display unit, ready for submission. And it was precisely this file which he had sent to Durand earlier.

It took about an hour. But at the end of that time, Petty Officer Samples stared back at him in the mirror.

Altered Egos

Samples entered the base without a problem at the gate; his personnel file was already in the system, apparently thanks to Admiral Durand. He stopped by a particular fire station, then made straight for the Planetary Tactical Office.

Once there, he stuck his head into the empty inner office, briefly feeling the slight sting of something in the air that shouldn't be there, then ducked back out, scanned the bullpen, and headed straight for Commander Gnad.

"Sir," he said, making sure to keep his voice in the lower pitch and rougher quality that characterized Samples' speech patterns. "I'm here t' report for the CSS *Aluna Kamau*, sir."

Gnad looked up from his corner desk and gave Samples a cursory scan.

"Who the hell are you?" he asked, blunt.

"Petty Officer First Class Phil Samples reporting from th' CSS *Aluna Kamau*, sir," he said, saluting, then he added, "'Er tac officer got caught up in some bus'ness of the captain, an' asked me to pop by with th' data." He held up a small chip in his thumb and forefinger... which Durand had had left for him at the fire station; the CSS *Aluna Kamau* had truly just made orbit around Jablonka that morning.

Not, Samples knew, that this was the REAL report from the *Aluna Kamau*; certain key pieces of data had been either deleted, or replaced with reasonable but fake data. "No sense in them getting the actual tactical data," Durand had pointed out. "I'll feed the real thing through the appropriate channels so it gets where it's needed without... 'diversion.'"

Gnad gestured at Lieutenant Commander Glaub, his assistant, who sat at the adjacent desk. Glaub nodded, then pointed at a row of visitor chairs along the wall, fully twenty feet away.

"Have a seat, Mr. Samples," he said without preamble. "We'll get to you when we get to you."

"But I—"

"Have a seat, Mr. Samples. That's an order," Glaub responded.

CAMPBELL: THE SIGURDSEN INCIDENT

Samples slouched sullenly over to the chairs and sat in one, whereupon he was ignored. He spent the next two hours fidgeting and looking bored.

He was anything but, however. He spent the time watching the interactions in the office suite when the cat was away — though, he considered, perhaps that should have been mouse — and found it interesting. And potentially telling.

Per Campbell's research, out of the seven staff members in the PTO assigned under Rao, two were born citizens of the Commonwealth, and the other five were naturalized from various Outer Colonies. More, all five had connections to the Stadt embassy in some fashion... but the native-born staffers did not.

Now, as Samples watched, he noted that the two native-born staffers were kept busy running errands out of the office; Lieutenants Kooistra and Zinn were hardly allowed to sit down at their own desks before Gnad sent them off on another task. But the others — Gnad, Glaub, and lieutenants Powers, Weiner, and Burk all stayed in the office, from time to time exchanging paperwork and curt, succinct, and mildly cryptic commentary.

"Gnad, request incoming," Weiner noted. Gnad nodded and pulled up something on the VR.

"Okay, yeah, we can handle that," Gnad said after a moment. "Go ahead and approve it."

"Brian, you see the out-system report?" Burk wondered.

"No... when did it come in...?"

"I took a look, guys," Glaub interjected. "I got it covered."

"Thanks, Bob," Gnad said, shaking his head. "Things have been pretty busy the last few days... what with Captain Rao out of pocket."

Several of the staffers shot surreptitious glances at Samples, who pretended to be staring out the window in complete boredom.

For all the chit-chat among the PTO staff, Samples noticed that nothing was being said about what systems were doing the reporting or requesting... which meant it was NOT necessarily COMMONWEALTH systems.

'I'll have to make sure their computer systems get thoroughly examined once we get this over and done, so we can determine who's benefitting from their shenanigans,' Samples considered.

From time to time, and with permission from Gnad, Samples rose to stretch his legs, usually moving to one of four windows in the outer office, to look out on the sun-drenched Mall and its green, open spaces dotted with trees and shrubs.

"I'll bet that's a nice view after months spent spacing, huh, Mr. Samples?" Powers wondered, the second time he did so. She came over to stand beside him, looking out for herself.

"Not t' put a fine point on it, hell yes, ma'am," Samples said, turning to offer her a slight smile. "There's more room right there than in my whole damn squadron!" He turned back to look out again. "Never mind all the green..."

"Aw! You stand there and enjoy it as long as you want to, then," she said, sounding sympathetic.

Powers patted his shoulder in a friendly fashion, then moved back to her desk.

Nearly two and a quarter hours after Samples had first taken his seat, Glaub and Gnad exchanged meaningful glances, shooting sidelong looks at Samples. Finally Glaub rose and moved to Samples.

"You said you had a ship report, Mr. Samples?" he asked.

"Sure 'nough, sir," Samples said, producing the chip again. "Got it right here. Sorry to bother; I gather you guys are pretty damn busy right now. But I got orders an' all, so here I am."

"All right, Mr. Samples," Glaub said with a friendly smile... that seemed slightly forced to Samples. "Sorry to keep you waiting, but our boss has been out of the office a good bit recently, and we've had to play whack-a-mole in her absence. Thanks for being patient." He held out his hand, palm up.

"Not a prob," Samples said, placing the chip in Glaub's palm. "I got my orders and duty, and you lot have yours. There ya go."

"And I can keep this, right?"

"Sure 'nuff."

"All right, Mr. Samples; thanks. Anything else?"

"Not that I know of."

"Okay, you're dismissed, then. Go check back in with your folks, and... I assume you have some shore leave coming up?"

"A little," Samples said with a wicked grin. Glaub laughed.

"Go enjoy it, then."

"All over that, sir! Thank you, sir!"

Samples stood and saluted, then departed the PTO with a jaunty swagger.

No one in the PTO knew he'd left behind more than a dozen audiovisual bugs.

From there, Samples headed to an adjacent building, which happened to be a barracks, the barracks to which Samples had been assigned... except that, unknown to most, it was controlled by the Intelligence Division. Instead of going to the berth Durand had assigned him, however, he hit the stairwell and headed down...

...Below the basement.

There, the stairwell appeared to dead-end, but some — including Samples — knew better. He went to the wall under the stairs, sought out a particular masonry block, and pulled out the façade, revealing a tiny touch screen.

A quick thumb print gave him access to the 'maintenance hatch' at that lowest level, and he opened it, entering a dimly-lit tunnel. Closing the hatch behind him, he set off down the tunnel.

Five minutes later, Samples emerged in the sub-basement, one floor down from the Class 1 basement facility in the Intelligence Division's headquarters building. He repeated the thumb-swipe to enter the stairwell, and climbed up one flight, provided another thumbprint, and entered the Class 1 facility.

As he moved to what passed for a reception desk in that classified center, he encountered two familiar faces, one standing, the other in a mobility chair.

"No, Admiral," Captain Rao averred, "I'm feeling much better, and I wanted to tag back up with you face to face — don't worry; I had really good help getting here, so no one knows I'm here that shouldn't. But I felt I needed to talk to you in person. Especially... well, especially when your office put out that announcement on Bill Campbell." She bit her lip. "I... I feel responsible. He's dead, on account of me."

"No, Captain," Admiral Durand corrected her. "You did nothing except fight to stay alive and to keep doing your job. Which was the same thing he was doing. He died because the same people who want you dead decided he needed to die, too."

Rao's shoulders slumped, and she bowed her head, staring at the floor with an empty gaze. Samples surreptitiously bit his lip, then eased past Durand to the commander behind the desk.

"Petty Officer First Class Phil Samples reportin', sir," he said, ensuring his tone was just loud enough for Durand to hear. "Have ya got a Class 2 work room reserved for me?"

"Did you say Samples?" Durand queried, turning. "Phil Samples?"

"That's me, Admiral sir."

"Ah!" Durand said, as a puzzled Rao watched. "Yes, Commander, I put in that request for Mr. Samples last night. He should be in corridor H, room 5, if memory serves."

"Mm..." the commander manning the secure reception hummed, as he scanned the roster. "Oh, here we are. Yes, corridor H, room 5, Mr. Samples, just as the Admiral says."

"Thumb swipe?" Samples confirmed.

"Thumb swipe."

"All right. Thanks much." Samples turned to Durand and Rao. "So, Admiral. Is this Captain Rao, that my friend Campbell told me about?"

"Oh, pardon me," Durand said smoothly. "Captain Mary Rao, this is Petty Officer First Class Phil Samples. Samples is — was — a friend of Lieutenant Campbell, who kept you safe... until this spy ring we believe he uncovered took him out. Now, with Campbell... gone... Samples will be taking over the case."

"But..." Rao began, patently puzzled. "He's a petty officer. He's Tactical, not Intelligence."

"Looks can be deceivin', Captain, ma'am," Samples pointed out. "Yeah, I started out in Tactical. But... well, let's just say I got recruited."

"Oh," Rao said, then, "OH!"

'This is weird,' Rao decided, watching the interaction between Samples and Durand. 'This Mr. Samples doesn't look like any intelligence officer I've ever seen. He's not even an officer! What gives?'

About that time, she saw Samples throw a concerned glance at Durand, who subtly waved the younger man off.

And that was when she noticed his eyes.

They were a distinctive pale green.

Just like someone she had kissed recently... who was supposed to be dead.

'Oh thank God!' she thought, suddenly understanding. 'Bill isn't dead, he's just under cover!'

Both men saw recognition flash into Rao's gaze, and they glanced at each other again.

"Well, Mr. Samples, you'd best be getting to it," Durand said then, anxious to hustle him away from Rao. "And Captain, I think we need to get you back to the safehouse. We want you off-base and out of sight. Campbell is enough of a casualty; we don't need to lose our planetary tac officer."

"Yes sir," Rao said, suddenly meek. "Um, Mr. Samples?"

"Yes ma'am?"

"I, uh, thank you. For taking over Bill's task, I mean," Rao tried.

"Bastards killed a pal I've known since he was a kid, ma'am," Samples declared in an almost-growl. "I ain't gonna let this one go."

"No... but I appreciate it, too, just the same," she pressed.

"Then... you're welcome," a sober Samples said, nodding.

And she was gone.

Once Rao was out of sight, Durand personally escorted Samples to his Class 2 workspace room, entering with the younger man. Once the door was closed and locked, he turned to Samples.

"She nailed you, you know," Durand pointed out.

"Well, it's the first time Samples has gone for a drive," Samples pointed out. "And she an' Campbell were together a lot in recent days. It isn't really surprisin', if you think about it. I guess I need to beef up a few things, but this right here," he jabbed at the floor, "running the deception live, is what it's gonna take to do it."

"Just don't get yourself killed before you get it 'beefed up,'" Durand noted.

"I won't," Samples declared, then dropped the below-decks patois. "But if I caught it all correctly, I think it was my eyes that gave me away. Either that, or this damn pimple I've had on my cheek for the last week," he fingered the blemish, "but I hope it was the eyes, because without a shit-ton of spackle, there's no way to effectively hide a pimple — it's all about contour, rather than coloration, and the wrong angle undoes all your efforts. And once you start using that much makeup, the makeup itself becomes obvious, especially in sunlight."

"I hear you, but I didn't even notice the pimple until you said something," Durand noted, "and I don't think she would have noticed it either, not from the other side of me, sitting on her scooter. Your skin is pretty damn clear, for your age."

"Oh, really? What did you see, then?"

"Mm," Durand considered for a moment. "Yeah, I'd agree with the eyes, I think. She saw us glance at each other, then she focused in on your eyes. Which are rather a unique shade of green, son. We need to do something about that. Tinted lenses are probably our best bet."

"Well, I didn't have any access to..."

"Aha. As well as you've been handling it, I keep forgetting this is your first real case. We need to get you set up with some supply lines, as it were. All right, I can take care of this in about ten minutes," Durand said with a grin. "Let me hit the VR in this room and a package will be delivered to you in a little bit."

"Be my guest," Samples said, waving a hand at the VR connections.

Five minutes later, Durand came up for air.

"There," he said, "it's done. I've set you up with a supply line for the long term. Meanwhile, a batch of brown, non-prescription contact lenses will be delivered in a plain brown-wrapper package, to this room, in about another five or ten minutes. Along with some saline, and the means for properly caring for 'em." He paused. "You know how to put 'em in?"

"Yes sir. Had the handling of all that, back in the special makeup class," Samples noted. "I just haven't had access to a means of getting more, SINCE then."

"Right. Well, we'll see to that, from now on."

"Thank you, sir. I'll put 'em in as soon as they arrive."

The ensign who delivered the package was as good as Admiral Durand's word. Before he could finish a quick debrief with Samples, there was a soft chime at the door. Samples rose and opened it.

"Petty Officer First Class Philip Samples?" the young ensign asked; judging by his young age, he was part of the latest batch of Academy graduates.

"That's me, son," Samples answered, and the ensign offered a small touchpad.

"Thumbprint here," he said, and Samples complied — with his left thumb. The ensign raised an eyebrow.

"Oh," Samples said, thinking fast. "Right one's all scarred up. Don't scan no more."

"Ah," said the young man in understanding, whereupon the ensign handed over the package. "Here you are."

Samples accepted the parcel, closing the door behind the departing ensign, and turned back to the table, which Durand had cleared of items, putting out a canister of wet wipes.

"There," he ordered, pointing. "Put 'em in. Now."

Samples sat and reached for the saline.

After donning a set of the brown contact lenses, Samples verified with Durand that Rao was all right after the latest poisoning attempt, and was in fact being treated for the ongoing exposure to clear her system of long-term contamination, while she was "in seclusion," as Durand put it. Samples saw the admiral out, then returned and sat down in the VR chair. He settled in, leaned back, and entered full immersive VR.

He pulled up the video bugs he had just planted in the planetary tac office about forty-five minutes before, and began to watch events. From time to time he swapped his point of view between bug locations, and even backed up the imagery and replayed it from the new perspective, to make sure he missed nothing. The brain's ability to process such things nearly instantaneously meant he saw almost everything in real-time.

'It would sure be damn useful, though, if I had the higher-tech state-of-the-art VR shit,' he grumbled to himself as he continued to watch. 'I barely have ANY audio, and the resolution on the video would be higher. I have a damn decent tool kit, sure, but I don't think this is quite as sophisticated as a more senior intel officer would have, at least as yet. Then again, I guess I need to prove I actually NEED it. And this is my opportunity to do that. If I can successfully complete this case... and survive it with my client and my skin both intact... I'll be damned if I'm not going to DEMAND it, too,' he decided.

But his patience and his due diligence paid off about an hour later, when he saw Commander Brian Lee Gnad, Rao's XO who hailed from Guernsey, discussing something with the 'regular' housekeeper. The audio was nowhere near good enough to pick up what was being said, since they were being very quiet — even with no one else in the room — but Samples could read lips.

'It's the non-human-approved cleaner junk,' he realized. 'That's what they're talking about.' Instantly he double-checked to make sure the video was being recorded in full fidelity... or as full as his tool kit allowed, at any rate.

"How is it going?" the housekeeper wondered. "Is she... gone... yet?"

"Not yet," Gnad said, huffing in annoyance. "It was working great there, for a while. She was sick as twelve dogs! But now, she doesn't seem to stay in one place long enough, any more. I don't know if she suspects something, or if she's just on a classified project that keeps her busy, or what. From what I've seen, I think it's a classified project yanking her away, but it's damn sure getting in our way."

"What the hell?! She should be dead by now!"

"I know that, and you know that. But she isn't staying in her office."

"I know THAT much; Marcel called. I got the orders to scope out her secure facility and 'clean' it, too," the housekeeper noted. "I started on that yesterday. But I didn't see any sign of her today when I went in there to clean it."

"Really? Oh shit."

"I was kind of hoping that might have done it," the housekeeper said. "You know, last straw and all. So I thought I'd swing by and see what you'd heard."

"No, not that I'm aware. In fact, I think she pinged Zinn just this morning about something..." Gnad recalled. "So I guess she's gone again."

"Well, SHIT! Marcel is NOT gonna be happy! Where the hell IS she?"

Gnad merely shrugged, to the watching Sample's satisfaction.

'Bingo,' Samples thought. 'This Marcel ringleader, the housekeeper, the XO, and the kluged-up cleaning solution, all in one go. Now let's see what else I can find.'

Samples immediately set to work, looking for any connections between the housekeeper or Commander Gnad and Lieutenant Marc Huber, and how Huber could have tipped them off. But he found nothing. There simply were no connections between Huber and any of the suspects on his list. There was enough to demonstrate a strong correlation between the housekeeper and Gnad, and both with the Stadt embassy, but not to Huber, personally, except possibly through the Stadt embassy chief of staff.

'And that one is familial,' he realized. 'Which means it might be nothing of import. If Huber isn't connected up with this, then... shit. Well, let me check out a few other things, first. He might just be another operative, and the only connection IS to the embassy chief of staff.'

So he checked the brick-fall date, only to find that Marc Huber was demonstrably at home at the Stadt embassy, on shore leave... and had been, all day. With verifiable witnesses.

'And when I was attacked, Huber was on duty as a shuttle pilot, actually outbound to a spacecraft. Looks like he's been busy shuttling back and forth for the last several days, helping to populate the crew of two new battleships and a light cruiser, fresh in from The Yards. Mm. Whoa. He's barely had just enough time for exhausted sleep in the shuttle pilots' barracks in between some damn long shifts.'

Samples double-checked the time when Rao had been showing Bill the brick-fall site.

'Well, shit,' he realized, 'apparently I spotted him as he was walking from the bus stop over to his duty officer's desk, reporting in after the leave. And that was when he was given the shuttle ship-population duty, and he started essentially immediately... and hasn't even finished yet! He's still got one more shuttle load to deliver before being given a few days off. He couldn't have been involved in either the brick attack, OR the attack on me. And he couldn't have been involved in the chemical attack, either, because that required Housekeeping staff...'

He shook his head. 'This doesn't make sense,' he decided. 'What I know of him indicates he's a likely suspect. But there's nothing here that supports that.'

"Mm," he concluded aloud. "Maybe I need to get some advice from a mentor..."

"Durand here," came the voice on the other end of the line.

"Admiral sir, it's Mr. Samples."

"Who? Oh! Right. Samples. What can I do for you, Samples?"

"Our, uh, mutual friend wanted t' ask some questions of his mentor, I think. Any chance I can get into your schedule so's I can pass on those questions?"

"I think I can manage that, Samples," Durand replied. "Give me... let's see... can it wait half an hour?"

"I b'lieve so, sir. You know what we're workin' on, so I don't think it'll wait 'til, say, tomorrow. But half an hour? Shouldn't be a problem, sir."

"All right, then. Give me half an hour and then report to Commander Jones in the outer office. I'll notify her when I have my other classified matters properly tucked away, and she'll see you into my office."

"I'll be there in thirty, sir."

"Hm," Durand mused when Samples had finished explanations. "I see your point. But it may just be happenstance. Yo-um, Campbell may be a little prejudiced on account of the events when he was in the Academy. We're all inexperienced, raw recruits in school — academy or officer candidate, it doesn't really matter, we're all still more than half kid at that point — and still prone to snit fits and temper tantrums. It may be that he got over it as he got older and gained a bit of maturity and experience."

"But sir..." Samples broke off and pondered for a moment. "Eh. Maybe you're right."

"There's an old saying, Cam-erhm, Samples," Durand corrected himself with a slight grin. "I think it comes from some of the first detective novels that were written on Earth, but the way I always heard it was, when you pare away all the extraneous details and the impossibilities, you tend to be left with the truth. Of course, then you're ALSO left trying to explain it, so it isn't cut and dried, even so. But if the data indicates Huber didn't do it, then chances are, Huber didn't do it."

Samples gnawed his lower lip, thinking over what Durand had said. When he frowned, then opened his mouth to say something, Durand held up a hand.

"Look, let's dig a little deeper into the situation, you and I," he said. "Do you trust me?"

"Sir?!"

"Do you trust me to scout out Huber for you?" Durand pressed. "I'd offer to let you listen in, but my office is expressly set up for privacy and security, given the nature of this job..."

"Yes sir, I trust you," Samples told the admiral. "What did ya have in mind?"

With Friends Like These

"Lieutenant Marc Huber reporting as ordered, sir," Huber declared, saluting as he stood before Durand's desk.

"At ease, Lieutenant," Durand said, looking up from an invisible VR screen.

"Yes sir. What can I do for you, sir? Do you need a shuttle ride somewhere? I'm just about finished up with an extended mission, filling out the crew for those two new ships from The Yards, but if you can wait a few hours until I catch a bit of sleep, I'll be happy to take you wherever you want to go, though you may need to ping my supervisor to have someone else ferry that last load of crew up to the new ships. If you need something quicker, I'm probably not your pilot; I'm pretty tired, and if I go much longer without some down time, safety will be a serious concern. But I can call my supervisor and have someone sent over right away."

"No, no, son, nothing like that," Durand said, holding up a staying hand. "And this shouldn't take long, though there might be something I need from you once you catch some sleep. No, I needed to ask you some things — you, specifically."

"Um, all right, sir." Huber was patently puzzled, per Durand's experienced eye.

"Have a seat, if you would." Durand gestured to the visitor's chair. Huber sat, and Durand studied him for a few moments. "I looked up your personnel records, you know. You have a fine record as a shuttle pilot, Mr. Huber."

"Ah, thank you, sir," Huber responded, surprised. "My supervisor expects me to receive a promotion in the next six months or so."

"Lieutenant commander? Excellent. Have you ever thought about transferring over to the Tactical Division, proper?"

"Um, no sir, not since OCS," Huber said, flushing. "That's when I, uh, got moved into the shuttle pilot track..."

"Oh? Not the starship pilot track?"

"...No sir. I'm afraid not, sir."

"Why not?" Durand sat back, at a loss. "I'd have thought an OCS pilot graduate would be a shoe-in for starship pilot."

"Not to put too fine a point on it, sir, I didn't have what it took, and eventually I figured that out," Huber admitted. "Though I had to be told, first. It seems I don't think... multidimensionally... enough."

"Ah. Now I see. Any friends over in Tactical?"

"One or two, from my OCS days. Nobody important, really. When I got sidelined, most of 'em kinda... moved on."

"Mm. Any tactician friends?"

"Not at all, sir!" Huber laughed. "I don't move in that kind of smart circle, and never did. You need real brains to do proper tactical studies. We were bright enough for what we wanted to do, but we didn't have that!"

"What about Intelligence?"

"I used to know a couple of people, but I'm ashamed to say that the one I probably knew best, I wasn't on great terms with. I believe I saw him on the street just the other day, and I'd been thinking about seeing if he would be willing to have a drink with me, and maybe start over."

"It wouldn't have been William Campbell, would it?"

Huber blinked, then stared at Admiral Durand.

"Are you a mind-reader, sir? That was exactly who it was."

"Well, I'm afraid you won't be meeting Mr. Campbell, Lieutenant Huber, now or ever — he's dead."

"DEAD?! But-but I thought he was on leave!" Huber exclaimed. "Away visiting relatives! I saw a status report..."

"No, that was a bit of a cover my office put out about a week back, to try to divert attention from what was his assignment at the time. Unfortunately, it didn't work as well as I'd hoped. No, he had no relatives left," Durand murmured. "Not close, not ones he knew, anyway. His grandparents died when he was a young boy, and his parents and sister died in a commercial shuttle accident right after he graduated from the Academy; I thought most of the base personnel at the time knew about that, especially given his sister had just finished her plebe year. It was considered quite the tragedy at the Academy. Anyway, he has a few offworld cousins that he doesn't actually know — only met a handful of them once, when they moved to Jablonka — and that's it."

"But... then why...?" Huber began, then broke off. "Wait. THAT'S why you called ME in! You think someone at the embassy — or at one of the embassies, at least — killed him. You're keeping it quiet while you investigate. Because he was on some investigation of his own, probably something to do with that captain he was with the other day when I saw him — they were questioning the repair contractors — and he got too close, maybe?"

"I thought you said you weren't smart enough for intelligence work," Durand said with a slight, wry grin. "That deduction belies the statement."

Huber flushed.

"I'm NOT that good," he murmured. "I just... I was on Becker through my mid-teens, and I saw a lot of... shit, begging your pardon, sir."

"Mm. I see. Well, in answer to your question, it's possible," Durand agreed. "What do you know about that captain you saw with Campbell?"

"I saw Campbell and the captain — Rao, wasn't it? I saw the news reports of the accident with the bricks — at the construction site, where the news said she had the accident," Huber noted. "I'd just come back from family leave of my own, and was about to report in and get my shuttle assignment. My chief is in the next building over, and I walked right by 'em on the way. Given the news report about how she'd gotten hurt, I immediately knew Campbell had to be looking into what happened. And since he's not in the MPs, I knew it had to be something more serious than an accident."

"Mm. Well observed," Durand decided. "Did you tell anyone?"

"Huh?"

"Did you tell anyone? Who might have known what you saw? After all, Campbell is only an ensign," Durand noted, conveniently overlooking the mid-investigation promotion. "And his assignment to our department is not commonly known as yet, in any case."

"Oh, that," Huber said with a shrug. "Nobody important. And I only said I saw him, not what he was probably doing."

"WHO?!"

"My mom," Huber said, adding another shrug. "I'd forgotten to put my personal VR link back in my kit, and she found it in my room and brought it over to the base; met me at my desk in the shuttle command bullpen to hand it to me. She asked if everything was going all right, and I said sure, nothing new, except I'd seen the guy I used to hate, back in OCS days, while I was walking from the bus drop-off to my building." He shook his head. "Nothing to worry about there."

"Your mother wouldn't be a gossip or the like, would she?"

"Nah. You've never met my mom. She fades into the furniture or something. Oh, I guess she mighta told my step-dad, and maybe some of the other embassy staff if they were there when she told him, but nobody else; I don't think she has any friends. I never did figure out why Frank fell for her in the first place. She's a good mom, don't get me wrong; she just doesn't have a lotta... pizzazz." He considered. "I suppose, though, it's likely that somebody overheard me tell her, someplace there or maybe back in the embassy; I expect she told my stepdad, too, all things considered, like I said. I didn't make a point of secrecy on it or anything; at the time, I didn't see a need."

Durand pulled up his VR display and typed in a few entries. "All right, son," he said, looking up. "I want you to do something for me. I just had you temporarily reassigned to me as my personal shuttle pilot, effective immediately — your supervisor will have to assign someone else to complete that crew complement shuttle flight — and I want you to work with a man I'm going to introduce you to in a few minutes. Don't worry, we'll give you a chance to get some sleep before sending you out on anything."

"Huh? Begging your pardon, sir, but... why?"

"You said you used to hate Bill Campbell. Do you still feel that way?"

"Nah, I don't think so," Huber decided, considering. "I don't think I've felt that way in a long time. Truth to tell, I was jealous of him... and kind of resentful of a, an incident that happened while we were in school. But I've long since gotten over all that."

"Oh? Do tell."

"Which?"

"Both. The jealousy and the resentment. And how you got over them. If you truly DID get over them."

"Yeah, I did," Huber averred. "The resentment, that came from an incident in school. Due to various scheduling conflicts, we wound up in the same battle training class together, and, well, he basically handed me my ass in some VR sessions where our ships went up against each other. And I was the one in OCS, and he was still in the Academy, and not even ready to graduate!"

"I didn't think that class was supposed to allow anyone to know who fought against whom," Durand pointed out.

"It wasn't. We used code names," Huber elaborated. "But I overheard a conversation by some of his bridge crew after the last simulation, and they called him by name. And then one of 'em let slip the code name of the captain he fought... and it was me. In both sims. Midterms AND finals."

"Aha. I see. So it was the merest happenstance that you found out. Very well, then. Go on."

"Anyway, where I was raised on Becker, that was a big deal, that he'd whipped my ass, not just once, but TWICE," Huber explained. "On Becker, your pride was everything. And he'd slapped me aside like a gnat. More, he got me sidelined from a Tactical slot into the shuttle pilot corps, because he showed up a weakness I didn't even know I had — I tended to think in two dimensions, not three or four, like a starship pilot has to." He broke off and chuckled, rueful. "I hate to think what woulda happened if that up-and-coming tac officer, Childers, had got hold of me; I probably wouldn't have had an ass left to hand back! Anyway, I had a real chip on my shoulder where he was concerned for a good year or so, there. If I even spotted him, I saw red, and I tried to find a way to give him grief... which was damn immature of me, and I know that now. But then I finally realized that I wasn't on Becker any more, and I was glad of it... so why the hell was I still going by Becker's rules? Given we're provided access to the recordings of our individual simulator flights for as long as we want it, I decided to go back and look at the simulations we'd fought, and see if I couldn't actually LEARN something from it," Huber admitted.

"A very wise decision. And did you?"

"Yeah, I did," Huber said with a grin. "I saw what Campbell did, and WHY he did it, and figured out what I SHOULD have done. He came at it with an intelligence analysis kind of thought process, it looked like to me, rather than a standard Tactical Ops thought process, like what I was used to seeing. And when I realized that, it opened up a whole new means of strategic analysis for me. I started applying it to my job, and..." he shrugged, "I got better. And I got promoted. So... I expect I actually owe my promotion to lieutenant to Campbell. And maybe the upcoming promotion to lieutenant commander, too, 'cause I've kept at it, and it's making more and more sense to me." He shrugged. "I'll probably never be up to being a tac officer anywhere, but my piloting skills are definitely improving."

"All right. And the jealousy?"

"Was stupid. I encountered him with his family one time, shortly after the simulation course fiasco. Well, as you can imagine, he didn't stop to introduce us," Huber said, wry, "but I went off and looked 'em up, 'cause I was curious. His parents were college professors! BOTH of 'em! His sister was beautiful and smart, like him. I guess, with those two for parents, it's no wonder they both had looks AND brains." Huber shrugged again. "Anyway. He had great parents, but me? Not so much. Mom is a mouse and Frank—"

"Frank?" Durand wondered.

"Oh. Frank Lang. He's the Chief of Staff to 'His Excellency, the Ambassador to the CFP from Stadt.' Geez, what a mouthful! He's also my stepdad, and he was... well, we weren't getting along great back then. I resented having him around instead of my real father. But I don't even know who my real father was!"

"Why not?"

"Mom won't tell me... or can't, I never figured which," Huber said with a rueful, slightly embarrassed shrug, as his face flushed. "All she'll say is that he wasn't worth knowing. It's one of the few times I ever see her show much emotion... and it's all bad. Angry. She hated him, I think, whoever he was, at least by the time their relationship ended. And I don't even know if he knew she was pregnant with his baby... me."

"I see."

"Anyway, Frank said I had a chip on my shoulder, and I needed to get rid of it if I wanted to get anywhere in life. I thought he hated me... but he was right; I just couldn't see it then. I think I was angry at damn near the whole universe, back then. And Campbell was smart, and good-looking, and quick-witted, and..." Huber sighed. "I felt like he had everything, and I had nothing. And I was jealous of it, and I resented him because of it. Which... was stupid. And I realized it when the transport accident took out his folks, though I didn't realize, at the time, that it left him all alone. I didn't know that until you told me, just now. But I could see, even from a distance, that it devastated him. He was pale, and... distracted... and, and sad, for a long time, there. And it didn't take a good buddy to see it. It made me... sit up and think, you know? Made me look around at what I DID have, and appreciate it more. The very next time I went back home to the flat in the embassy compound, I went to Frank and... and made up with him, for all our fights and shit. I apologized, and told him I respected him, and I wanted us to start over, if he was willing. And he was. So we've been great buds ever since, him and me. He's a straight arrow, as the old Earth saying went, and he's helped me become one, too. He may not be my genetic father, but now? I think he's my dad in every other way that counts. I don't think I've ever told Frank that, and I guess I probably oughta; maybe when I finally get time to go home for a few days, I will." Huber met Durand's gaze, and his eyes were clear. "So... no. I don't have a problem with Campbell, not any more. To be honest, I wasn't even sure that was Campbell, the other day when we passed on the street. It's been a few years. I had to kinda stare at him for a few moments to make sure." Huber blinked. "Oh damn. I hope he didn't mistake that for me glaring at him, like I used to do. I'd like to think he went out thinking halfway decently of me..."

"Would you like to help us find his killer?"

"Oh!" Huber said in surprise, eyes widening. "Oh, now I get it. You're pretty sure it was out of the Stadt embassy, huh?"

"Very sure," Durand said. "The incident that took him out occurred right outside the embassy, in a side street. More, he did manage to take out the assassin, before staggering back to his quarters, where he collapsed and died... and the assassin was an off-duty Stadt bodyguard; I think the name was Zinn? And with your connection there, you're in a good position to help us do it."

Huber considered for a long moment, then scowled.

"Yes sir," he agreed then, jaw setting hard. "That doesn't belong in that embassy! Frank and the ambassador have always been about doing things right and proper and diplomatically, not all this skulking around shit! Damn straight, I'll help you find his killer. Like I said earlier, I'd actually been thinking of hunting Campbell up, apologizing, and seeing if he wanted to join me for a drink or something, on account of how he made me sit up and learn to be grateful for what I had. Now... I guess I never will. But maybe I can pay him back for that, by helping you now. I want to try, anyway."

Durand studied the young man, then nodded and hit an intercom button. "Jany, send in Mr. Samples, if you would."

"Right away, sir," Commander Jones' voice replied on the intercom.

"Mr. Huber, this is Petty Officer First Class Phil Samples. Mr. Samples, this is Lieutenant Marc Huber," Admiral Durand provided a formal introduction, as Samples entered the office and Huber stood. Both younger men shook hands, then Huber resumed his seat, and Samples sat in the visitor's chair next to Huber.

"I'm afraid I don't quite understand, sir," Huber said then. "Mr. Samples is in the Tactical Division, not the Intelligence Division."

"Officially, I am," Samples noted with a sly grin. "That don't mean I stay there."

Durand laughed, as Huber looked surprised.

"That's right," Durand agreed. "Looks can be deceiving, Mr. Huber. Which, in this instance, is just what we want. Trust me when I say that Mr. Samples, here, is on top of what we need. I'll let him tell you how he finds himself working this particular case, though."

"Eh. No big deal," Samples said, making sure to keep his voice pitched low and slightly rough; he couldn't be sure how much Huber might recall or recognize. "I met Bill Campbell a couple years back; Intel used him as a courier f'r somethin' he couldn't talk about, an' I was a petty officer aboard the ship what carried him. Rather than stayin' up top with the commissioned officers, an' with his superiors' orders, he modified his rank pips an' came 'below decks' with us noncoms. I guess it kept him more outta sight that way."

"Exactly," Durand interjected.

"So I got a chance to get to know 'im on that trip," Samples continued, "and he and I became friends. He's the reason I do stuff for Intelligence Division from time to time; Bill recruited me, see. We don't always get to see each other that much any more, given I'm here an' there dependin' on ship assignment, and he's mostly based on Jablonka. But we get together when we can, him and me, if it's only f'r a drink. Or we did, I guess." Samples sighed, and looked down briefly. "Guess we won't be doin' that no more. But I'm back at

Sigurdsen between ships, and Admiral Durand, here, called me right away when things went south f'r Bill, and pulled me in on the case. Damn, I was sorry to hear what happened to that boy." Samples paused, chewing on his lower lip for a moment, as if in annoyance and anger. "So Admiral Durand didn't hardly have to even ask me to step in an' finish the job Bill started. I'm here, an' I aim to see that, not only does the mission get completed, but my ol' pal Bill gets avenged."

"And Lieutenant Huber is here, because I think he can help," Durand pointed out. "You know we talked about what Mr. Campbell found out, Mr. Samples."

"Yes sir, we did. So this is that potential contact you mentioned?" Samples said, turning to Huber.

"I am," Huber averred. "I knew Bill Campbell too, though we weren't always friends. In fact, back in his Academy days, I was kind of a pain in the ass to him. But, well, let's just say I've grown up since then, and I'd been looking to find a way to start over with him, become friends." It was Huber's turn to sigh. "I guess I just waited too long, dammit. That's gonna be a regret I'll live with my whole life, I suppose."

"Aw," Samples said. "That's a fine sentiment there, son. Don't take it too much to heart, though. The Bill Campbell I knew didn't hold grudges much. He'd 'a given you another shot, I feel sure."

"That's... good to know," Huber decided.

"So. Do the two of you think you can work together to solve this case?" Durand asked.

"Yes sir!" a determined Huber affirmed, squaring his jaw.

"I expect as how we'll do fine, Admiral," Samples said, giving Huber a grin. "Ya want we should get started right away?"

"Not quite yet, Mr. Samples," Durand cautioned. "Mr. Huber has been in the midst of ferrying the crews up to those two new ships in orbit; he's been extremely busy, with a heavy schedule of shuttle flights, and what he needs most right now is sleep."

"Amen to that," Huber murmured, running a hand over a suddenly-weary face; his shoulders slumped as he admitted it.

"In fact," Durand added, "I pulled him off that assignment for this; the Shuttle Office is handing the last few flights off to another shuttle pilot."

"Ohhhh," Samples said, sitting back and looking at Huber with wide eyes. "So you need some serious down time, if we're gonna do this safely."

"Not long," Huber declared. "I've had breaks throughout the assignment, and I've generally chosen to crash during my breaks. But I'm on..." he glanced at the clock on the wall, "I'm on my fifteenth hour since my last sleep period, now, and was only coming off duty as I got the summons from Admiral Durand, here. So if we can wait until tomorrow morning, I'll go home straight from here and crash, sleep straight through, and be fine by then. Hell, that'll be more sleep in one block than I've had in over a week!"

"Does that work for you, Mr. Samples?" Durand asked.

"I think that'll work out pretty well, sir," Samples said, considering. "I got a few more things I can spend the rest of the day lookin' into, maybe have a bit more intel data to work with, by then, anyhow."

"Oh good," Huber murmured. "I was afraid I was gonna slow things down by needing to rest."

"Nah," Samples said, offering the other man a grin. "Better you're well-rested and awake, never mind alert, in case things go weird on us."

"This sounds like it's going to be exciting. And not in the good way."

"I hope it won't be, but you know 'bout battle plans meetin' the enemy," Samples pointed out. "It never goes quite like you think it will."

"Ain't THAT the truth," Huber agreed.

"All right, then," Durand decreed. "Mr. Huber, you're dismissed; go home and get some sleep, son. Mr. Samples, if you'd stay for a bit, I want to discuss a few details of the case with you that I forgot to mention the other day."

"Yes, sir. Thank you, sir," Huber said, standing and heading for the door. There, he paused, and asked, "Oh. Where shall I meet you tomorrow morning, Mr. Samples?"

Durand shot a glance at Samples. "Downstairs?"

"That should work, sir," Samples agreed. "Th' conference room, I think."

"Come back here at 0800, and I'll take you there, Huber," Durand said.

"Aye, sir."

And he was gone.

The office was silent for several moments after Huber's departure.

"So I take it, you were satisfied with him, sir?" Samples asked.

"I was," Durand agreed. "More, he seems very anxious to make up past behavior to Campbell. He LEARNED from past mistakes. Which is more than many people can say."

"True," Samples agreed, thoughtful. "So he's gonna be my 'in' to the Stadt embassy?"

"I think that's probably the best plan," Durand said. "He can get in, and go almost anywhere inside, and take you with him. Because he lives there, when he's not on base."

"Then that's what we'll try, as soon as we get a good opportunity," Samples decided.

While Huber went back to his quarters and collapsed after such a long shuttle assignment, Samples went back to his workspace in the Class 1 facility and resumed watching the PTO. As he had noticed earlier that day, Kooistra and Zinn were still being kept hopping, running hither and yon on errands for the PTO, while the others stayed in the office proper.

However, unlike that morning, when he had sat in that office himself and the staffers had said next to nothing, now they proved rather more loquacious.

"Hey, where's the bitch these days?" Lieutenant Burk queried. "Is she dead yet?"

Gnad and Glaub exchanged glances.

"Dunno," Glaub admitted then. "She's apparently gone to ground."

"What? Where?" Lieutenant Powers demanded to know.

"We. Don't. Know," Glaub repeated, annoyed at the question he had already answered. "She's vanished."

"WHAT?! Then we need to find her!" Powers pressed.

"WE need to continue doing the job we're in this office to do," Gnad noted. "Marcel is on the job of locating Rao. Our job is to gradually gain control of the Jablonka PTO."

"I'd say we already had," Weiner pointed out. "She's not here, and we're doing her job."

"Not so," Gnad said. "She's still on the job. I keep getting notifications from her, so they have her someplace, out of sight but not out of the ability to keep working. Which also means they probably have someone treating her, or she'd be too sick. And she isn't going home at night, either."

"Should we be talking like this, here?" Burk wondered. The others tensed, and glanced around in unease.

"Nah, we're fine," Glaub noted. "I swept for bugs last night before I got off duty. I do that at least once every few days."

A general sigh went through the group as they relaxed, and Samples smirked to himself as he watched. Not, he considered, that what Glaub was likely using was going to find THOSE bugs, in any case.

"Who is 'they,' anyway?" Powers asked.

"Not sure. Probably Intelligence Division," Gnad said with a shrug. "At least our guys took out Campbell."

"They DID?!" several of the others exclaimed.

"Yeah," Gnad averred. "Didn't you see the announcement a day or two ago, that Intel put out? According to them, Campbell was struck by a ground car, off-base, while coming home from visiting a friend. He made it as far as his quarters, then collapsed and died, apparently of internal injuries. They only knew about it when he didn't report to his duty station the next day, and his C.O. sent somebody around to his quarters, looking for him. Now, how many people do you know of that can be hit by a ground car hard enough to kill 'em and still walk all the way home before biting it? Nah, one of ours took him out. I got word that a bodyguard, out of uniform, was found dead over by the Stadt compound the next morning. He had a knife in his hand, with blood all over it that wasn't his, so there musta been a fight."

"Oooo," the others hummed.

"Which bodyguard was it?" Burk asked.

"Mm. Zinn, maybe?" Gnad considered, thinking back. "Yeah, I think that's right."

"Wait," Burk said, surprised. "The boy toy killed ZINN? Zinn was one of their best people. One of OUR best people, at least at that sort of thing."

"Lucky shot," Gnad said with a shrug. "Though I did hear someplace that the boy toy kept in shape with martial arts — I guess he thought it was more fun and less work than pumping iron — so maybe some of the training actually kicked in with the adrenaline of getting stabbed."

"Huh. Maybe," Burk agreed, if reluctantly.

"I still think that was about as stupid a thing as we coulda done," Weiner protested. "It only gave Intel a heads-up that something was going on! That boy toy of hers wasn't an investigator! He was a stylus-necked desk-jockey analyst suck-up!"

"He was Intel," Gnad pointed out. "Marcel felt we couldn't afford to risk it. And if the bodyguard was found where I heard, then Campbell was on Embassy Row anyway. Who the hell was he visiting there?"

"I can think of half a dozen innocent options," Weiner countered. "If he was as much of a night-life guy as it sounded like to me, he probably has friends all over that he met in the bars." He shrugged. "After all, that's how he met Rao."

Gnad shook his head.

"I can't argue that one with you," he agreed, "and I'd lay odds he was two-timing Rao — maybe three-and four-and five-timing her — but it wasn't our call, either. Marcel wanted him gone, especially after he went snooping on Embassy Row, I expect."

"So Campbell is dead, Rao isn't, Rao's hidden and still on the job?" Burk summarized. "Damn, I bet Marcel is NOT happy about that."

"No. But give 'em time," Gnad said. "The disadvantage to being undercover is that your own people don't know where you are either, for the most part. So, other than what few guards she may have around her, she has NO backup."

"Wait. You're not saying she's off the base, surely?" Powers wondered. "If she's sending in her work, she has to be ON base. In which case, she DOES have backup."

"No, that's correct," Gnad said, "and we don't see her being off the base. As you say, it's far more probable that she's on base somewhere. But she's undoubtedly in a very classified, very hidden location. Which means that only a handful of people know where she is. And we have Housekeeping in our pocket. Or at least, we have enough to count, where we need it. And they're all looking. Sooner or later, they have to hit paydirt. Just wait, and be patient."

"So eventually they'll find out where she's hiding, and somebody takes her out?" Wiener asked.

"Exactly," Gnad confirmed. "Now it's just a matter of time."

"Not hardly," Durand chuckled, when Samples gave him a warning about the search. "They're about as off in their assumptions as they CAN be."

"Well, that works, I guess," Samples decided. "And as this data comes in, I'm havin' it recorded, an' then shippin' it to you under ultra header. I've also assigned you an' Byrne to the group of people who can view it in real-time, if you feel like ya need to."

"Much appreciated, and that might be something for me to keep an eye on," Durand agreed. "I'd suggest you put April on it, but she's not back yet from a little assignment I gave her last week, so for the time being, that's moot."

"What, your chief of staff, Senior Captain Kardas?"

"Yes. So for now, what you have is good. Certainly we'll have access to it for the courts-martial, once we get to that point."

"Exactly, sir. And if you want someone added to the permissions goin' forward, just let me know."

"Very good, then. So you and Huber are going to start working on finding this 'Marcel' first thing tomorrow?"

"That's right, sir. Bright and early in the morning."

Offensive

"...No, I can get you that information," Huber said in a small conference room in the Intelligence Class 1 facility the next morning. "Until I took the exam for Commonwealth membership, I was considered a dual Becker/Stadt citizen, because of my mom being from Becker — and I was born on Becker — and Frank Lang, my stepfather, being chief of staff to the Stadt ambassador. Even now, since I'm family to the embassy chief of staff, I have almost complete access." He shrugged. "But you're not gonna find anything. The entire compound is clean. Frank wouldn't have it otherwise."

"That sounds real good, Huber, and I hope you're right, for your sake an' his," Samples said. "So if you can log inta their system an' let me know if the ambassador, your stepfather, or the head of th' bodyguard corps is home or on duty today, it would be real good right now."

"You suspect him, don't you? Frank?"

"Well, I don't NOT suspect him," Samples pointed out. "Way I figger it is, chief of staff prob'ly has t' know if something this big is going on outta his embassy, right?"

"Mm," Huber murmured, unhappy. "I see your point. But I've always thought Frank was a real straight shooter."

"Well, anything's possible," Samples noted. "It may be somebody close to him, instead of him. But if we're gonna go have a look-see, we need those three out of the way, for sure."

"Point." Huber sighed. "All right, let me see the VR link."

It took a couple of hours for Huber to locate all of the people for whom Samples wanted whereabouts. Once Huber located the ambassador — at what was likely to be an all-day meeting in Council Tower, negotiating a new trade deal; his stepfather — with the ambassador; and the chief bodyguard — also with the ambassador — Samples wanted to try to locate what bodyguards remained at the embassy compound.

"But they're mostly with the ambassador and Frank," Huber observed.

"Yep. More," Samples said, looking at the displays, "th' Commonwealth Council is in session an' the majority o' the embassy staffers are there to see what's gonna go down, I s'pose."

"Pretty much," Huber agreed.

"How many are left?"

"Not many, just the usual entry guards, it looks like," Huber finally decided. "Maybe half a dozen, all told. And I can get us in past those, no problem."

"Then let's go. Now," Samples decreed. "While we have time."

"Without any time to strategize or prep?!"

"Who said I hadn't already? Follow my lead; we'll be all right. Now let's GO."

They went.

As they walked toward Embassy Row from the bus stop, the pair were relatively silent except for some sporadic conversation. Huber appeared worried, probably about the possibility of his stepfather's participation; Samples mulled over the situation.

'It has to be someone that Huber tipped off about matters,' Samples decided, 'though from the look and sound of it, Huber had no idea that he did so, and didn't MEAN to do it. But that someone has to be in the Stadt embassy; all the connections go there. It's a multi-planet operation, for sure, but the headquarters — at least on Jablonka — is at the Stadt embassy. If it's not his stepfather, it's still going to be someone he knows in the compound. Knows and trusts. The question is, when push comes to shove, where do Huber's loyalties lie? If I have to confront somebody, will he side with me, or against me?'

That thought churned around in his head, but eventually Samples decided there was no way to decide based on the data he currently had about Huber.

'I guess I'd better be ready for anything,' he finally concluded.

He extracted his personal comm unit and fired off a quick message.

Moments later, a beep heralded the response, and he checked the message. He studied the device for long seconds, then replaced it in a pocket.

"Hey, Huber," one of the door guards greeted the man as Huber and Samples approached. "Who's your new friend, there? I'm sorry, but you know the rules; I gotta know before I can let him in."

"Oh, this is Petty Officer First Class Phil Samples," Huber explained. "I'll vouch for him. And yeah, he's a new buddy; he's gonna be the new chief petty officer over my shuttle wing, soon as his promotion goes through. I met him while I was ferrying people between ships on my last shuttle assignment, and we got to talking about hobbies. I wanted to show him my collection of antique film posters, that I keep in my rooms here."

"Ooo, right," the guard noted, as the other guard logged their entry on his electronic display unit. "That's an awesome collection, Huber. You're in for a treat," he added to Samples. "This guy has some really great stuff. It's hard to believe you used to have to go to a big building to watch that shit."

"But it was good shit," Huber said. "They made great entertainment on old Earth. They just didn't have the tech we've got now to experience it like we can."

"You guys go on in and have fun," the second guard noted. "Cook has the day off, while most of the embassy staff is at the negotiation, but there's a skeleton staff in the kitchen if you two get hungry. You should be able to get snacks sent up, at least, though anything fancier than sandwiches for a meal is probably out."

"Right," Huber said. "Thanks for the heads-up on that. C'mon, Phil. You're gonna love this."

"I'm lookin' forward to it," Samples declared with enthusiasm, following the other man into the Stadt embassy main building.

"All right," Huber said, sitting at the desk in his closed bedroom while Samples sat on the bedside; at Samples' insistence, Huber really had shown him his collection of antique movie memorabilia, in case anyone queried them later. "Now what?"

"Stand by," Samples said, producing an electronics sniffer and scanning it around the room. "They actually have NOT bugged y'r

184

room," he declared. "That's good... an' unexpected." He adjusted the settings. "There. Now they ain't gonna be able to intrude on our activities, no matter where we go in the compound. Just don't get farther away from me than about five feet."

"Oh. Um, okay."

Huber watched as Samples pulled out a certain electronic display unit — that had once belonged to a bodyguard from Stadt named Zinn, now deceased — from a pocket of his shipsuit. From another pocket he brought out a tiny pouch, extracting a chip and plugging it into the electronic display unit. A few taps and swipes across the screen, and he nodded.

"Good. All right, then lemme add this..." He pulled out another chip from the pouch and installed it on the electronic display unit, then swiped down the screen, pulling down the decryption overlay he'd managed to find by dint of thoroughly hacking the electronic display unit a couple of nights before.

Samples typed in a single punctuation mark, then entered it, sending it to 'Marcel,' and watching the three-dimensional readout that had popped up in a separate window.

"Here," he said, gesturing for Huber to come look over his shoulder. "Where is this?"

"Damn," Huber breathed, "what's that?"

"That's the location o' the device that received the message I just sent," Samples explained. "An' since I just replied to 'Marcel,' the leader of this sabotage an' assassination ring, if we can find it, it oughta tell us who 'Marcel' really is."

"I don't get it," Huber murmured, as he led Samples through the dark, quiet building — most of the Outer Colonies embassies were short on windows, in order to try to prevent eavesdropping and external monitoring. And with most of the staff away, there were very few lights on anywhere within the building. Both men employed as much stealth as possible as they progressed; just because the security system couldn't pick them up didn't mean human guards couldn't, or might not get curious about what they were doing. "How did you know how to contact this 'Marcel'? Surely you didn't..."

"This," Samples waved the electronic display unit. "The guy what killed Campbell? He was carryin' it. The last message on it was an encrypted order from this Marcel... to kill Campbell."

"But how did YOU get it?"

"Admiral Durand told ya that Campbell an' me were old friends, right? 'Member that?"

"Oh. Yeah. Okay. So... did Campbell give it to you before he...?"

"No. I... didn't see him before he... passed. But he managed t' contact Durand."

"...Who then knew to give it to you, to finish the case for Campbell," Huber murmured, realizing — or so he thought. "Okay. Um... oh shit."

"'Oh shit' what?"

"Up here and to the left," Huber said, obviously unhappy. "Your target device is in my parents' flat. Looks like you were right to suspect Frank."

"Wait — your room isn't in, or even directly connected to, your parents' home?"

"No. Used to be, when I was younger. Once I made lieutenant a few years back, Frank said I needed a place of my own, so he arranged for me to have that little flat we were in just now. It's only, like, three rooms — a den-slash-kitchen, my bedroom, and the bathroom, like you saw — but it suits me, for when I have a little leave time. And it's private, 'cause sometimes I need that. There's a communal laundry downstairs, for the staff, that I can use if I need to wash clothes an' shit."

"Is your mom at home?"

"Don't think so. This is usually her day to go around and visit all the other wives on Embassy Row. There's a... whaddaya call it... kaffeeklatsch. It's a ladies' club sorta thing. They take turn about meeting at this or that embassy."

"Will it be locked? Your parents' flat, I mean?"

"Yeah. They're pretty consistent about that."

"Mm. Can you open it?"

"Oh, that's not a problem."

Huber extracted an electronic key, and in moments they were inside the darkened apartment. Samples kept tracking the location of Marcel's electronic display unit as they moved through the flat's rooms, and eventually they moved into a utility room off the main living area, toward the back of the flat. Samples looked around the room, scanning it with the app in the display unit, then moved...

...Straight to the cat box.

"Down there," he said, gesturing at the top of the hooded litter box. "Does y'r mom have a cat?"

"Yeah. It's probably sleepin' on their bed at the moment; Mom says she likes it when it purrs her to sleep. An' please don't TELL me we gotta dig through the cat poop an' piss," Huber grumbled, then started rummaging quietly in the cabinets and drawers of the utility room. "Wait an' lemme see if I can find some nitrile cleaning gloves..."

"I don't think we'll need that," Samples said with a grin, crouching down.

He tipped up the front of the cat box, slipped one hand under it, and produced another electronic display unit.

'Oh shit, this is NOT good,' Samples thought, as he stared down at the newly-discovered display unit. 'This means it probably isn't Lang at all; it's—"

"Well, well," a voice all but snarled behind them. "Someone's been sticking noses in where they don't belong. I'm surprised at you, Marc."

The two men spun.

A mousy, rather homely woman stood there, attired in a beige pantsuit, dishwater-blonde hair pulled back in a tight, austere ponytail. Even her makeup was bland; her entire appearance seemed washed-out...

...Except for the pistol with silencer in her hand.

Aimed at Samples.

"MOM!" Huber cried.

"Now, now, look here," Ida Huber Lang said, face twisting in an expression of hate. "Who have you brought home, Marc?"

"I, I, Mom, someone's been trying to kill people on base," Huber explained. "He's not breaking in, I swear! He's with me! Mr. Samples was, um, I was trying to help him find..."

"Idiot!" Ida Lang snapped. "I KNEW you'd turn out to be no good, given who your father was!"

"Who WAS he, Mom?" Huber said, pleading. "Please, put the gun down and just TALK to me!"

"None of your damn business, Marc!" she snapped. "And no way in hell."

"She seduced either an enemy agent, or an adversarial ambassador, f'r information, Marc," Samples murmured, "only she wasn't as careful as she mighta been, an' went an' got 'erself pregnant with you."

"YOU shut the hell up, Mr. Samples," Mrs. Lang ordered, waving the pistol at him. "And put the display unit down, if you please. You're going down shortly, yourself, anyway."

"Mom! NO!" Huber exclaimed. "He's a friend!"

"He's a SPY!" Mrs. Lang hissed. "He's Sigurdsen Intelligence Division, and you brought him right in here, like the fool you are!"

"Because we're looking for someone," Huber began.

"An' we found her, Marc," Samples noted, waving the electronic display unit he'd just found, before laying it carefully on top of the nearby counter, along with the one Campbell had taken off Zinn's body. "There's only one person who woulda gotten notice that a message 'uz waitin' on this unit — the person it belongs to. 'Marcel.' Your mother is the assassin team leader."

"Mo-MOM?!" Huber cried, gaping. "Mom's a spy? An assassin? MY mom? No way!"

"What, because I'm so mousy and unassuming?" she sneered. "Shy and dull and plain?"

"Well... yeah."

Mrs. Lang rolled her eyes.

"You got your father's brains, too, I see," she fairly growled. "Damn, I am so glad I killed that imbecile. Marc, you are SUCH a disappointment." She shifted her weapon to cover both men. "What better way to infiltrate than by blending in? Being as nondescript, as bland, as boring as possible? How better to disappear in plain sight? Do you think I always looked like this? How could I have seduced your father if I looked like this, acted like you're used to me behaving? How else would I have convinced your stepfather to marry me?" She smiled. "You'll find I can be... VERY... persuasive."

"I... I don't..."

"Look, Marc," Mrs. Lang said, trying to reason with her son. "Help me out here. You'll be a hero at home on Becker. Help me get rid of Samples, finish our task, then we can leave here and go home. We'll be heroes, son. You and me. Heroes. You can pilot one of Becker's starships, not one of the damn little shuttles the arrogant bastards have you flying here. Eventually, you'll be a captain of one of those ships."

Huber blinked, and Samples' heart sank.

"Captain?" he murmured. "Becker..."

"Exactly," Mrs. Lang said, smiling brilliantly, as she eased her weapon away from her son and back toward Samples, and suddenly Samples saw a glimpse of the beautiful seductress beneath the colorless, self-effacing disguise. "Captain in the Becker fleet. Hell, if we successfully manage to put one of our allies in as PTO for Jablonka, forget pilot. I can probably arrange to have you installed as captain of your own ship as soon as we get home."

"But... what about Frank?" Huber wondered.

"What about him?" Mrs. Lang shrugged, callous. "He was a means to an end, Marc. No more, no less. Needless to say, I didn't make the same mistake with him that I made with your father, so you have no siblings. Marrying him got me to Jablonka, right outside Sigurdsen, and perfectly situated in between Sigurdsen and the Council complex."

"He won't come with us? Frank wouldn't leave with you?"

"I doubt it," Mrs. Lang noted. "I checked him out early on. He never had the stomach for this work."

"But... I like it here," Huber murmured, thoughtful.

"Better than home?"

"This IS home," Huber declared.

"Aw, come on, Marc, son," Mrs. Lang grumbled. "Forget that sentimental shit and just come with me. There's a job to be done. For the Homeworld. For Becker." She waved the barrel of the gun back at her offspring. "Don't make me have to do THIS. You're my SON. Even if you did have a misbegotten pig for a father! SOME of those genetics are MINE. I don't want to have to take you out, too."

"Who are ya workin' for?" Samples asked, deliberately interrupting, trying to give Huber a chance to process matters, to realize that his mother was willing to kill him if he didn't go along with her demands, her mission. He jammed his hands in his pockets, lightly fingering his personal communications unit. Fractions of a second later, his fingers found what he was looking for, and he pressed a certain button.

"None of YOUR damn business!" she retorted. "And get your hands where I can see 'em! Nice and slow, now. No funny shit."

"No, Mom," Huber said then, clear and calm. "I'm not going along with it. You're going to have to kill me... if you really mean that. And I don't think you do."

Fury washed over Mrs. Lang's face, and she scowled as she turned toward her son.

"Damn your rebellious ass!" she snarled, turning her weapon on him. "If you won't do it voluntarily, you'll do it because I say so! Get the hell over here!"

"No," Huber reiterated.

"GET OVER HERE!"

"I said... no."

Mrs. Lang raised her pistol.

Just as Mrs. Lang made the mistake of turning away from him, Samples flicked his wrist, and a small handgun slid out of his sleeve into his palm. It had exactly two projectiles and didn't have the greatest targeting because of its size, so he had to make it good. He stepped forward, raised his hand, and fired both projectiles into Lang's head, right behind her temple, from only about a foot away...

...Even as another discharge came from his left.

Just as Ida Lang's body dropped to the floor, Samples glanced left, to see a white-faced Huber, personal-issue weapon in hand, staring at the hole in his mother's chest, where he had shot her.

Within some thirty to forty-five seconds, three Stadt guards barged into the room, weapons drawn, attracted by the noise of three weapons discharges. Samples made a mental note that, if he survived this, he needed to acquire quieter weaponry. An air gun would do nicely, he thought.

"Oh shit!" the first guard exclaimed. "They got Marcel!"

"Really," Samples drawled, raising an eyebrow. "Not Mrs. Lang, eh?"

"Dumb ass," another hissed, waving his weapon at Samples and Huber. "Now we HAVE to kill 'em."

"No, I don't think so," came a quiet, firm voice behind the three guards. "Not if you want to live to see the morning. Drop your weapons, all of you, and put your hands on your head."

The guards spun.

Commander Ryan Byrne stood there, personal firearm drawn and pointed at the nearest guard, with a dozen of his own people around him, weapons aimed. All the Sigurdsen personnel had their index fingers inside the trigger guards; they meant business.

The three guards blinked in surprise, then eased their weapons to the floor, as the members of Counter-Intelligence swarmed around them, taking them into custody.

"I... I..." Huber stammered, still white.

"Stay calm, Marc," Samples told him, putting a steadying left hand on the other man's shoulder, even as his right hand slipped the tiny derringer-like pistol out of sight. "Easy does it, son. She drew down on ya. You didn't have no choice."

"I... I just..." Huber tried again, as his eyes filled with water.

"Go," Byrne murmured to Samples. "Get out of here. I'll take care of Huber. We got this. Get your ass out of sight."

Samples gently patted Huber's shoulder once more, then spun and headed for the side entrance of the Langs' flat, to escape through the heavily-landscaped gardens to the back street.

Consequences

In very short order, Samples had disappeared from Embassy Row, headed back to the bolt-hole Campbell had established.

There, he pulled out a bottle of makeup remover, another of contact cement solvent, mineral oil, and several similar items, and began removing makeup. The scar came off, the crow's feet and naso-labial folds dissolved, the forehead lines removed. The used brown contact lenses went into a special container so that they could be disposed of in a discreet manner.

Everything else went into a special kit that Durand had sent along for his use, and which had been tucked into his duffel until that moment.

Then he trimmed down and shaved his entire head to allow the hair to grow back in his normal color at a uniform rate. The shaved hair was carefully cut into smaller bits, then flushed down the toilet.

"That's gonna itch," he decided, staring at his smooth scalp in the mirror.

He stripped out of his dirty shipsuit and removed all the petty officer insignia, tucking them into another pouch that went into the special kit alongside the makeup and contact lenses. The shipsuit, which might now contain traces of bloodstains, was rolled up and placed into yet another special pouch, which would be tucked into his duffel next to the disguise kit; Durand had already promised to handle the disposal through a special channel he had.

Then Campbell took a long, leisurely hot shower, dried off, and stretched his nude body on the bed for a much-needed — and, he decided, well-earned — nap.

Two hours later, Frank Lang arrived home, to find the medical personnel carrying a sheet-draped body on an emergency gurney from his flat, Sigurdsen investigators everywhere, and a white-faced stepson standing nearby.

"What the hell is going on here?!" he demanded.

"Frank," Huber began, and choked. "It... it's been... bad, Frank! Oh, dear God!"

"What happened?" Lang wondered, shocked.

"It's Mom," Huber said, pointing to the covered body.

"Oh NO!" an appalled Lang exclaimed, running to the medics. "Let me see!"

They paused in wheeling the gurney, and the medic at the head of the gurney tugged back the sheet, exposing Ida Huber Lang's face. The hair at the left side of her head was caked in blood, but the exact cause was not immediately obvious.

"Oh, God help me! NO!" Lang exclaimed, horrified. "Honey! Oh, sweetheart! Don't leave me like this! Don't leave US like this! Say something!" He ran trembling fingers over the white, still face, caressing; when she didn't respond, he buried his face in his hands and began to weep. "Oh, dear God," he keened, "oh, dear God! Help me!"

"Frank, I... I'm so sorry!" Huber began, but Byrne laid a hand on his shoulder and gestured for him to be quiet; Huber silenced, deeply upset but obedient to the senior officer.

By this point, Senior Captain April Kardas, Durand's chief of staff and Commander Byrne's immediate supervisor, had arrived on the scene — having returned only that morning from a brief assignment of her own — and she took control of the situation.

"Mr. Lang," she asked in a soft voice, "did the Ambassador come back with you?"

"Yes," a confused and distraught Lang replied. "He went to his office, and I came straight here to see Ida. I promised... we were going out to dinner tonight... it was the anniversary of our first date..."

"All right," Kardas said. "I'll go talk to the Ambassador; Byrne, you explain things to Mr. Lang."

Byrne nodded, then stepped forward to lay a light hand on Lang's shoulder as Kardas headed for the office of the ambassador from Stadt, led by one of the bodyguards who had returned with the embassage.

"Mr. Lang," Byrne asked, keeping his voice low, "is there someplace you, your stepson, and I can go to talk in private?"

They had retreated to Lang's private office inside his flat, standing in a tight circle, where Byrne proceeded to explain the entire situation.

"She WHAT?!" Lang exclaimed, when Byrne had finished. "You're lying!"

"No, Frank, he's not," Huber confirmed. He had been quiet up until this point, at Byrne's instruction and order, but now interjected his confirmation. "I wish to high heaven he was. But he's not. I was there, Frank; I think she woulda killed me if the investigator hadn't taken her out first."

"She... would have killed YOU, Marc?" Lang breathed, staring at the younger man in horror.

"Yeah, Frank," an unhappy Huber admitted. "She... she was trying to convince me to work for her on this, this spy and saboteur ring she'd put together, and... and when I wouldn't..." He broke off and swallowed hard. "Frank, I was staring down the barrel of her gun when the investigator... when he... and I..."

Lang's knees buckled, and he collapsed into his desk chair, which spun and nearly flung him into the floor; Byrne leaped to grab and steady the chair, thrusting out an arm to keep Lang in it, and a light-headed Lang shot him a grateful glance. Huber knelt by his chair.

"I... I... she wasn't what we thought she was, Frank," Huber said, patently miserable. "She wasn't WHO we thought she was. She said my genetic father... see, it turns out he was an enemy of Becker that she slept with to try to get information, except she... she got pregnant with me in the aftermath, and..." His voice broke. "She said I was a disappointment to her, because I was just like him and she evidently hated him... and then she KILLED him... my mother killed my real father! How can you sleep with someone you hate, Frank? How can you kill 'em? It's called LOVEmaking! I.. I don't..."

"Did... she say anything about me?" Lang asked, his voice low, and hoarse with dread.

Huber nodded.

"Do I want to know?"

"...Probably not."

Lang drew a deep breath. "Tell me anyway," he ordered.

"She said..." Huber began. He steeled himself and finished. "She said you were just a means to an end."

Lang put his face in his hands.

"It... it gets worse, Frank," Huber admitted after several seemingly endless moments, silent, uncertain, and hesitant.

"How can it possibly get worse, son?" Lang wondered, miserable and grieving, on several levels.

"I... well, the investigator wasn't the only one who shot her," the young man confessed. "I... she had her gun pointed at my chest! They trained me good in OCS, Frank; I drew and fired before I had a chance to think about it. I DIDN'T even think, until it was too late. I..."

Lang swallowed. Hard.

"It's called self-defense, son," he murmured.

"You... you don't hate me? Because I think I hate me..."

"...No. I don't hate you, Marc. I don't like it," he conceded, "but I don't like the fact that she pointed her gun at you and threatened to shoot you, either. I don't like the fact that she admitted to killing your real father. I don't like the fact that she had one of your friends killed. I don't like the fact that she was trying to kill the tactical officer for Jablonka. But I ABSOLUTELY HATE the fact that, apparently, the woman I loved was only using me! Oh, God help me, the pain of THAT... She was so beautiful, Marc! You were probably still too young to notice such things, but surely you remember? She only started dressing down once I brought her to Jablonka as my wife, on account of my position, she said. I was head over heels for her! If I only thought she loved me, I..." He bowed his head. "So... no. I... I can't fault you for reacting to defend yourself, son. And don't you get down on yourself, either. I... I don't know what I'd have done in your shoes. Evidently your mother just... wasn't who we thought she was, at all."

It took a while, because Lang wanted to know everything, or at least everything he was cleared to know; when once he'd finally managed to satisfy Lang, Byrne found himself exhausted. He left Huber and Lang alone together, to process what had happened in their own way and in their own time.

He stepped out of the private office, to find the investigative team that Durand had assigned; they were fairly swarming over the flat, processing the crime scene, branching out into the rest of the embassy to locate collaborators among the staff, and arresting them — with the

Stadt ambassador's full permission; he did not want a war with the Commonwealth, and had been shocked to find out what had been going on in his own embassy, under his own nose.

Byrne continued out of the flat, into the embassy proper, to find Kardas waiting for him.

"Bad?" she wondered, studying his face.

"Not good, I'll put it like that," Byrne noted with a grimace. "She had everybody fooled, by the look of things."

"Damn. Including the son and the husband?"

"Especially including them, if that was anything to go by." Byrne jerked his thumb over his shoulder. "And I've been doing this long enough now that I've got a pretty good feel for real versus faked grief, no matter how good the fake. Besides, I had a little gadget in one pocket, and it agreed with me. There's enough pain and grief in that one room to supply the entire base. And then some."

"Ah. Well, I did a full-on interrogation of the ambassador — with his complete cooperation — and he wasn't part of this, either. He was NOT happy."

"There's that, I guess."

"Yes." She paused. "Is the crime scene processing occurring properly?"

"It looked like it. Minton was heading it; he said it seemed pretty straightforward."

"Good. Come on; let's go back and report in to Admiral Durand about how it went," Kardas said.

"I... could get into that, right now," Byrne decided. "Anywhere away from here is good."

"No shit," Kardas replied.

They fell into step together as they exited the Stadt embassy, headed back to Sigurdsen and the Intelligence Division building.

"Lang, I must insist that you explain," the Stadt ambassador demanded only a couple of hours later, "or I may have to remove you from embassy employ. What did you know, when did you know it, and how much were you involved?"

"Your Excellency, I..." Lang's voice cracked, "I didn't know anything until just a few hours ago. I found out about the same time you did. I swear to you, I did not know! I had no involvement at all, nor did Marc. She tried to SHOOT Marc! Her own son! What kind of woman WAS she, really?! I... I loved her, or I thought I did, but... but I'm beginning to realize... I didn't really KNOW her... at all."

Lang bit his lip, then closed his eyes, scrunching the lids tight, but a droplet escaped them nevertheless, and tracked down his cheek. He dashed the water away with an angry hand, even as his face contorted with grief and pain.

The ambassador studied the man in front of him, the man he had known — known, and trusted — since they had arrived on Jablonka together, more than a decade before. Together they had tried hard to construct a workable peace between Stadt and the Commonwealth; though Stadt was by no means in a peaceable place where the Commonwealth was concerned, the two men saw no reason why such a peace could not be constructed, and had worked hard to lay the foundations. The very founders of the Commonwealth itself had been their models.

Unfortunately, the ambassador was now realizing, not everyone around them agreed with them. So when a potential leader, antagonistic to the Commonwealth, had infiltrated their envoy... and Lang's heart, he grasped... quite a few had fallen under her sway.

And that meant he needed to either sweep the embassy staff and clean house... or go home himself, and let someone else become the ambassador in such a tricky location.

And he might not get a choice in the matter.

"I see," he said then, modulating his voice and temper to something that might help soothe his chief of staff. He knew Lang far too well, he decided, to think that the patent grief and pain he was seeing was any sort of attempt to sway him. No, it was heartbreak, pure and simple and deep. "Sit down, my friend."

"I... I'm sorry, Ben," Lang breathed, taking the seat that the ambassador indicated, then leaning forward and putting his face in his hands, despairing. "I brought a wolf into the fold. I had... no idea... she was, she would..." He broke off, then blurted, "I thought she loved me, too!"

"Sshh, my friend, let it go if you can," the ambassador murmured. "I understand. But when you're able, as SOON as you're able, we're going to need to plan how to respond to this."

"Wh-what?" Lang raised his head to stare at the ambassador.

"There will be repercussions, Frank, and you and I will have to deal with them," the ambassador pointed out. "It's entirely possible that, once this gets back to Stadt, I'll be recalled. Either we need to figure out what to do to counter that before it happens, or you need to decide if you'll come back with me."

"But we were trying to..."

"I know. But your wife may have ended our opportunity to try."

"Damn. Ida, what were you THINKING?!" Lang grumbled. "I..." He drew a deep breath. "Do I even have time to try to deal with this on a personal level, Ben?"

"I'll do what I can to give you that time, Frank," he replied, "but I don't know. I'd think hard about what you want to do next, if I were you. And as much as it pains me to say it, don't let it take a back seat to your grief, or you'll likely find yourself in a bad situation by the time you come up for air."

Early in the afternoon, the day after the confrontation, Durand contacted Campbell on a secure call.

"Bill, I thought you'd want to know, the autopsy came back," Durand noted, careful to avoid identifying the young intelligence officer on the call. Campbell knew that his own comm unit had been in secure mode from the time 'Samples' had appeared, and he also knew that Durand would not have made such a rookie mistake, so even though they were careful not to use easily identifiable names, there was little likelihood of anyone overhearing, let alone decrypting, the ciphered, secure communication.

"Oh. And?" Campbell followed through.

"Three projectiles, of two different calibers, were found in her. One in the chest, two in the head; the projectiles found in the head were a different caliber, smaller than the one in the chest. The one in the chest did puncture a lung, but missed the major structures — heart, aorta, and such; she would have survived it, though it would have taken her down. Maybe not out, though; she could still have fired HER weapon, according to my sources. The two in the head were both in the brain, and that was what killed her."

"Ah. I see," Campbell said, thoughtful.

'So the bullets that killed her were mine,' he thought. This case was, he realized, the first time he had ever had to kill another sentient being, for any reason... and now he had killed two. 'But they'd both have cheerfully killed me, and I swear it looked like SHE was ready to kill Huber,' he decided. 'Her own son. Maybe she would have, and maybe she wouldn't have... but she tried multiple times to have Captain Rao killed, she tried to have me killed, and she would have killed 'Samples' in a heartbeat within a few more moments, even if she didn't kill Huber. So... no. I don't think I feel remotely bad about it.'

"Are you all right, Bill?"

"Mm. I was just mulling that over, Jake. Yes, I think I'm fine. But you might want to pass this information on to Marc, just so he knows."

"Oh damn. The chest...?"

"...Yes."

"Why?"

"She tried to talk him into switching sides, and he wasn't having it," Campbell told his mentor. "You were right about him, in spades. He's loyal as the day is long, and a dedicated citizen and soldier of the Commonwealth. But she was getting ready to take him out for it. At least, that's what it looked like to me, which was one reason for the, um, timing of things."

"Ah. I see. All right; I'll get on that as soon as we're done here."

"Sounds good, Jake. Anything else?"

"No, not for the moment. Let me know if you change your mind about being all right, though. We have people for that, and it's not that uncommon. Especially on... firsts, if you get me."

"All right. And thank you. But I believe I'll be fine."

"That's good, then. Okay, talk to you later, Bill."

"Thanks for the heads-up, Jake."

"Not a problem."

Campbell broke the call connection, then sat for a while and stared at his comm unit, thoughtful.

Campbell holed up in his hideout for a couple of days more, staying in contact with Durand via secure means, and waiting for the admiral's notification that it would be safe for him to resume 'living' status.

Meanwhile, he took it easy, letting his body — and skin — rest and allowing his beard to grow back in; it was not especially heavy, but it grew fast, and within the time spent in the bolt-hole, he had grown back enough of it to shape, so it would look mostly normal. But he kept his head shaved for that time, as it might look odd if he came back with head stubble; however, there were several offhand, and a couple of serious, excuses he could make for a fully-shaved look.

Partway through his sojourn in exile, Durand pinged him again.

"Hey, Bill," the admiral said.

"Hi, Jake. What's up?"

"I just wanted to let you know that I talked to Marc, like we discussed the other day. I made sure he knew it wasn't him that did it. He made a wounding, take-down shot only."

"Oh. Okay. Um, does... does he feel hard at 'Phil' because of it?"

"No, I don't think so. He honestly thought she was getting ready to take him out, so he feels that 'Phil' likely saved his life," Durand explained, "but... well. He's not in the greatest shape, and he's taking things hard. I got him a few sessions scheduled with that help you and I discussed, the last time we talked."

"Under the circumstances, I think that's a really good idea," Campbell agreed. "You think he's gonna be okay?"

"Eventually, yes. Though I expect this is going to be a painful part of his personal history for the rest of his life. But we're going to do our damnedest to help him get past it and move on with what looks to be a promising career."

"That sounds great, Jake, and I'm very glad to hear it."

"I rather suspected you would be, Bill, school events notwithstanding."

"Oh, that? That's all water under the bridge, Jake. I never quite understood what the problem was, anyway. I never had a problem with him, I just knew he had an issue with me." Campbell shrugged, despite there being no one there to see. "I kinda learned to avoid him when I saw him coming, but other than that, no big deal."

"Think you can unlearn that habit? I gathered, when I brought him in, that he wanted to start over, if possible."

"I probably can, sure."

"Good man."

"I try."

"You do well at it, then."

"Are you saying you need me back there now?"

"Not quite yet. I'll ping you when things are ready for that."

"Got it."

"Later."

Finally, two days after that call, almost a week after Samples had vanished, he got the word from Durand that it was safe for him to reappear, and Campbell slipped quietly back onto the base, making straight for Durand's office.

Commander Jany Jones stopped him in the outer office.

"Wait," she said. "He has someone else in there with him. But he knows you're coming, so I'll ping him, and he'll let me know when you can come in." She offered him a prim smile. "I have to admit, I'm glad you're all right, Mr. Campbell."

"Me too," he said, returning her smile. "Speaking of — how is Captain Rao doing?"

"I think she's better, though I haven't seen her myself," Jones said. "The admiral said she's off crutches and the scooter now, though, and just using a cane to stabilize herself. AND the Intel docs were able to clear her system of all the noxious chemicals — they're better than ninety percent sure — already. So there shouldn't be any future repercussions from this little incident."

"That sounds really good," Campbell said, pleased, as Jones sent Durand the signal that he'd arrived.

"So," Durand said, as Marc Huber sat in front of his desk. "Are you doing a little bit better after... recent events, Mr. Huber?"

"I... I guess so, sir," Huber said, subdued. "Under the circumstances, I have to be honest and say I'm not really sure. My own mom... and I..."

"Easy, son," Durand murmured. "I understand, and I'm sorry. I never meant for it to work out like that. We none of us realized the spy ringleader was your own mother, or we'd never have asked you to get involved. We'd have found another way to get where we needed to go, there."

"I know, sir. I don't think anybody thought it might be MOM. Even Mr. Samples was kind of startled, too, when Mom showed up like that, already drawn down on him... well, on both of us. Which also didn't do me any favors."

"I can imagine."

"Though, now that I think about it," Huber said, thoughtful, "he maybe didn't startle as much as I'd have expected; maybe he'd just figured it out, and he only startled 'cause she was suddenly right there behind us."

"That sounds... astute of Mr. Samples," Durand decided. "I'm sure it was an altogether uncomfortable situation, all around."

"Yes sir. But... well, I guess I don't have a choice but to keep on keepin' on," Huber observed, downcast. "Don't worry. I'll... manage. Somehow."

"Well, I have some good news for you, if you want to hear it."

"I'm definitely up for some good news right now, sir."

"Good. Well, I've wangled a couple of career options for you, Mr. Huber. The first involves a transfer to the Intelligence Division, where you'd become my personal shuttle pilot. I'm in the line to head the Division one day, and I could use a good, trustworthy pilot. And you fit that description to the proverbial T. Right now, I pretty much get whoever's on rotation when I need a shuttle... but having someone specifically assigned to me would make for a much better situation for you, especially as I move up in the hierarchy. And," he added, "it would mean a bit more training of the sort like Mr. Samples had, in order to keep an eye out on things for me."

"Oh," Huber said, sitting up straight, his eyes widening. "That sounds... intriguing."

"And the other would allow you, after some bereavement leave time — which you'll get, either way — to re-test your command skills for the Tactical Division. If you pass... and based on what I've seen of your personnel file, I think you would, now, because you've been open to learning new ways of thinking... you'd have the option of moving up through the ranks of starships in the Fleet."

Huber's jaw went slack.

"Don't worry about giving me an answer right now," Durand said with a smile, "though I'm betting I know which one you want. And for what it's worth, if you decide to try testing for starship pilot and still don't pass, the other offer will still be open. You proved your loyalty to me, son, in an amazing way, and I wouldn't be unhappy in the least to have someone like that for my personal shuttle pilot."

"I... thank you, sir. I don't know what... I mean, which..."

"I know that. You don't have to make a decision until you come back from your bereavement leave, and under the circumstances, I managed to negotiate several weeks for you; I expect your stepfather will need you, too."

"Um, all right. Again, thank you, sir."

"If you find that, given your participation in your mother's death, you need more counseling, that can be arranged, as well," Durand said, sympathetic. "Come back to me and I'll see it happens through my people, so it doesn't have to be made public."

"I... think that's an excellent idea, sir, and I think maybe we should go ahead and, and..."

"Got it," Durand said, making a notation on his virtual computer terminal. "I'll have the counselor ping you to work out a new appointment time."

"Yes sir."

"Ah, there we go," Durand said, as his VR unit beeped twice. "That's what I've been waiting for. I have one last bit of what I hope will be good news for you." He toggled the intercom to the outer office. "Jany, send him in, please."

"Right away, Admiral," came the reply.

Moments later, the door opened, and Lieutenant William Campbell walked in, alive and apparently healthy.

Huber gaped.

"Lieutenant Huber, I believe you recognize Lieutenant Campbell?" Durand noted.

"Wait," Huber said, shocked, as he stared at Campbell, "he's not dead? I thought..."

"No, no," Durand said to Huber. "I know the report we put out, and I know what I told you — and forgive me for lying through my teeth to you — but Campbell was in hiding for his safety, while you helped a friend he met some years back, Samples, scope out the situation and clear things up. After he survived the attempt to kill him, Campbell contacted me and I sent him into cover, but he was feeding

Samples information he'd already dug up, from the safehouse. Samples is very good, but he's originally out of Tactical Division, after all, and doesn't have quite the skills or tools that Intelligence Division staffers have... because we're trained on those from the very beginning."

"Oh," Huber said, still a bit dumbfounded. "Well, I'm awful glad you're not dead, Campbell."

"And that's appreciated," Campbell said with a smile. He moved to Huber and offered a hand; Huber took it, and the two young men shook.

"Now, if memory serves, Lieutenant Huber, didn't you want to take Lieutenant Campbell out for a drink, by way of apology for old behavior?" Durand asked.

"Um, yeah, I did," Huber confessed, flushing. "I, uh, I wanted to apologize for being a real jackass when we were in school, Campbell. It... it was resentment, because you whipped my ass in the simulator course — and I accidentally FOUND OUT it was you — and, and a little jealousy, too, if I'm honest. Because you had such a great family... and I... didn't." He laughed once, a bitter sound. "I just didn't know how truly not-great my family was."

Campbell gaped for a moment at the revelation, then nodded.

"Uh, okay," he said, hoping that didn't sound as lame to the others as he thought it sounded. "Well, it's good to know what that was all about; frankly, at the time, I had no clue what I'd done to piss you off. And... I didn't MEAN to whip your ass in the simulators, you know. To be honest, I wasn't even sure if they were putting us up against real people or not. It could have been just more simulation, though I didn't say as much to the others."

"Yeah, I wondered about that, too, later," Huber admitted. "Anyway, I thought maybe a brew or two might chase away old memories an'... an' give us a new start? I'll buy; I owe ya."

"I think that's a plan," Campbell said with a smile. "I only just got back from being in the safehouse, so I have a few things yet to do before I can go off-duty — reports and debriefs and stuff like that — but I can meet you at Don's in about three, three and a half, hours?" He glanced at the admiral. "If that's okay with my commanding officer?"

204

Durand nodded permission, and Huber and Campbell both grinned.

"Done," Huber declared. "See you there."

While Campbell waited in Don's pub for Huber to arrive, he took a table in the corner and ordered a double shot of whiskey, chilled, neat; he'd decided he had earned his favorite beverage, but it wasn't cheap, and he didn't want to start off a budding friendship by putting that on Huber's tab. Just then, he saw Lily Martell come into the bar, and he sat up straight with a smile, then held up his hand. He caught her attention, and she froze, staring at him, before her eyes narrowed and she headed toward his table.

"Hey, honey," he said, as she neared the table. "Have a seat, here. You want your usual?"

"What the HELL did you do to your hair?" she demanded. "Did you SHAVE it?! ALL of it??"

"New look. You like it?"

"Oh HELL no."

"Oh. Well, it'll grow back. It was a dare. For some kind of kid's charity, I think. Be patient."

"PATIENT?! How. DARE. You?" she snarled. Then, before he could react, she grabbed his old-fashioned glass and tossed the whiskey in his face.

"Ow!" he exclaimed, as the alcohol stung his eyes. "What the hell was THAT for?!"

"I thought you were dead!" she hissed. "Your bosses put out that release that you'd been killed in a traffic accident while running errands off base, and all this time, I thought you were dead! I cried my eyes out! And now here you are! What the hell were you doing?!"

"What? That I'd been killed in a traffic accident?" Campbell dropped into his 'dumb-bunny' cover for the benefit of the bar; quite a few of the patrons had turned to watch as she tossed his drink into his face. "Huh, no, I'm fine. What, did Intelligence say I was dead? Wow. Somebody sure got their wires crossed someplace."

"Wires crossed, huh?" Martell grumbled. "I'll just bet, you bastard. There never was a 'case,' was there?"

"I told you what to do if something strange came up, back at the beginning of the thing, Lily," Campbell said, groping for a napkin to wipe the worst of the alcohol off his face, even as his eyes teared profusely from the burn. "Please keep your voice down."

"Yeah, right," she growled. "You were two-timing me with her the whole time, weren't you?"

"Is that really what you think?"

"Then why didn't you tell me where...?"

"Let me repeat, honey. Once things started getting serious, and I already knew that I could trust you, I gave you instructions for how to find out things like that," Campbell pointed out. "Didn't you follow them?"

"What, you mean you actually expected me to barge in on a rear admiral, demanding to know what happened to you? When his office was the one who put out the release that you'd been killed?"

"You should have done it. He told me to tell you to."

"Oh HELL no! Like I believe THAT!" she exclaimed, and several of the bar denizens glanced their way again. Fortunately, Campbell thought, they only saw a pissed-off girlfriend and a hapless boyfriend; except for that last exclamation, Lily hadn't been loud enough to hear over the jukebox. And that had fit right in with a girlfriend accusing her boyfriend... which she was doing, after all. "We're done, Ensign Campbell!"

"It's Lieutenant Campbell now," he murmured.

"What?"

"I got a promotion," he pointed out, tapping the silver bar denoting his new rank.

"I don't care if you got named President of the Commonwealth!" she cried. "I never wanna see you again!"

And before he could say more, she spun on her heel and stalked out of the bar.

"Oookay," Campbell said with a sigh, as his eyes teared worse. "I guess that ends that."

'Maybe... maybe it's just as well,' he added in thought. 'In my line of work, it's probably too dangerous to take a wife anyway. She's good at her job, and she's pretty, but no matter how good she is, a grease monkey in the Maintenance Division probably isn't cut out to be the wife of an Intelligence Division investigator.' He sighed again. 'I'll be surprised if I ever find someone who could cut it as my wife.

Not given the kind of shit that Admiral Durand said he was sending my way. Oh well.'

Just then, he felt a touch on his arm. Looking up through blurry vision, he saw that Don, the bartender, had come out from behind the bar with a tray... something Don almost never did.

"Here," Don said, picking up a clean bar towel. "Close your eyes a minute, and I'll blot the worst of it off you. That cocktail napkin you had didn't begin to handle a double shot."

"Thanks, Don," Campbell murmured, complying even as the bartender cleaned away the dripping whiskey on his face, scalp, and neck. "Umph. That helps."

"Good. This'll help more." Don peeled the shrink wrap off a fresh bottle of eye drops, removed the cap, and handed it to Campbell. "Flush your eyes out with this. Use the whole thing. Half in each eye."

"Wow." Campbell stared from the bottle to Don and back. "You came prepared?"

"What, you think I've never seen this happen before?" Don said with a chuckle. "Oh hell no. I've got you set up here, son. Do what I tell you, and you probably won't even have bloodshot eyes in the morning... unless you drink too much to forget her."

"I hate to say it, 'cause I really liked her, but it was a fairly new relationship — we've only been seeing each other for, what, two, MAYBE three months — and that reaction just told me she wasn't the right one for me anyway," Campbell noted, taking the eye drops and tilting his head to the left. "Okay, keep that towel handy; I'll need both hands for this, and I'm gonna flush 'em out pretty thoroughly, like you said."

"Exactly what you should do, and I got this," Don said, lightly holding the bar towel against the bridge of Campbell's nose. In turn, Campbell held the lids of his right eye open with his left hand, then squeezed the dropper bottle in the fingers of his right, letting the fluid run into the outer corner of his eye until the fluid ran out the inner corner, across his nose, and into the towel, thoroughly flushing out the alcohol. "Good," Don said. "Now swap."

Campbell tilted his head to the right and swapped the dropper bottle to his left hand; Don adjusted the towel positioning, and they repeated the process.

"There," Don said, as Campbell straightened his head. "How's that?"

"A lot better — whoa," Campbell said, blinking, then grabbing another cocktail napkin from the small stack the waiter had left earlier with his now-defunct drink, and mopping at his suddenly-running nose. "I can actually see you now."

"I bet you regret THAT!" Don said with a grin, and they both laughed. "Here," he said then, placing the last two items from his tray on the table; one was a thick stack of dinner napkins, the other a fresh old-fashioned glass with a double shot of his preferred whiskey, chilled, neat. "Some bigger napkins, and I'll leave this towel here too, so you can try to blot up some more of what got on your uniform. And a replacement for your drink, on the house. And there's another when you're ready, on me, on account of the girlfriend walkin' on ya."

"Thanks, Don," Campbell said, grateful. "I appreciate that. I'm afraid I didn't see that one coming."

"We never do, I think," Don said, then put the empty old-fashioned glass on the tray, took the tray, and headed back for the bar.

Ten minutes later, Huber arrived. "Whoa, what happened to you?" he wondered. "Your face is all flushed, your uniform is wet, and you reek of booze. You spill your drink?"

"Nah, not exactly," Campbell said, as Huber sat down and signaled Don, who nodded and began preparing Huber's drink. "I HAD a girlfriend before all this shit went down. When that assassin from the Stadt embassy tried to take me out and I went into hiding, she apparently believed the story that got put out about my getting killed, and never bothered to follow my instructions to find out if I really was dead or not."

"Uh-oh," Huber said, as a waitress swung by with his stein of beer.

"Yeah," Campbell said, a bit morose. "Evidently she popped in here after work tonight, saw me all hale and hearty, and hit the roof. My own drink wound up in my face. And my uniform," he said, glancing down. "I did my best to clean up a bit, and Don helped, but I guess there's only so much you can do, short of going home, stripping, showering, and changing clothes. And I didn't have time to do that before you were scheduled to get here."

"Aw. I'm really sorry about that, man."

"Sorry seems to be going around, I guess," Campbell decided.

"Yeah," Huber said, mood dropping. "Yeah, it does." He all but belted his beer, chugging three-quarters of it at a go before even slowing down. When he finally set down the nearly-empty beer stein, Campbell laid his hand on Huber's shoulder.

"I know, Marc," he murmured. "I know."

"I know you do," Huber said, voice choked. "Let's, um, let's not talk about it. I'm not here to talk, really, anyway. I need... I need to forget, for a little while."

"Right," Campbell said, raising a hand. "Don? Another round, here, please."

"All over it," Don replied.

About an hour and a half later, while Huber was in the necessary ridding himself of all that fluid from the beer — by that point, he'd had at least four half-pints, maybe six; Campbell had lost count — Captain Mary Rao entered the pub, making good time on a cane. She spotted Bill and made a beeline for his table.

"There you are," Rao said, walking up. "Whoa, chrome dome."

"Yeah. It was a dare. For some kind of kid's charity, I think."

Rao eyed him with a knowing smirk.

"Yeah, right."

"What, you don't believe me?"

"Right. I heard you were 'on leave' or something."

"Or something," Campbell noted, bland. "Better that than dead."

"No joke," Rao agreed. "I'm sure you had time for a dare while you were in hiding."

"Ah. Well..."

"Uh-huh. So where's Samples?"

"Hm? Who?"

"Mr. Samples. Where is he?"

"I'm afraid I don't know who you're talking about, Captain Rao."

"Heh. I just bet you don't. And I thought it was Mary and Bill."

"Well," Campbell tried, and sighed. "It's done, and I thought..."

"All right, Lieutenant Campbell. But that offer of friendship is still open if you want it. I gather the whole matter is tied up, after your people carted off more than two-thirds of my staff in handcuffs? And Rose sent me word through her C.O. that about half a dozen people were arrested in Facilities Division, too?"

"We believe so, yes, ma'am."

"Stop that."

"Stop what?"

"We're both off duty, and you... and 'Mr. Samples'... probably saved my life, a couple of times over. After all that, you can't deny that we have a good friendship in the making. So I'm MARY. Deal with it." She smirked. "I'll make it an order if I have to, Lieutenant."

"...All right, all right. And I'm Bill," Campbell said with a smile. "I'm with another friend — his mom was the ringleader, only he didn't know it, so watch what you say, but he did help us with it all, including when we had to take his mom out, so REALLY, watch what you say, 'cause he's in a lotta pain — but you're welcome to join us for drinks."

"Where is he?"

"Necessary. He's been, uh, drowning his sorrows. He'll be back in a few."

"Ah. Can I buy?"

"I won't argue that in the least."

"Then you can introduce us when he gets back."

"I'll be happy to."

"Sounds good, then. Don...?"

The Loose Threads of a Life

Two days after that, and at Huber's request, Campbell attended the memorial service for Ida Huber Lang. He was a little uncomfortable; if anyone there — other than Marc Huber — had known he was the man who had killed her, to say the interaction would become very awkward really damn fast would be putting it mildly.

'And,' he thought, 'if ever Huber needed a reason to hate my guts, he'd sure have one now.'

But no one save Marc knew who had killed her, and even he thought that Samples was a different man, so Campbell put aside the thought and concentrated on helping his new friend through the service; he remembered, entirely too well, struggling through a similar service all by himself only a few years before.

As the small group of mourners and those who had come to pay their respects filed into the chapel, Huber grabbed Campbell's arm and towed him into the chapel with himself and his father.

"Marc, I'm not family..." Campbell began.

"We're friends, right? I need a friend right now," Marc breathed into Campbell's ear. "Stick by me, please."

Campbell nodded, and followed the two men to the front pew of the chapel.

Marc Huber sat next to Frank Lang, his stepfather and the previously-suspect chief of staff to the ambassador from Stadt, with Campbell on his other side. Lang said little, but offered a slight smile when Campbell took his seat beside his stepson.

To judge from his demeanor immediately before the service began, however, a still-bewildered and deeply heartbroken Lang was not a little puzzled over what exactly had happened — not to Ida Lang; that had been obvious. No, Campbell adjudged he was confused over why she had done what she did — why she had felt she had to, to begin with. Lang was also mystified about Ida's feelings toward him and toward her own son; it seemed, Campbell decided, that Marc had told him of the hateful things his own mother had said to him in her last moments.

"I can't think she didn't love us, in her own way," Lang had told Marc. "Not for all the years she had lived with us beside her."

"I dunno, Frank," Marc had said. "She never would tell me who my father was. If she was really a spy for Becker — and it looks like she was a good one — then it's entirely possible she really did pull a Mata Hari. You know, slept with someone to get information. And then ended up with me by accident. In which case..."

"Shh, Marc," Lang murmured. "Don't go there, son. Just don't even go there. I understand how you feel, though. I have to wonder now, did she ever love me the way I did, her? Or was I just a means to an end, like she said?"

"So... I mean... you really loved her?" Marc asked, wondering.

"I loved the Ida I thought I knew, yeah," Lang admitted, then shook his head. "But evidently the Ida I knew wasn't... wasn't real." He choked for a moment, and Marc laid a hand on his stepfather's shoulder. Abruptly Lang grabbed Marc and pulled him into a hug, burying his face in the younger man's shoulder. "In the end, you're... you're probably the only real thing she left me."

Marc Huber had put his arms around his stepfather as the older man began to weep.

The service was short and fairly succinct, as might be expected, given the true nature of the woman they memorialized, revealed in and by her death. The ashes were in a small urn on the altar of the chapel, and when the service was ended, most of the attendees — and even the chaplain — filed out somewhat awkwardly, leaving Campbell standing with Huber and Lang... uncomfortable with being there, but unwilling to leave Huber.

"So, um, Frank, what... what are you gonna do with...?" Huber wondered, gesturing at the urn.

"I... I'm not sure yet, Marc," Lang admitted. "I mean, I loved her, but... did she ever love either of us? Did you think she did?"

"I... I just don't know for sure, Frank," Huber said. "I... she was always kinda distant, but... but I think that was... just her way, you know? I mean, even when I was little, she always looked after me — when she could have given me up for adoption, or terminated before I was even born, or something like that. But she didn't. She never let anything hurt me, took care of me when I was sick, all that. Until... until the other day, I thought... I really believed she loved me. I just thought she was this... mousy, invisible mom, you know? And... and I thought she... loved you, the same way..."

"Then that's what we're going to keep believing," Lang declared. "I'll bring Ida's ashes home and put them in my study. You can visit her any time you want to, son. And... listen," Lang began, then broke off.

"What is it, Frank?"

"Several things, really. You remember the Stadt ambassador? My friend Ben?"

"Sure."

"Well, he and I had been working really hard on trying to lay a foundation for some sort of lasting peace, a good relationship, between Stadt and the Commonwealth," Lang explained. "Only... well, Ida may have scotched that. Ben's seriously looking at the possibility of being recalled to the homeworld, likely in disgrace. And given some of the feedback we've been getting, it might happen."

"Oh," Huber said, choking a bit. "So... you'll be leaving?"

"No, that's just the point — I won't," Lang continued his explanation. "On Ben's advice, I gave it a lot of thought. I've been on Jablonka a long time, and I find I've come to like it here. And... well, you're here. I'll keep working for peace between Stadt and the Commonwealth for as long as I'm allowed, but... if it comes down to it, I've decided that, rather than going back to Stadt, I want to apply for Commonwealth citizenship... or whatever they'll let me have, given my age. I'll need your help in that..."

"You've got it, Frank!"

Lang shot a querying glance at Campbell, who nodded affirmation, as well.

"And... there's one other thing. See, I... I may not be the genetic donor, but you don't know who that was, anyway," Lang pointed out, "and never will, now. Plus, Ida apparently didn't like him much, based on what you told me. I dunno, I thought maybe... you might like to think of me as your dad. I know I'd love it if you called me Dad, or Pop, or whatever you wanted, in that general vein..."

"Really?" Huber breathed, his eyes widening. "I always... I... I just... you mean that...?"

"Yeah, I mean it, son," Lang said, sincere. "I've called you 'son' for the last several years, ever since you came to me that time, right before you graduated from OCS, and made up with me, with all the fights and the arguments and all, and I've meant it, all this time. I think of you as my son, and to tell the truth, I always have. I'd... really like it if... if you'd think of me as your dad. I know," he held up his hands, "I know you think of me as your stepdad, and we have a good relationship now. But I want us to have a better relationship. We're all we've got, now... just you and me. And whatever comes in the future, we're gonna stay here together... or wherever you get sent, in the course of your duties, 'cause I'll go with you, if you say the word. Can you..." Lang broke off, then tried again. "Can you deal with that? Can you handle making me your actual family? Making me your father?"

Huber tried to speak, then choked. Campbell produced a bottle of water from a pocket in his shipsuit, and offered it to the other lieutenant. Huber took it, opened it, and sipped from it for a moment before handing it back with murmured thanks. Then he turned back to Lang.

"Yeah, I think I'd like that... Dad," he said.

The two men embraced.

A week later, Campbell received an official summons.

"Lieutenant Campbell reporting as ordered, Admiral Durand." Campbell saluted the gathered officers: Admiral Durand, Admiral Birken, Senior Captain Kardas, and Commander Byrne, all in Durand's office.

"At ease, Lieutenant," Birken ordered. "Jake, you have the floor."

"Well then," Durand said, "we wanted to let you know that you done good, Mr. Campbell. Very good, indeed. We still have our loyal planetary tactical officer, even if we did clear out most of her staff; we cleaned house of a damn vicious spy ring; and we — er, I suppose that should be 'Mr. Samples' — took out the head of that ring." Durand smirked, giving Campbell a meaningful wink. "And all of that was done at your analysis, discovery, and instruction. And for at least two of those, it was your personal hand in action. Or that of an alter-ego."

"The only thing we don't have in hand is the power behind the ringleader, and that's because they're in the Outer Colonies, not within the Commonwealth," Birken pointed out. "Give us time, though. With the information and connections you provided, we're even starting to track that down. And we have operatives in place that can be used to, ah, return the favor, let us say."

"That's seriously excellent detection, Lieutenant," Byrne interjected.

"It sure sounds like it," Kardas agreed. "I rather wish I'd been here to see."

"It was, and is," Durand agreed. "As I said when all of this started, you're going places, Campbell. And as I told you in private a few days ago when it ended, I have a shit-load of cases I plan to direct your way. You are now considered an experienced intel officer-slash-agent investigator, with all that that entails."

"And 'that' entails the top-of-the-line 'tool kit,'" Byrne added, handing Campbell another packet with several small items within. "Including the OFFICIAL beta test version of the correlation software. You'll be kept up to date on it; each time a new version of the software is released for testing, you'll get a copy. Stay on it; I have the feeling it'll be useful."

"THANK you, sir!" Campbell exclaimed, pleased, as he accepted the packet. "All of you! That'll make things a lot easier!"

"Very good, then," Birken said in satisfaction. "You should also know, Campbell, that we did seriously discuss a promotion for you, based on this work. Unfortunately, it hasn't been a full month since your LAST promotion, and that puts you so far out of the zone that we didn't feel we could get away with another promotion so soon..."

"Understood, sir, and I appreciate the thought," Campbell said, saluting, "but seriously, the move to the active investigator listing, with the top-line tools, means just as much to me, under the circumstances."

The four ranking officers exchanged glances.

"Told you, Pavel," Durand murmured. "He's in this for the long haul."

"You did, and he is," Birken agreed. "Byrne, take good care of this one. He's going places."

"I know, sir," Byrne acknowledged, "and I will, because he is. I figured that out a while back. And," he added, turning back to Campbell, "I apologize for scorning your abilities in the beginning, before you'd had an opportunity to even show them. I've learned a few things myself, on this case."

Campbell smiled, then nodded.

"Now," Durand said, "we can't give you a promotion, and for obvious reasons, Intelligence Division isn't much on handing out awards; it has a nasty tendency to give away our operatives' work, and usually ends up getting them killed. But we CAN do a couple of other things. Such as give Mr. Samples an official promotion. Effective immediately, Phil Samples is now a Chief Petty Officer; I'll see you get the appropriate rank designations for the uniform, for the next time you need him."

"Um. Samples, sir? A promotion?" Campbell blinked in surprise. "But..."

"...What, you didn't think he was going away, did you?" Durand wondered in amusement. "As well as that worked, and with the cases that are likely to come your way?"

"Especially given the designations we plan to make permanent," Birken added.

"I, um, I guess I just hadn't, uh, thought about that aspect of things yet, sirs," Campbell admitted, and Durand chuckled before he continued.

"Well, think about it, then. We can also give YOU a commendation, Mr. Campbell. And that's already been done, and placed in your personnel records."

"Not in the front part, though," Byrne added. "Only someone with a NOT LIMITED clearance will be able to see THAT."

"Your own clearance has now been upgraded to NOT LIMITED," Birken tag-teamed, "and as I alluded to a moment ago, your status as a 'fixer' has been made permanent. Your specialties now include infiltration, counter-intelligence, and neutralization... whatever is required." He eyed Campbell with a stern gaze. "Take that last bit DAMN seriously, son."

"I do already, sir," Campbell said, sincere.

"Very good, then," Birken said.

"Those designations have also been added to Samples' files," Durand added, "in the same fashion — to the NOT LIMITED back page — to ensure that we don't wind up with any SNAFUs going forward."

Campbell blinked again.

"That... works, sirs," he decided. Birken chuckled.

"Well, well," he said. "He blinked, but otherwise didn't even look cross-eyed. Yes, Jake, I think we have an excellent new operative, now. More," he added, "I think it's about time he had a proper duty assignment. And after this little investigation, I have just the thing. Lieutenant Campbell, starting tomorrow, you will begin a stint at Planetary Headquarters. It should be interesting to see what, if anything, you can root out there."

"Um, yes sir," Campbell acknowledged.

"Any questions, Bill?" Durand asked then, voice soft. "Are you up for all this? Do you understand what you're getting into, here?"

"Absolutely," Campbell answered, firm, "and no sir, not at this time."

"You're good with it?"

"Positively."

The four ranking officers glanced at each other again. Birken nodded; the others responded in kind.

"All right then," Durand said. "Dismissed, Lieutenant Campbell. Very good. I look forward to seeing what you can do."

"Thank you, sirs, ma'am," Campbell said, doing his best to make his gratitude obvious.

He turned smartly on his heel and headed for the door.

Epilogue — Meetings

After the year's assignment in the Planetary Headquarters was over, Campbell found himself back in Intelligence Division. Chief Samples had come out to play once or twice, keeping things straight, but even so, Campbell had discovered that Planetary Headquarters kept him busy. He had gotten out of shape in the last year, given everything that had been going on, and now that he was back in ID, it was high time to get back to his routine.

Around a month after his return to ID, and with some time to get his body in better shape, Bill decided to head for the gym to get in an Enshin workout. He ducked into the locker room and changed into his gi, then headed for the dojo.

But when he arrived in the dojo proper, there was already a bout under way, so he stood along the wall with several others and watched. The pretty, petite brunette on the mats was mopping up those mats with her opponent.

'Wow,' he thought, as, within minutes of his beginning to watch, she put down her opponent, kneeling on his shoulder blades, one of his arms pulled behind him, firmly held in her grip.

"A thousand one, a thousand two, a thousand three!" she called, and her opponent slapped the mat with the other hand, then held it up in an acknowledgement of defeat. She stood and released him, helped him to his feet, and as he shuffled, shamed, in the general direction of the locker rooms, grabbing a lone towel off a kickboxing bag as he went past it, the brunette called, "Next?"

"Damn, is she fast," Campbell murmured to himself. He eased over to a friend from Academy days, Lieutenant Travers Adamson. "Hey, Trav? Who's the cute little brunette mopping up the floor with Pete?"

"Oh, Little Miss Lightning over there?" Adamson wondered. "She's just back on planet. That's Jan Childers."

"Jan Childers? You're kidding. From all I've heard about her, I thought she must be seven feet tall."

"Nah. Barely five."

"Hm. I could use a little work on my speed. I wonder if she'll spar with me?"

"Glutton for punishment, eh? As far as I know, she'll spar with anybody... once. That's usually all it takes. You lose your taste for sparring with her real fast once she's embarrassed the hell outta ya."

"Ohhhh-kay."

Campbell watched her through two more bouts, growing ever more impressed as she took down her opponents with speed, craft, and skill.

When she took a break to sip some water from her insulated bottle on an equipment rack nearby, he approached her.

"Hey there. You're really good."

"Thanks. Given my size and my personal history, I've kinda had to be."

"I always like to try myself against someone who's good; it's the only way to get better, in my opinion. Could we maybe spar, see how I do against you?"

"Sure. Why not?" She offered him a wolfish grin. "I can always call Housekeeping to come over and finish mopping the floor with you." Then she paused and looked him up and down, and Campbell realized she was giving him a once-over, taking in his muscular but lithe build, and the worn gi and somewhat-frayed black belt. Her eyebrow shot up, and she decided, "Or maybe not. This could be interesting."

"I hope so," he averred. "I try to give as good as I get. But I try never to hurt a friend."

He grinned back, and the wolfishness faded from her expression as he held out his hand, and she took it and they shook.

"I'm Campbell, by the way. Lieutenant William Campbell. My friends call me Bill."

"And I'm Commander Jan Childers. Call me Jan."

They smiled.

Please review this book on Amazon.

STEPHANIE OSBORN

Author Notes

I'd like to deeply thank Richard Weyand for allowing me to play in his series; I enjoyed the other books in the Childers series immensely, and hope his fans think I have done due diligence to his universe and his characters in this one. I've certainly tried my best to do so! Each author is unique, however; style, focus, direction — no two of us write alike. So while I'm sure it's a little different, I hope you can still point and say, "Yup! That's Bill Campbell, all right!" It's been a lot of fun, and I love the characters as much as anyone. Richard's been very patient with me, and put up with innumerable questions, as I picked his brain about this or that aspect of his universe! I think I was constantly coming up with questions, until I was at least halfway through the manuscript! Then it became a case of, "Now where the heck was that in the other books...?" And of course, he knew where to look.

I'd also like to thank friend and fellow author Dan Hollifield for a bit of brainstorming battle scenarios with me. Sometimes what I need is just to bounce ideas off someone else, and toss concepts back and forth, before the whole thing gels in my head. One of my beta readers who reads REALLY fast, Evelyn Zinn, had a quick look-see, too, with an eye toward general feel and catching any errors, and that was appreciated.

In any case, here's the flashback story of Mary Rao's adventure on Sigurdsen, with the help of Bill Campbell! I hope you enjoy it!

Stephanie Osborn
Huntsville, AL
July 2019

STEPHANIE OSBORN

Appendix

Inhabited systems mentioned (capital city)

Earth (New York City)

Members of the Commonwealth of Free Planets:

Anders
Bahay (Kabisera)
Bliss (Joy)
Boomgaard
Calumet
Courtney
Hutan
Jablonka (Jezgra)
Kodu
Meili

Mountainhome
Natchez
Pahaadon
Parchman
Saarestik
Shaanti
The Yards [Doma]
Valore
Waldheim

Outer Colonies

Alpen
Arramond
Becker
Brunswick
Coronet (Jewel)
Drake
Duval
Epsley
Feirm
Ferrano
Grocny
Guernsey
Lautada
Melody

Mon Mari
New Carolina
Nymph
Oerwoud
Paradiso (Corazon)
Refugio
Samara
Seacrest
Stadt (Dorf)
Svobodo
Tenerife
Villam
Wolsey

Notes on Navigational Notation

The Commonwealth Space Force uses the following standards with respect to navigational bearings and distances.

Navigational bearing and distance are specified as:

rotation mark/minus elevation (on point) (at distance)

All such references are with respect to a point, a baseline, and a plane.

- If no point is specified, the point is the ship, the baseline is the long axis of the ship projected through the bows, and the plane is defined by the plane of the ship with the command cylinder(s) considered to be 'up'.

- If another ship is specified as the point, such as 'on the enemy', the point is the enemy ship, the baseline is the vector of the enemy ship's velocity, and the plane is the plane of the ecliptic.

- If a planet is specified as the point, the point is the planet, the baseline is a line from the planet to the sun, and the plane is the plane of the ecliptic.

- If a sun is specified as the point, the point is the sun, the baseline is a line from the sun to the primary inhabited planet, and the plane is the ecliptic.

- If the galactic center is specified as the point, the point is the galactic center, the line is the line from the galactic center to the ship, and the plane is the plane of the galactic lens.

Bearing angles are always specified as 'number-number-number'. Designations such as 'ninety-three' and 'one-eighty' are not permitted. These are correctly specified as 'zero-nine-three' and 'one-eight-zero'.

An exception occurs for 'zero-zero-zero', which may be stated simply as 'zero', such as in 'zero mark zero' or 'zero mark one-eight-zero'.

rotation is specified as 'number-number-number' in degrees clockwise from the projection of the baseline onto the plane when viewed from above. Leading zeroes are included, not dropped. number-number-number runs from zero-zero-zero to three-six-zero.

- If the point is the ship, 'above' means from above the ship with the command cylinder(s) considered to be 'up'.

- If the point is an enemy ship, a planet, or the sun, 'above' means from the north side of the solar system as determined by the right-hand rule: with the fingers of the right hand in the direction of orbit of the planets, the thumb points north.

- If the point is the galactic center, 'above' means from the north side of the galaxy, as determined by the right hand rule applied to the rotation of the stars about the galactic center.

elevation is specified as 'mark/minus number-number-number' in degrees up/down from the plane. 'mark' is used for bearings above the plane, and 'minus' is used for bearings below the plane. 'Above' is defined as for rotation. Leading zeroes are included, not dropped. number-number-number runs from zero-zero-zero to one-eight-zero.

distance is specified in light-units, most frequently in light-seconds.

CSF ships mentioned, by class
First ship in class is underlined

Battleships (BB)
CSS Amazon
CSS Artemisia
CSS Boadicea
<u>CSS Cleopatra</u>
CSS Jean d'Arc
CSS Kriegsmädchen
CSS Lakshmibai
CSS Tomoe
CSS Zenobia

CSS Akbar
<u>CSS Alexander</u>
CSS Belisarius
CSS Genghis Khan
CSS Georgy Zhukov
CSS Hannibal
CSS Julius Caesar
CSS Marlborough
CSS Napoleon Bonaparte
CSS Scipio Africanus
CSS Sun Tzu
CSS Ulysses S. Grant
CSS Zheng He

Heavy Cruisers (BC)
CSS Aluna Kamau
CSS Anderson Lail
CSS Donal McNee
<u>CSS Gerald Ansen</u>
CSS Guadalupe Rivera
CSS Hu Mingli
CSS Ikaika Kalani
CSS Jane Paxton
CSS Jacques Cotillard

CSS Manfred Koch
CSS Matheus Oliveira
CSS Mineko Kusunoki
CSS Nils Isacsson
CSS Patryk Mazur
CSS Roman Chrzanowski
CSS Sania Mehta
CSS Willard Dempsey

Light Cruisers (CC)
CSS Aquitaine
CSS Caribbean
CSS Catalonia
CSS Great Plains
CSS Gujarat
CSS Kansai
CSS Midwest
CSS Provence
CSS Schwarzwald
CSS Sichuan
<u>CSS Tuscany</u>

Destroyers (DD)
CSS Bennington
CSS Brenau
CSS Clermont (DD-ST)
CSS Elmhurst
CSS Emery
CSS Hamilton
CSS Howard
CSS Knox
CSS Maryville
CSS Middlebury
CSS Pomona
CSS Whittier

CSF ship capabilities, by class

Battleships (BB)

Classes: *Cleopatra, Alexander*
Crew Complement: 2400
Maximum Acceleration: 1.1 gravities
Guns, number: 6
Guns, type: 'battleship-grade', 'super-heavy'
Guns, range: 10 light-seconds

Heavy Cruisers (BC)

Classes: *Gerald Ansen*
Crew Complement: 1200
Maximum Acceleration: 1.4 gravities
Guns, number: 3
Guns, type: 'heavy'
Guns, range: 7 light-seconds

Light Cruisers (CC)

Classes: *Tuscany*
Crew Complement: 800
Maximum Acceleration: 1.7 gravities
Guns, number: 3
Guns, type: 'medium'
Guns, range: 5 light-seconds

Destroyers (DD)

Crew Complement: 400
Maximum Acceleration: 2.1 gravities
Guns, number: 3
Guns, type: 'light'
Guns, range: 3 light-seconds

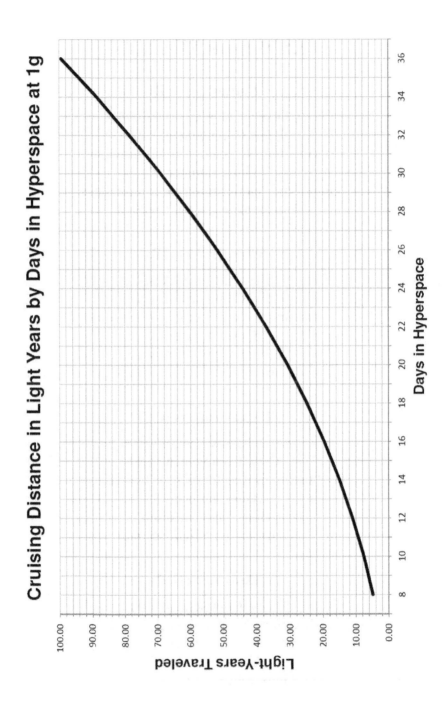

Cruising Distance in Light Years by Days in Hyperspace at 1g

Acronyms and Terms

AAR – After Action Report.

AO – Area of operations.

ATO – Assistant Tactical Officer.

ATS – Advanced Tactics School.

below decks – cylinders on a ship containing enlisted quarters and mechanical areas such as propulsion, weapons control, etc.

blue team – defender in a war game exercise.

BMS – Brunswick Merchant Ship.

bogey – an unidentified contact, such as on radar.

BSF – Becker Space Force.

BSN – Brunswick Space Navy.

BTS – Basic Tactics School.

building book – designing a book of maneuvers.

bulkhead – wall on a spaceship.

CCM – CSF decoration, Commonwealth Charter Medallion.

CCS – ship prefix, Commonwealth Colony Ship.

CFP – Commonwealth of Free Planets.

CIC – Combat Information Center.

Class 1 secured facility – the highest rated facility for the use or discussion of classified materials.

CM – CSF decoration, Combat Medal.

CNO – Chief of Naval Operations.

Commonwealth – Commonwealth of Free Planets.

CPS – ship prefix, Commonwealth Passenger Ship.

CSF – Commonwealth Space Force.

CSL – Commonwealth Star Lines, commercial passenger company.

CSS – ship prefix, Commonwealth Space Ship.

deadhead – make a trip aboard ship while not serving; guest; ferry.

deck – floor in a spaceship.

deckhead – ceiling in a spaceship, with a room directly above.

division – half of a squadron; in CSF, four ships.

DNA – deoxyribonucleic acid; a molecule of genetic instructions.

door – physical closure on a doorway; may not be airtight.

229

doorway – opening in a bulkhead.

DSM – CSF decoration, Distinguished Service Medal.

DSN – ship prefix, Duval Space Navy.

ENS – ship prefix, Earth Navy Ship.

Enshin – martial art combining karate and judo, founded in 1988.

Exam – Citizenship Exam of the Commonwealth of Free Planets.

Fleet Book (of Maneuvers) – CSF standard book of maneuvers.

flotilla – two squadrons under one command; usually destroyers.

g – one gravity, the amount of gravity one feels on Earth.

GMD – Galactic Mail And Defense Corporation.

geosynchronous – west-to-east orbit in 24 hours; geostationary.

Goat Locker – Chief's Mess on a ship.

hatch – airtight cover on a hatchway in a deckhead or overhead.

hatchway – opening in a deckhead or overhead, with a hatch.

HQ – Headquarters.

inner envelope – calculated volume inside the published system periphery allowing hyperspace cruise but not transition.

IS – interstellar.

JAG – Judge Advocate General, the legal arm of the CSF.

JTO – Junior Tactical Officer.

ladderway – opening in a deckhead or overhead, without a hatch.

light-second – distance light travels in one second; 186,282 miles.

light-year – distance light travels in one year; 5.88 trillion miles.

low-g – low gravity; gravity under 0.2 g.

metroplex – city and its suburbs; metropolitan area.

LNS – ship prefix, Lautadan Navy Ship.

MP – Military Police.

NOC – Naval Operations Center at Sigurdsen Fleet HQ.

OCS – Officer Candidate School.

outer envelope – calculated volume inside the published system periphery allowing hyperspace cruise and transition.

overhead – ceiling in a spaceship, without a room directly above.

PhD – Doctor of Philosophy; the most advanced degree in a field.

ppm – parts per million.

PR – public relations.

PSS – ship prefix, Paradiso Space Ship.

PTO – Planetary Tactical Office, Officer

red team – attacker in a war game exercise.

R&R – Rest and Recuperation.

SM – CSF decoration, Science Medal.

SMH – Sigurdsen Military Hospital.

section – half of a division; in CSF, two ships.

squadron – group of ships under one command; in CSF, eight ships.

SSN – ship prefix, Samaran Space Navy.

STO – Senior Tactical Officer.

system periphery – published boundary inside which hyperspace cruise and transition are dangerous to the ship.

topside – cylinder(s) on a ship containing officer's quarters and command & control areas like the bridge, CIC, etc.

TNS – ship prefix, Tenerife Navy Ship.

UCS – Unarmed Combat School.

UJ – University of Jablonka.

VA – CSF decoration, Victorious Action ribbon.

VR – virtual reality.

XO – Executive Officer, First Officer.

zero-g – completely weightless; in free fall.

Made in the USA
Middletown, DE
21 December 2021